c/o The Royal Australian and New Zealand
College of Ophthalmologists,
94-98 Chalmers Street, Surry Hills,
N.S.W. 2010, Australia

Nick Arvin grew up in Michigan. He has degrees in mechanical engineering from the University of Michigan and Stanford, and is a graduate of the Iowa Writers' Workshop.

THE RECONSTRUCTIONIST

Finishing college, Ellis Barstow drifts back to his hometown and into a strange profession: reconstructing fatal traffic accidents. He seems to take to the work, forming a bond with his boss, John Boggs. Yet Ellis harbours a secret. Haunted by the fatal crash that killed his half-brother Christopher, he is drawn to the reconstructionist's grisly world. Boggs, in his exacting way, would argue that if two cars meeting at an intersection can be called an accident then anything can — where we live, what we do, even who we fall in love with. For Ellis these things are no accident. He harbours a second, more dangerous secret, which will shatter both their lives and lead to a desperate race towards confrontation, reconciliation and survival.

NICK ARVIN

THE
RECONSTRUCTIONIST

Complete and Unabridged

ULVERSCROFT
Leicester

First published in Great Britain in 2010 by
Hutchinson
The Random House Group Limited
London

First Large Print Edition
published 2011
by arrangement with
The Random House Group Limited
London

British Library CIP Data

Arvin, Nick.
   The reconstructionist.
   1. Traffic accident investigation- -Fiction.
   2. Secrecy- -Fiction. 3. Brothers- -Death- -Fiction.
   4. Traffic accident victims- -Fiction.
   5. Detective and mystery stories 6. Large type books.
   I. Title
   813.6–dc22

   ISBN 978–1–4448–0820–9

Published by
F. A. Thorpe (Publishing)
Anstey, Leicestershire

Set by Words & Graphics Ltd.
Anstey, Leicestershire
Printed and bound in Great Britain by
T. J. International Ltd., Padstow, Cornwall

This book is printed on acid-free paper

For Rachel and Cade

0

At the sound of shrieking tyres the boys stop and hold. Ellis is nine and Christopher, his half-brother, is eleven. They stand anticipating the resonant crash of large metal bodies at speed, but even so, when it comes, they startle. The glare on the television glass quivers. A lingering metallic sound, like a rolling paint can, drifts away.

Silence resumes.

The boys stampede the door.

A high wooden fence surrounds their subdivision, and on the other side lie what they call *the big streets*. They run nearly a quarter-mile to reach an opening in the fence and turn into the big streets where a line of unmoving traffic is already forming, car behind car, drivers staring dully toward the intersection. Ellis wheezes and feels the shortness of his legs relative to Christopher's, but he keeps up. A pair of teenagers stand on the sidewalk hand in hand, peering toward the stop lights, and the two boys spin around on either side. A siren's howl draws toward the intersection from across town.

Two boxy American sedans — a Chevy and

a Plymouth — have a startling appearance: they lie in unnatural postures, pointed in oblique directions, damaged in dark inversions, their black guts exposed, their glossy surfaces crushed, twisted and torn. An acrid odour cuts the air, and for a minute Ellis holds his breath against it. A green Kool-Aid-coloured fluid glistens in an arc on the asphalt. Across the intersection a chrome hubcap lies shining. It matches the chrome hubcaps on the nearest sedan, the Plymouth, where a fat man and his fat wife stand. The husband peers toward the approaching sirens while his wife glances at her watch, repeatedly, and Ellis wonders why she is barefoot. In the Chevy are two women. One, older, is comforting the other, a young woman with heaps of hair who holds her hands over her face and intermittently moans, a sound Ellis hears faintly, muffled by distance.

A few people gather on the corners. Two more boys from the neighbourhood arrive. A third. They punch one another on the shoulder. A policeman picks up the hubcap and directs traffic around the damaged vehicles. Another policeman talks to the women in the Chevy and scribbles on a notepad. An ambulance arrives. The woman holding her face is placed onto a gurney and swallowed by the ambulance. A wrecker with flashing amber lights backs up to the Plymouth while the ambulance moves off with its siren alternating yowls, bleeps and squawks.

The twins trot in, and they get punched on the shoulders, too.

The sedans are trundled away behind a pair of wreckers. A cop remains, taking notes, talking with people. He measures distances with a wheel on a stick that he rolls from point to point. He retrieves a camera from the trunk of his cruiser and takes photos. 'Go home,' he shouts toward the boys. They sidle a few steps down the sidewalk and loiter there. Only when this cop, too, has climbed into his car and driven away does Christopher start to saunter down the sidewalk, and the others follow. The short twin trips and stumbles, and someone giggles. 'It was an accident,' the short twin protests, and the others laugh. They pretend to trip, flail around, clutch one another. One of the boys jogs backward in front of the short twin and chants in his face, 'Accident, accident.' Christopher steps a little further ahead, waves a fist in the air and shouts, 'Ax-E-Dent! Ax-E-Dent!'

Ellis shouts, 'Ax-E-Dent!'

Christopher screams, 'Ax! E! Dent!'

The boys parade along the sidewalk, chanting, 'Ax-E-Dent! Ax-E-Dent! Ax! E! Dent!'

The tall twin screams, 'Crash!' A boy shouts, 'Smash!' Another hollers, 'Blood!' And another, the son of a mechanic, yells, 'Glycol!' They beat one another on the shoulders and shake their fists skyward as if on a team that has won. Soon they begin to sprint and strain for speed.

The next day, Ellis rides through the intersection with his mother in her Oldsmobile. The damaged vehicles are gone, of course, and the splash of green fluid has vanished, too. The only indications of the collision are a couple of short dark tyre marks on the road and, at the corners of the intersection, near the kerbs, shards of glass and broken ruby-coloured plastic, pushed by passing tyres into long shallow piles.

PART ONE:
CAREER

1

When Ellis Barstow finished college he took a job in a plant that manufactured axles and driveshafts for pickup trucks and SUVs. His workday began and ended with a journey across the plant floor, and curiosity took him on circuitous routes through the drills and lathes, assembly lines, clapping stamping presses, robot arms manoeuvring weld pincers, and a heat-treatment area where tubular furnaces glowed and flamed under the care of hunched, thin old men wearing goggles and asbestos gauntlets. Ellis liked these walks, liked gawking, liked the spectacle of a mechanised world where the sprawl of machines spread out of sight to all sides, conveyor systems criss-crossed overhead, and grates underfoot showed milk-coloured lubricants coursing in streams. And he liked how sometimes, as if to sharpen the strangeness, a sparrow swooped down from some dark nook overhead and worried at a stray Cheeto or muffin paper on the blackened floor.

But the rest of the job was more difficult.

He had earned a degree in mechanical engineering without developing any concrete ideas about what he wanted to do with it. He had thought maybe he would like to work with things that made things, so he had taken a job where things were made. His particular realm was a 10.5-inch differential assembly line with twenty-two manned stations that pieced together a set of gears and then secured them into a housing, called a pig-head because it looked like one. The line workers accomplished their work by fitting parts into fixtures, then pressing buttons to engage a press, or spin down a set of bolt drivers. Then they pulled out the result and put it on a conveyor to the next station, until it reached the end of the line, went onto a pallet, and a forklift carried it away.

He was, ostensibly, an engineer. The human resources department had given him a box of business cards that said *Ellis Barstow, Engineer*. And on Ellis's first day a bearing-press operator had come over, shaken his hand and said, 'Great to meet a new engineer.' The man grinned. 'Know why I like engineers?' He then — while Ellis stared with lagging comprehension — dropped his coveralls and danced a naked jig. 'Because,' he shouted, 'they suck great dick!' Then he pulled up his overalls and went back to work.

But Ellis soon began to understand that his own work here had little to do with engineering. Instead he supervised his line in much the way that one would manage a franchise restaurant. He needed to schedule deliveries of parts, and he needed to manage the crew. And while he was soon orchestrating the deliveries of parts with reasonable success, he didn't know how to deal with the people. Every one of them had fifteen to forty years on him. They ignored him. He tried to be nice, tried to be funny, tried to be stern. He gave them gifts — doughnuts, birthday cakes, and for Christmas he bought everyone a toy model of one of the trucks that their axles went into. He was an introvert and none of this was easy for him. And none of it worked. The day after Christmas, the toy trucks he had given away lay piled on his desk. He knew he was doing poorly at this. His jokes weren't funny. His sternness was tainted with meekness. They had been here before him — they had black in the creases of their skin where years of airborne oils and dust had collected — and they would be here after he left. Ellis spent more and more time at his desk, which stood in a little low-walled office near the line. He executed pointless manipulations of columns of numbers in Excel spreadsheets and waited for the days to end, his mind filled with the noises of parts clanking, impact wrenches clattering, forklift engines roaring, the number eight station sputtering and number fourteen grinding. From time to time a loud buzzer sounded to indicate line halts. Several of the machines on the line broke down routinely, and then everyone sat chatting while an electrician fiddled around, joked with whomever happened to be nearby, and eventually told Ellis that a pipe fitter was needed. When the pipe fitter showed up, he worked for a while, then announced that a millwright was needed. The millwright came, tinkered, muttered that the problem appeared electrical. The electrician had departed long ago, of course. One day, after the buzzer had been clamouring for a full five minutes, Ellis left his desk and found no mechanical problems, only the man who'd pulled down his coveralls asleep at his station, forehead against a bearing press. Ellis lost it. He grabbed him by the shoulder and shook him, yelling. The man's eyes opened wide with surprise and fear, and Ellis shoved him away and circled to yell at several of the others.

When the adrenalin had faded, however, he collapsed at his desk, feeling disturbed, less at what he had done than at how it had happened, in an abrupt loss of control. In losing that, it seemed to him, he lost everything.

To his surprise, for the rest of the week he had a relatively efficient line. But after a weekend the crew resumed old habits and became, if anything, more uncooperative. It struck Ellis that if the only way to do his job was to yell at people who grew negligent about repetitious, numbing work, then probably he didn't want the job.

Monday of the next week he watched a pair of sparrows hop around in his office doorway. They pecked and preened, observed him with one eye then the other, doubting and verifying. Ellis pulled his earplugs, and faintly in the general roar he heard a chirp. He stood from his desk and approached, hoping to move them toward a building exit, but they only flew into the dark overhead. He turned a circle, then came to a resolution and crossed the plant floor to his manager's large, clean, quiet office.

A stamping-press accident years ago had taken the ends off two fingers on his manager's right hand, and he fidgeted with a micrometer in this hand while Ellis uttered a few irrelevant phrases, then finally blurted, as if an admission of guilt, that he intended to quit. The manager boomed, 'I'll see if we can find you another position!' He was half deaf.

Ellis shrugged, then shook his head. 'I guess I don't think the manufacturing

11

environment feels right for me.'

'OK! What kind of job do you think is right?'

'I don't know.'

The manager set both hands on the surface of the desk, as if to keep it down, and held them there while he stared at Ellis. Then suddenly he smiled and stood and extended his hand. Ellis stared at the two nub fingers, then realised that this was an invitation to shake, and to leave.

He cleaned his desk and escaped through a side door.

Then it seemed as if he had reached the edge of a cliff over a sea. He didn't see any sign of how to move forward.

★ ★ ★

Over the next years he worked various jobs, none of which were in engineering. He spent a great deal of time reading. As a child he had fed on books, and now he continued to read — mysteries, science fiction, Calvino, Eco — books to carry his thoughts from his own life to someplace else. He contemplated returning to school for a degree in English, but couldn't imagine what he would do with it. Teach? He doubted whether he could inspire kids, or even merely control a classroom. He felt he lacked a vocation, and that if he had one, his life would gain direction. For consolation he read and grew lost in du Maurier, Chandler, Lem, Borges. *The Big Sleep* and 'The Garden of Forking Paths'.

One winter he spent his savings on a two-week trip to India, which he'd become interested in through reading Rushdie. He was twenty-five years old. He travelled alone, and he found himself anxious and over-whelmed by alienness and sensory density. And, diarrhoea. At the end of the trip he could hardly say what he had seen except a swirl of colours, gods over doorways, filthy toilets, tattered clothes, outstretched hands. To beggar after beggar he had given away more rupees than he could really afford. He kept thinking that, but for the accident of where he had been born, this life might be his own. After landing again in the US he had to wait for one more flight to carry him home, and he sat in the airport terminal feeling flaccid and ill. His head contained a miasma and the objects around him trailed green auras. As he watched through the windows snow began to fall and soon gathered into a white, obscuring storm. Periodically he trooped to the restroom to discharge his sickness and sip at the water fountains.

Flights were delayed. He sat queasy with his bag between his legs and dozed. Delay passed into delay. People around him collapsed to the floor and slept or gazed at windows where the snow fell fast and straight down.

After an indeterminate sleep he stood and began to walk. At the food stalls uniformed employees served the trapped with grumpy languor. Along the hallways travellers lay propped on bags and one another. The fluorescent lighting blued their lips, yellowed their eyes.

Seeing Heather's face here jolted him, and he stopped in the traffic of the hallway and let people push by. He had last seen Heather Gibson a decade earlier, when he was fourteen and she was sixteen. His memories of her were surrounded by glinting, uncomfortable emotions. She sat with her back against a painted concrete wall, head tilted, eyes closed. A small woman. The skin of the left side of her face bore a slight shine of scar tissue, and Ellis wondered if he would have noticed it at all if he hadn't been looking for it. Her dark hair, which had been curled when they were in high school, now fell straight and neat around her face. But aside from this and the scarring, something more in her face seemed strange, although he could not identify it. Perhaps only age. She had one

14

arm propped on a duffel bag and a small blue blanket lay over her feet. She appeared to be alone. Memories crowded in, of her, and of his half-brother Christopher, who had been her boyfriend — so many memories and of such varied feelings that they crowded and confused one another. She had been burned in the aftermath of the accident that killed Christopher, and as Ellis stood staring with a sensation of wide confusion his attention returned again and again to the alteration of her face.

Then a passer-by struck Ellis's bag and spun him a quarter-turn, and his illness became urgent again. He ran to the restroom.

He returned to the gate for his flight. The chairs were full, so he sat on the floor, put his bag on his knees and rested his head on it. The electronic display at the gate showed yet another delay. He dozed. Then he stood.

Heather, in her sleep, had not moved. He edged himself into an opening between people seated against the opposite wall, and he watched her in the spaces that flickered between passing bodies. She stirred once or twice but did not look toward him. He saw that her eyelids had no lashes. Those, too, had burned away. He still could hardly separate his emotions from his dizziness, his muddled senses and his abused internal organs, but he knew that he felt, at least, wonder.

Perhaps as much as an hour passed before he moved on again. The snow had slackened, and soon he boarded his flight.

★ ★ ★

Talking on the phone with his mother about the trip, Ellis mentioned that he had seen someone who looked like Heather Gibson in the airport.

His mother wanted to know why he hadn't approached her, and he said that the woman he saw was asleep and at a distance, and he was sick, and he wasn't entirely certain whether it had been her at all. He asked his mother if she knew anything about what had happened to Heather in the years since Christopher died. She said she didn't.

He guessed that not knowing would bother her. And two days later she called back — she had talked to a friend who knew the Gibsons. Heather lived in the same sprawl of downstate suburbs where Ellis lived, and she had married a man named John Boggs.

This was information enough — he found an address and drove out, to a neighbour-hood of two-storey homes, each on a quarter-acre of lawn, each with a two- or three-car garage, each with bits of brass around the front door — knob, knocker, porch light. Maybe a wrought-iron or picket fence. No sidewalks. The last snowfall had melted away except for a scatter of white scraps pocketed in the grass. Near the address he slowed. An asphalt driveway led to a garage on the side of the house, which was faced with brick on the first floor and wood-sided on the second. The garage door stood open. The lawn looked neatly kept, though it remained winter-brown. Several leafless trees scratched at the void. From one hung a brightly painted birdfeeder made from soda cans. A red Taurus wagon rested in the drive; a sticker on its rear bumper had a few words that he could not read and an image of an Egyptian mask, sketched with simple lines. Ellis had slowed almost to stop when he noticed, in the gloom of the open garage, a large, bearded man with a grocery bag in one hand. The man waved.

Ellis drove away determined not to return.

But weeks passed, and still he recalled again and again the interval of watching Heather's face as she slept against the airport wall. Then on the interstate he happened to glimpse the Egyptian mask, stickered on a Lincoln Navigator a couple hundred feet ahead. Pulling nearer he saw that it advertised the city's art museum.

For half a day he wandered among pieces by Picasso, Bruegel, Donatello, Van Gogh. Sarcophagi and medieval armour. A collection of snuffboxes. A few days later he returned. He came back repeatedly, through that spring and summer, sometimes two or three times a week. He often brought a book, and he liked the empty open peace of the place, where he could sit for an hour or two, alternately reading and watching an object of art, in a hush only rarely interrupted by one or two people strolling by. As he read, as he studied a sculpture, as he walked a high-ceilinged gallery, as he edged nearer to a canvas, a fraction of his attention was always listening for her, watching. Sometimes he sniffed the air for the trace of her presence — as he had years before, when she had visited Christopher in their house in Coil.

Then, stepping from a roomful of paintings — misty images labelled 'Luminist and Tonalist' — into an echoing marbled hallway, he saw her. Loose linen clothing, sandals, sunglasses on her head, as she never would have dressed in high school. She knew him immediately; she smiled, and with enthusiasm she hugged him and looked up at him. The scars. The eyelashes. A clotted feeling in his lungs. 'How have you been?' she asked.

He coughed. He forced himself to speak

18

and told her that he had studied engineering in college but had done little with it. He mentioned odd jobs, reading books. Now he held a floor job in an appliance store, in the television department.

If that disappointed her, she showed no sign. She said she had majored in art, and since then she had been working on obtaining her teaching certificate. But she had also had a job in graphic design, shelved books at a library, written copy for an advertising firm. 'I guess I'm not entirely focused,' she said. She had been married almost five years. 'He works in automotive stuff,' she said of her husband.

'An engineer?' Ellis said.

'They're a dozen for a dime around here.' She shrugged apologetically.

'Do you think he could get me a job?'

She pulled her sunglasses off her head and folded and opened the temples. 'John's work is unusual.'

'Unusual is OK.'

'I don't know.'

'It has to be better than selling TVs.'

'Forensic engineering,' she said. 'He examines car accidents, to see how they happened.' She inclined her head forward as if they might be overheard. By whom? By Christopher, was all he could think. 'Or maybe the preferred term is accident reconstruction,' she said. 'They hire out to insurance companies and attorneys. I don't know. I should have a better sense of it, but it's pretty dark. I don't really like hearing about it.'

She changed the subject, and they talked of a few people they had known in Coil. Where his mother had kept track of people, Ellis was able to give news, and he could even make Heather laugh. But then she looked at her watch. 'Well, hey,' she said, 'it's good to see you.'

His heart fisted. 'Let me — ' Everything gyred. 'Let me give you something,' he said. He groped into the backpack he carried, and his hand came on pens, books, a calculator, and then a computer mouse pad that he had bought some weeks earlier, here, at the gift shop. A stupid thing, he thought, but he held it forward.

She turned it over and back again. It showed a detail from an oil painting — a grey mouse on rough floorboards, looking upward, a red ribbon around his neck. Ellis couldn't tell what she thought of it and feared she would try to press it back. 'For mouse-on-mouse action,' he said. 'Or, I guess, for the best-laid pads of mice and men.'

She rolled it between her hands. 'You could

talk to my husband,' she said, 'if you're serious about looking for a job.'

'Yes. Yes.'

'Maybe it's OK if you can get past the ugliness. He's mentioned that he might take on someone to help with his caseload. I don't know if he's serious, but it won't hurt to ask.' On a slip of paper she wrote a phone number. At the top she wrote 'Boggs'. She said, 'Everyone, except for me, calls him Boggs.'

2

A large aqua-blue SUV lay in the corner of the parking lot, terribly mutilated — windows broken out, front and rear lamps gone, bumper covers hanging, grille missing, wheels settled on flat tyres, doors twisted out of door frames, hood bent like a potato chip.

But otherwise, the place looked like an ordinary suburban office building, with ordinary cars clustered in the parking spaces nearest the front door. Ellis had arrived early. He sat in his car, looking at his résumé. It seemed a document built from scant and shabby materials.

'*He is in the old labyrinth,*' said a deep voice. '*It is the story of his gambling in another guise.*'

A shining green Volkswagen convertible had come into the parking lot, top down though the weather was cool. '*He gambles because God does not speak. He gambles to make God speak.*' It took Ellis a second to connect the voice to the convertible and its stereo. '*But to make God speak in the turn of a card is blasphemy. Only when God is silent does God —* ' A large, bearded man in a dark

22

blue overcoat stood out of the Volkswagen and stalked toward the office door. His sand-coloured hair held itself out from his head like frayed hemp rope, and he carried a bright orange bag stuffed to overflowing with papers and binders. Ellis felt pretty sure it was the same man he had seen in Heather's driveway.

A few minutes later, as Ellis stared again at his résumé, he was startled by a knock on his window. The man from the Volkswagen peered down. 'Ellis Barstow?'

'Yes, sir.'

'You're early. I'm Boggs.' He appeared to be in his middle thirties, with crow's feet beginning at the corners of vivid blue eyes. Ellis stood out of his car, and Boggs shook his hand and grinned. If he recognised Ellis or his car from the drive-by half a year ago, he offered no sign of it. He only tilted his head. 'Come on.'

He led Ellis to the battered aqua-blue SUV and nodded at it. 'What do you suppose happened?'

'Hit by an avalanche.'

Ellis meant it as a joke, but Boggs only shook his head, as if he had encountered avalanche-struck vehicles from time to time, but this was not one. Looking at the vehicle again — the terrible dents and tears and missing windows and lamps — Ellis didn't know how to begin to make an intelligent guess. He said, 'Um — '

'Rollover damage,' Boggs said, 'at highway speeds. Happens every day, more or less. The left rear tyre blew out, and the causes of that are being argued, but whatever the reason, it blew out and induced a leftward drift. The driver attempted to steer back to the right but over-corrected, and very quickly the vehicle had turned almost sideways. The left-side wheel rims bit into the roadway, the right-side wheels lifted, and the whole thing vaulted. After that, it spun and bounced along like a punted football.'

'How many people were inside?'

'Five occupants. Two fully ejected, three partially ejected. Five fatalities.'

'All of them?'

'Dead before the vehicle stopped moving. A matter of seconds.'

'That's horrible.'

'It is. It really is. And now it's part of a very expensive lawsuit.' He put a hand back through his hair, and it stood out yet more from his head. 'So. Let's say that you are a reconstructionist. You've been asked by an attorney involved in a very expensive lawsuit to examine this vehicle. Could you tell him how many times it rolled over?' After a

24

second he amended, 'At least how many times.'

Ellis touched a scarred door, the metal cold and abrasive. He stepped back and examined the forms of the damage, the denting, scraping and tearing. It looked as if it might have been spun inside a concrete mixer. He admitted, 'I really have no idea.'

'Look at the scratch patterns,' Boggs said.

Ellis wasn't sure what he meant by patterns. Random scratches seemed to be everywhere — single long scratches, scratches in pairs and threesomes, groups of light scratches and areas that looked as if they had been attacked with a power sander. Boggs pointed to a location on the passenger-side fender. 'Like these.'

Here was some scratching of the power-sander variety, gouged deep into the sheet metal, while above and coming down into the deeper ones at a slight angle ran a second set of scratches, longer, less deep. Ellis moved a finger over them. He crouched to get out of the sun's glare and saw that almost perpendicular to the longer scratches lay yet a third set, very light, little more than minor disruptions in the paint.

'Three?' he said.

'Three?' echoed Boggs.

'Three rolls?'

'Three rolls? Why three?'

Three sets of scratches. Could that mean three rolls? Why?

'Think about it,' Boggs said. 'Let me know.'

Stacks of cardboard banker's boxes filled the corners of Boggs's office and paperwork sprawled over the desk. Littered among the papers, as if stranded in snow banks, were toy cars — a Ferrari, a Land Rover, a GTO, a milk truck. Beside the banker's boxes stood a shelf lined with textbooks, technical manuals, collections of conference papers. They talked through Ellis's résumé in about fifteen minutes — college engineering classes and projects, and the supervisory job at the axle plant, which Ellis tried to gloss. He ticked through other jobs: a lawn service, a coffee shop, running deliveries, selling appliances. The conversation began to wallow, Boggs seemed subdued, and Ellis grew embarrassed. He had an engineering degree that he'd hardly applied and no useful skills. He sat here only because years ago his now-dead half-brother had been the boyfriend of a girl who was now this man's wife. Absurd.

Yet he wanted this job. He saw an opportunity to set his life on a new path. He felt he badly needed a new path.

From the clutter on the desk he picked out the toy Land Rover and turned it. Like a bouncing football. A thought came. 'At least three times,' he said. He moved the Land Rover slowly over the desk, as if rolling. 'Each time this corner hits the ground, it picks up new scratches.' Growing excited, he elaborated: a vehicle couldn't slide in two directions at once, so each set of overlapping scratches indicated a different time that that part of the vehicle had been on the ground. He had seen three separate sets of scratches in the area Boggs had pointed out, so that fender had hit the ground at least three times.

Boggs smiled. He took the toy and illustrated some other aspects — that the orientation of a set of scratches indicated the direction the vehicle had been travelling as it struck the ground; the deeper scratches were made when the vehicle hit asphalt while the lighter ones came as it hit softer soil off the roadway; looking closely, one could see the sequence in which the scratches were made, because the cutting of a new scratch pushed paint into the existing scratches that it crossed.

'We do lots of reports for our clients,' Boggs said. 'Can you write?'

'I won a prize for something I wrote in college.'

'Really? Why isn't that on your résumé?'

'Well, it was fiction. And it wasn't really so

much an award as an honourable mention. And, in retrospect, it sucked.'

'You like to read? Have you read Coetzee? I've been listening to him on tape.'

'In your car.'

'Yes.' Boggs grinned. He talked happily for a few minutes about books, of Dostoevsky, of *War and Peace*, which he loved and which Ellis had to admit he had never read. 'I like the Russians,' Boggs said. 'Do you know this one?' he turned to his computer and clicked and a voice began —

' . . . *why, where in the world has his character gone to? The steadfast man of action is totally at a loss and has turned out to be a pitiful little poltroon, an insignificant, puny babe, or simply, as Nozdrev puts it, a horse's twat* . . . '

'Poltroon!' Boggs laughed happily and turned it off. '*Dead Souls*. Did you know that Gogol could pull his lower lip up over his nose?' He grew distracted in straightening the vehicles on his desk. 'This job,' he said, 'is emotionally odd. Are you ready for that? It's analytic, and you sometimes have to remind yourself: people died.'

'I don't know if — ' Ellis stalled and let the sentence lapse.

'Well, there is no way to know. I'm just warning you, it's odd. You look at terrible

28

events and analyse them minutely. It's not normal. It's strange. Then, after you've done it for a while, what's also strange is how you get used to it, and even how much you forget. It seems a little indecent to forget. That's what bothers me, now. It's as if, if I were a better man, I'd go back to tour the old accidents from time to time. Like those old soldiers revisiting the Somme or Gettysburg or Vietnam. Austerlitz. But no one remembers Austerlitz any more.' He looked hopefully at Ellis, as if he might be the exception.

Ellis admitted that he didn't remember Austerlitz.

By the time he left, Boggs had offered the job outright, and Ellis had accepted. In the parking lot he stopped to look again at the aqua-blue SUV. He scrutinised a few of the scratches, then leaned through the vacant space where a window had been. A strand of gleaming purple and green Mardi Gras beads was wrapped around the gear shift. Black tyre shards and an empty can of diet soda littered the cargo area. Dry leaves lay on the back seat, along with a yellow receipt that was, he saw, from Babies R Us. He returned to his car and sat, lightly touching his hands together, hesitating now to drive into traffic, onto the streets, the interstate. But after a minute he started the engine, and he drove.

★ ★ ★

Ellis had largely fallen out of touch with his father, so that was easy. He spoke regularly with his mother, but he waited until he had already accepted the job and begun working before he told her about it. He worried that she might think of Christopher's death and disapprove of this work; perhaps she would articulate certain objections that he had not yet articulated to himself. But she only asked what his salary would be. He told her, and she sounded happy, and soon she was complaining that the neighbour's cottonwood was dropping branches onto her lawn, and Ellis thought, maybe that's all it needs to be — a job.

Later, after years, it seemed to him almost as if he had always been a reconstructionist, and he recalled only with effort that at one time it had been new to him, that it had felt like entering an obscure nation with its own language, customs and peculiar manner of thinking. On his first day Boggs had handed him a stack of technical papers — 'A Comparison Study of Skid Marks and Yaw Marks', 'Physical Evidence Analysis and Roll Velocity Effects in Rollover Accident Reconstruction' and 'Speed Estimation from Vehicle Crush in Side Pole Impacts'. Even the word *reconstructionist* felt odd in the mouth.

Ellis sat at a desk in a cubicle with five-foot-high foam-core walls, two shelves for books, two file drawers, a computer and a telephone. It was one cubicle in a grid of twelve, each occupied by an engineer. 'Eggheads in a carton,' Boggs called it. Around the periphery of the room were a handful of walled offices where the senior engineers sat. At the rear of the building a wide door accessed an underground garage where items of physical evidence were stored: car seats burned down to their internal steel frames, pieces of exploded tyres, dismantled disc brakes, shatterproof windows glittering with cracklines, a fuel tank cut into halves for examination, a Honda motorcycle improbably twisted, a Dodge pickup truck blooming with front and rear collisions.

Ellis had projects occasionally with some of the other engineers, but for the most part he worked directly with Boggs, and he acquired the skills of the job by doing the job with Boggs. Boggs was at once boss, mentor and co-worker, and he performed these roles with patience and humour. Ellis never felt as if he were being tested or made a fool of. From the day he started, he never seriously feared for his job. He grew used to the word reconstructionist. He learned the nomenclature. When Boggs, as testifying expert, went to have his opinions taken outside of court it was at a deposition, which was called a depo, or sometimes just a dep. The pillars connecting a vehicle's body to its roof were named alphabetically from front to back: A-pillar, B-pillar, C-pillar, and sometimes a D-pillar. A change in velocity due to a collision was a delta-V; conservation of linear momentum was COLM; primary direction of force was PDOF. The people in a vehicle were occupants. Anyone thrown from a vehicle in the course of an accident was ejected. The dead were occupants or pedestrians who had sustained fatal injuries, or, simply, fatalities. He learned the methodologies of crush-energy analysis and momentum-based analysis, how to calculate speed loss during braking, how to incorporate perception-reaction time into a time-space analysis. He learned photogrammetric techniques for identifying the locations of objects on the roadway that the police had failed to record, and he learned how to download data from airbag modules, how to examine tyres and brakes for evidence of defects or improper maintenance, how to look at light bulbs and seat belts for indications that they were in use at the time of a collision, how to document the damage to a car, how to build computer models of vehicles and terrains, how to generate data describing motion and impacts.

There were slow days, and days spent reading maddeningly useless depositions, days spent working out some trivial but necessary and elusive problem of mathematics or physics, days spent trying to find a source for obscure information on decades-old frame rails or fuel tank designs, days spent travelling between obscure towns amid empty plains in order to take a few photos and measurements of dubious utility. But even these days held at least a possibility of discovering something of significance, of seeing a problem in a new way or coming upon some small, critical, overlooked evidence. Ellis liked the work. It reminded him of the books he enjoyed, stories of sharp-eyed detectives, stories of worlds a little separated from the usual one. At intervals he came across an accident-scene photograph — a bloodstain on the road, a tooth alone on a car seat, a body burned past recognising — that made him cold in his bones and reminded him of his reservations, and at these times it again seemed possible that this was the last job on earth that he should have. But this feeling came to him less often as time passed, as case files accumulated and accident-scene photographs overlaid one another and grew indistinct.

★ ★ ★

Ellis discovered that Boggs didn't generally keep friends — he could be too overbearing, too blunt, too indifferent, too silent. But somehow, because Ellis worked for him and because Boggs loved working, Ellis was largely shielded from these traits. Moreover, they were often seated side by side for long periods — in airports, airplanes, rental cars and hotel bars as they travelled to inspect accident scenes and vehicles — and the travel demands of the job curtailed other relationships even as the two of them were pushed together. They joked easily, and they could be silent easily. As years passed and Ellis came to understand the work and to participate in it with the efficiency of familiarity, they also began to go together to occasional baseball games, or pike fishing, or funny car races. They had a habit of long, desultory conversations called from desk to desk late in the office when everyone else had left. Sometimes these seemed to Ellis almost a dream of voices in the head.

'One of the problems between my wife and me,' Boggs said once, out of a long silence, startling Ellis, 'is over kids. What do you think about kids?'

'I don't know. They're pretty cute. I guess sometimes I get tired of their noise on airplanes.'

They were in the middle of the inspection of an exemplar Silverado, an undamaged pickup of make, model, year and option package identical to that of another pickup which had been struck head-on and burst into flames when a drunk drifted across the double yellow line. They would use measurements from the exemplar for comparison purposes. Boggs stood on a ladder, above the hood, shooting photos downward while Ellis held a measuring tape against the vehicle one way, then another. They were interested in the precise curve of the bumper. Boggs called, 'I really don't like them when they're little. Like village idiots. You can't have a real conversation.'

'They're cute, though.'

'Cute, but they don't even know how to wipe themselves. Who wants to spend day after day hanging out with a room-mate who can't wipe his own butt?'

'Someone did it for you.'

'Bless her, I have no idea why. Look at

what Mom got out of it. A son who sent her a case of beer at Christmas.'

'Mindless propagation of the species,' Ellis said.

'You're being sarcastic, but you're right.'

'You're being sarcastic.'

'Nope.' Boggs grinned, took another photo, then dropped the camera and let it hang on its cord around his neck. 'The other thing is, I'm sure that any kid I have will die before I do. Hit by a bus, drowning in a pool, SIDS, finding a gun in the neighbour's closet, leukaemia, drafted into some dick-swinging war, whatever. How could the kid possibly survive? Most do, somehow. But I'm stuck inside my own lizard brain, and whenever I think about having some idiot kid, I get these chills. Dead kid. It would be horrible. I would go to the nearest steel foundry and jump into a batch of molten iron.'

Ellis looked up at him and said nothing.

'I'm sorry.' Boggs frowned. 'I wasn't thinking of your brother. I hadn't made the connection. I'm the idiot.'

'My dad's life did go pretty much straight to hell after that,' Ellis said. Trying to give nothing away. He already knew Boggs's position on the topic of children, through Heather, because he was conducting an affair with her.

36

'I don't know what an accident is, really,' Boggs said.

This — or a version of this — represented one of Boggs's themes. And after the third or fourth time, Ellis had developed a standard response: 'Everything's got a name, but not every name's got a thing.' Or a version of this.

'Everything,' Boggs would say, 'depends on the contingent and the adventitious, and if the meeting of two vehicles in an intersection can be called an accident, then what can't be called an accident? Where my footsteps fall, where I place my hands, where I sit, where I stand, how I appear in the world, who I speak to, the kind of work I do, who I befriend, who I fall in love with?' Boggs pouted. '*Accident?*'

Some of these conversations occurred in Boggs's office, and Ellis had grown exquisitely familiar with the backside of the photograph of Heather that stood on Boggs's desk — the black cardboard, the little rotating latches, the triangular folding stand, the stainless-steel frame edge. But if he came around the desk to point out something on Boggs's computer screen, he wouldn't let himself glance at the photo. Instead he closed his attention on the computer screen, sometimes examining it pixel by pixel. He had an attitude of awe before his yearning toward her. And anger, because that yearning appeared so irrational and futile.

Every few weeks, despite himself, he went again to the art museum and wandered. He could not deny his hope, which amazed him. Sometimes he paced a slow circle around the spot where he'd encountered Heather before, looking, smelling the air, as if he might find some evidence of her, as if by detecting her in the past he might summon her into the present.

And years passed. Then, on a late-spring afternoon when Boggs was across the continent, participating in a mock trial that a client had arranged, Ellis's phone rang. Boggs, in a growly tone, said, 'Do me a favour?' Heather — he said — was stranded in her father's RV in a grocery store parking lot. The engine wouldn't start. 'Do you know what it costs to get an RV that size towed?' Boggs asked. 'And I wouldn't be surprised if it's just a bad connection at the battery.'

Ellis went.

★　★　★

The RV — a Coachmen Leprechaun, running a Ford V8 under the hood — lay at the edge of the parking lot, big and

38

rectangular as a fallen megalith. The problem was just as Boggs had suggested. Ellis retrieved pliers and a wire brush from a hardware store down the street, cleaned the battery connections and tightened the leads, and the engine keyed on. Heather, in the driver's seat, clapped. She climbed down and peered at the burbling engine. 'All good,' Ellis said.

'Want some iced tea?' she asked. 'Want to come in?' she added, in a satirical tone, gesturing at the RV's fibreglass side door. She apologised several times for the mess before letting him enter.

Marbles, toilet paper rolls, electrical wires in many colours, seashells, dryer lint, blackened sheets of aluminum foil, quartered tennis balls, Dixie cups, images of children cut from magazines, moulded plastic zoo animals — these were gathered in coffee cans and shoeboxes all over the floor. On the little dining table lay a large set of watercolours and an old anatomy textbook with holes drilled through and plastic flowers sprouting from it. She cleared a seat for him and poured iced tea in repurposed yogurt cups. He sat with anxiety bobbing inside. Beside her, loosely arranged on the bit of counter space beside the sink, stood a few strange objects. A pair of little alien creatures

— assembled from pen caps, wires, pieces of cellphones, bits of shining broken glass for teeth — looked at themselves in dollhouse mirrors. A spiky ball had been built from cigarette butts and painted an unnaturally bright sun-yellow, making it a pretty little object. And flooding from the double door of a plastic toy barn came a blob-like collection of pieces of things, arranged as if oozing into all directions. Looking closer, he saw that the blob-thing was made of many plastic soldiers, or pieces of plastic soldiers, assembled to present a surface of weaponry — pistols, rifles, bazookas, mortars, machine guns, aiming everywhere.

Heather said, 'Don't touch!' But then she reached with a finger and prodded it. 'It's too delicate. Some day I'll hit a pothole and destroy it.' She apologised once more for the clutter. 'Dad doesn't use the RV any more, so he lets me borrow it, and it's kind of evolved into a storage unit.'

As if conditioned by the photo on Boggs's desk, he could look toward her only in fretful glances. 'I should thank you,' he said, 'for helping me to meet Boggs, for the job.'

'Should you? Do you like it?'

'It's always interesting. Every case is different.'

She talked about her father's love of his

job, as a cop. Ellis picked a roll of tape from the table and tested the stickiness of its edges. He tapped with his foot a box of toothpaste-tube caps and matchbook covers.

Into a silence he blurted, 'That's a lot of toothpaste caps.'

'You can find the strangest things at garage sales. I once saw a shrunken head, set out on a blanket beside some cheap flower vases. A price was stickered onto the nose. Ten bucks, I think.'

'It was real?'

'I think so. I tried to buy it, but the woman decided she didn't want to sell it after all. I offered fifty, and she started yelling at me.'

'She lost her head?'

Heather didn't reply, and Ellis, in anxiety, glanced at her again. 'It's more like she kept her head,' Heather said, 'but decided that she'd gotten ahead of herself.'

'Stuck her neck out?'

Now she grinned. 'Way out.' She searched in a pile of construction paper. 'I was just sort of experimenting with Popsicle sticks for Christmas tree ornaments.' She held up a star shape, decorated with glued bits of coloured cellophane. 'The trick is to remember to pretend that you have the clumsy hands of a child.'

They sat quietly while she fussed with the cellophane.

She said, 'John's glad to be working with you. He likes you.'

'I like him, too.'

'But don't you wish sometimes that he'd just shut the hell up?'

Ellis laughed. But she didn't. She made a small adjustment to the position of the pitcher of iced tea. With a feeling of abandoning the shore he said, 'It wasn't a coincidence, exactly, when I ran into you at the art museum.' He told her about seeing her at the airport, about driving by her house, about going week after week to the museum.

'Why didn't you say something in the airport?'

'My mom wondered the same thing,' he said. He was trying to joke, but she only picked up a bit of amber-coloured cellophane on the tip of her finger. 'I was surprised.' He looked at the oozing blob of tiny weapons. 'I suppose I was scared.'

She set the cellophane onto a star. Was she waiting for him to go on? He couldn't go on. He ached and jittered with embarrassment, and then, looking at the aliens' broken glass teeth, he thought of Boggs. Abruptly he stood and said goodbye, and he fled. He saw that she was surprised; he went too quickly to see if it became disappointment.

For six weeks a pain seethed in his chest, as

42

if his blood were attempting to flow in the wrong direction. Until, on an afternoon when Boggs had again left town, the phone rang, and Heather said she needed help moving a set of shelving she had bought.

★ ★ ★

In great caution they didn't meet very often. Sometimes he did not see her for three weeks, four weeks, and he grew anxious. Then despairing. The architecture of his life began to look like lunacy.

Affair: the word astonished him every time it appeared in his mind. All he had done was rediscover and fall for a small, dark-haired, scarred, slow-smiling woman. That she happened to be married wasn't a part of the equation. That she happened to be married seemed simply strange. That she happened to be married to his boss seemed strange to the point of unreality.

Sometimes Heather said that things needed to change. On a couple of occasions, she grew angry. 'We all need to grow the fuck up!' she cried. 'I'll just tell him it's time for a divorce. It's not a big deal. A divorce.' She sounded very grim. It made him fearful. He wished he weren't, but he feared to sabotage Boggs, feared Boggs's reaction, feared the loss of his job, feared the end of his present life. He wished it could be done in some way that would not hurt Boggs. But she spoke of *soon*, and when *soon* might be remained undefined. He had decided that if she asked him to give up his job and his friendship with Boggs, he would. But finally she didn't ask, and he wondered, what did she fear?

The covert nature of the relationship amplified, he saw, its excitement. The sense that they were getting away with something, that they should be ashamed, that no one else knew the potent emotions flowing between them, that they created and inhabited a hidden world. When their relationship became public, it would become something different. So, after he'd been working for Boggs for six years and having sex with Heather for two, he still could not say when the situation would change. Shouldn't he want an ordinary life with her? He did. He did. And he had an obscure trust that it would come. And nothing changed.

And what was wrong with her relationship with Boggs? She said only that her husband had closed away the essential parts of himself. Ellis could see that being married to the man would be a different thing than being friends with him. There had been entire days on the road when Boggs didn't speak a single unnecessary word. And when they examined the result of some inexplicable driver action — a driver who attempted to pass in a blind curve, or run a red, or pushed a grocery cart full of concrete mix down the street with the front bumper of an IROC-Z — Boggs often displayed a daunting misanthropy. 'The only thing that makes humans different from animals,' he said, 'is that humans can be *creatively* stupid.'

One night, on a nearly empty highway, returning to civilisation from an accident location a couple hundred miles into the plains, Boggs had hung behind a semi-trailer for several miles and then, without a word, began edging nearer and nearer, until the front bumper of their rental was just two or three feet behind the trailer's blunt steel framework. At 75 mph, Ellis gazed in horror at the trailer's glowing tail lights, close and large. When he glanced at Boggs, Boggs reached down and adjusted the volume of the radio. Ellis said, as gently as he could, 'What are you doing?'

Boggs backed away. He didn't say anything.

Ellis intended to bring it up sometime when Boggs seemed more calm. But it didn't happen again, and nothing, really, had happened — there had been no collision, no physical evidence. It seemed almost as if he might have imagined the incident. And it was a tricky topic to raise with a man who was, after all, his boss.

★ ★ ★

He met Heather in cars and motels and in the duplex where he lived, but most often in her father's RV, in strip mall parking lots and highway rest stops. The RV's little windows were always shut, the lemon-yellow curtains drawn, so nothing outside could be seen, and nothing outside could see in. Still, traffic always ran nearby making its ceaseless noise, rising to a roar when the semis passed, and Ellis could imagine the vehicles and their motion quite clearly. On the RV's dining table lay Heather's experiments for her classes, or some of her own work — an Elvis bust made from peppermint drops, small gold Christmas tree bulbs glued together into a crashing wave. She intermittently worked for weeks or months on these things, then they sat around for a while, until she threw them away. If Ellis suggested they could be displayed or sold, she scoffed.

Nearer in memory, however, were the movements of Heather's ribs as she breathed, the touch of her fingers on his skin, the minty odour of her shampoo and her own human scent. She called his penis Detroit; her crotch was Los Angeles. And she called it the *recreational vehicle* in a tone that made it a double entendre. In memory, the RV meetings washed together warmly and settled into a few singular, wondrous impressions. She moved on top of him, and when he had come, she stilled him and held him inside her until he became hard again and she renewed her movements. He'd felt as if they might go on this way, the two of them, simply, lazily, forever.

'Tell me something you don't like,' she'd said once, lolling beside him.

'Moment.'

'What?'

'Just the word, moment.'

'Why?'

'It might mean a fraction of a second, or it might mean minutes, or days, or weeks. In a history book it might mean years. It's totally imprecise. What's worst are things like 'a moment or two', 'a few moments'. I don't know how anyone ever understands anyone else when we use words like that.'

'You should let your inner dork out more often,' she said. 'It's cute.' She rolled over and grabbed his penis with both hands. 'Just don't get cocky about it.'

'OK. OK,' he said. 'Let's talk economics — I have a theory that Detroit is about to experience an urban renewal.'

She asked, climbing onto him, 'What if joking is a substitute for real communication?'

'Detroit doesn't know what you're talking about,' he said, 'and Detroit doesn't care.'

Then, Heather's father died. For years he had been in declining health, a decline that failed to halt his habit of burning and inhaling three or four packs of cigarettes a day. Ellis learned of the death in a brief phone call from Heather, and he ached that he couldn't go to the funeral, couldn't see her, couldn't comfort her. She had not seemed especially close with her father, but he had been her only parent from the time she was four. When he did speak with her after the funeral, on the phone, she said that she was all right, more or less, that her father's long illness had helped her to prepare for the end. But she was angry with Boggs; without consulting her, he had sold the RV.

June passed into July, and Ellis still didn't have any opportunities to see her, until the company picnic.

The picnics were an annual, vaguely ritualised event where cold catered food lay on picnic tables and Ellis's colleagues stood drinking beer from cans or shepherding their smaller children through the adjacent playground equipment and the company CEO stood on a cooler to give a short, vacant speech. Heather generally skipped company events, but this year she made an appearance, and Ellis smiled at her and said, 'Hello,' and added, 'Boggs told me about your father. I was really sorry to hear about it.'

'Thank you,' she said.

Then he avoided her. Her presence made him anxious and wretched and a little ecstatic with secret knowledge. There were about thirty people on hand, most of the company staff. He talked and joked with the other engineers and the administrative personnel. He helped set up a volleyball net and hit the ball over a few times. He ate cold barbecued ribs, potato salad, and coleslaw with too much mayonnaise.

Boggs had wandered off and stood at the top of a grassy hill, alone, hands in pockets, looking away. The others had gathered in cliques of three or four, talking for some reason in hushed tones, and a half-dozen played volleyball. One of the newer engineers stood slouching at the edges, as if wishing someone would invite him to dance. Heather had vanished.

Ellis started up the hill, trying to think of

something to say that would make Boggs laugh. Boggs seemed to be looking at his feet. 'Hey,' Ellis called, and Boggs looked around, with a peculiar twist in his lips. Then he smiled, but too widely. And Ellis saw that Boggs wasn't alone, that Heather lay in the grass at his feet.

Ellis wanted to veer away, but it didn't seem plausible that he'd been heading anywhere else. Heather raised herself. 'Hi, Ellis,' she said. 'I was telling John that he should lie down and look at the sky with me.'

'She claims that I've never seen it before,' Boggs said.

Heather settled back into the grass. 'I'm just saying.'

'Come on,' Boggs said to Ellis, grumbling, lowering himself. 'Lie down. So I don't feel like I'm the only idiot.'

Lying side by side on the grass, Heather and Boggs looked as if they'd fallen from the sky. Boggs twitched his legs around. Ellis glanced back toward the picnic site, but then he lay down, beside Heather.

'I haven't done this since I was seven,' Boggs said.

Heather said, 'Just, quiet. Watch.'

The grass bristled coolly on Ellis's back, and the air here smelled wormy and sharp. In the south a rough head of cumulus expanded rapidly, changing form with unnerving speed. Below it, and all across the sky, scrims of haze moved from west to east. After a minute the entire sky began to advance and recede slightly before him.

'You can't paint it or photograph it,' Heather said. 'Canvases aren't big enough, and it's all about the third dimension anyway.' She moved her arm slightly, and the back of her hand came into contact with Ellis's hand.

After a minute Boggs said, 'Hey, Ellis, you've read Chekhov?'

'A few of the stories,' Ellis said.

'His plays are better,' Boggs said. '*Uncle Vanya* is on the schedule at the university, in a couple weeks, three weeks, something like that. I'm going to make Heather come with me. You want to see it? For you, it's optional.'

'I don't know — ' Ellis said. Then he began coughing, hard, for time to formulate an excuse.

'Inhale a grasshopper?' Boggs asked.

'It would be great if you'd come,' Heather said. 'It's running for a couple of weeks. I'm sure we can find a day that works.'

Ellis, set aback, said, 'OK.' Then he lay transfixed, waiting with shallow breaths for the next thing. Heather's hand still touched his.

'Good,' Boggs said.

A grass blade niggled his ankle, and a breeze shifted over his face, but these were only background to the touch of her hand on his, the point of pressure and warmth.

'I'm still pissed off about that depo last week,' Boggs said. 'Have you read the transcript?'

'Not yet,' Ellis said.

'I'll let you try to guess the point in there when he threw his pen at me. The fucker.'

Ellis pressed her hand. She, almost imperceptibly, pressed back. The grass clutched at him while the hillside careered.

Boggs said, 'When the wind shifts, I can smell the stink of that barbecue.' He sat up. Heather's hand departed. 'I need to stop at the office for a file,' he said. 'I'll see you at the airport tomorrow?'

'Tomorrow's Monday already,' Ellis said.

From the ground he watched Boggs and Heather rise. Their faces appeared against the sky. He couldn't read Heather's expression. 'I'm going to stay here,' he said. 'I like this.'

'Right on. Sleep here if you want,' Boggs said. 'Just be sure to get up in time to get to the airport. We're only doing inspections. You don't need to change clothes or anything.'

Heather gestured with one hand. Ellis listened to their steps in the grass until even

52

that faint sound was lost.

His inspections with Boggs the next day went fine. One of the accident's victims had been killed by a burning semi-trailer loaded with Life Savers candy, which inspired a few jokes. Life Takers. Life Enders. Life Whackers. Boggs claimed that the name and the hole in the candy had been inspired after a candy-maker's kid choked to death on a mint.

PART TWO:
POINT OF INFLECTION

3

Ellis plunged down a ramp into interstate traffic, merged left, and was moving with the great flows of red and white lights when his phone rang and Heather asked from it, 'Where are you?'

'I'm coming.'

'Are you going to be late?'

'I won't miss the start,' he said, although, when he glanced at the glowing digits of the clock in the instrument panel, he wondered. 'I have my ticket. You and Boggs can go in.'

'John isn't here either. His plane was delayed.'

'Then why are you yelling at me?'

'I'm not yelling. It's only that I hoped to see you first.'

'OK. I'm sorry. I'm sorry.'

As they hung up, he came off the interstate and when traffic slowed he made himself keep away from the bumper of the car ahead. Over the right side of the road floated an enormous sepia-toned semicircle moon. Chekhov. Ellis didn't care about the play, and he didn't like this arrangement — his sense of guilt was curling itself tight at the prospect of seeing

Boggs and Heather together. But Heather had re-expressed that she wanted him to come, and when he thought of skipping the event entirely his guilt wrapped around and urged him onward. He approached down into the city on a road with two lanes in either direction, and he drove in the left lane. Passing clusters of houses and apartment buildings made orangey by sodium lamps, his phone rang, and he thought it would be Heather again, but when he looked at the screen he frowned. On the third ring he answered. 'Boggs, are you with Heather?'

'She's already at the theatre,' Boggs said. 'We drove separately. My connecting flight was late. Actually, I think she probably could have given me a ride, but she said she wanted to stop at the store.'

'I could've picked you up. I can't believe we're all driving to the same place in separate cars.'

'Welcome to America. Where are you?'

'I'm just passing University Street.' He had almost reached the theatre, but he would have to circle past to reach the parking lot. 'Should I be wearing a tie for this?'

'I hope not. I'm not wearing one. You're running a little behind me. Look for us in the lobby.'

'Sure.'

'Bye.'

'Yeah.'

'Oh, wait, wait, Ellis,' Boggs said.

The light turned yellow, and in front of Ellis an older model C/K 1500 pickup began braking. Ellis cursed under his breath and glanced to the right lane for an opening. Mud was spattered over the rear of the pickup, so that the brake lamps glowed a strange, irregular pattern through clumps of earth. Then the driver changed his mind, and the pickup accelerated. Ellis, muttering again, followed through the intersection as the light went to red.

'What are you mumbling about?'

'Traffic,' Ellis said.

'On the Matteson job,' Boggs said, 'I was asked if we can calculate the Volvo's speed at the time he passed that thing, the warning sign — '

In later memory the instants now began to stretch apart, as if someone had touched a finger on a turning phonograph. On either side of the street people moved along the sidewalks, and, although Ellis didn't see Boggs's tall shape, through the phone he heard vehicles passing near Boggs. The columned face of the theatre imposed itself into view on the right. The mottled brake lamps of the pickup lit again. Ellis grunted,

59

'Turn signal, jerk.' He glanced over his shoulder and swung into the right lane to pass. His car hesitated for a few tenths of a second before it gave a rush of acceleration. In the left lane the pickup continued to slow, and Ellis glimpsed an unusual motion ahead. Unsure of what he had seen, of size or shape or location or direction, he lifted off the gas.

' — with the flashing — ' Boggs said. Traffic noise cut sharply behind his words.

Ellis still trailed to the right of the pickup when the motion appeared again, ahead and on the left, nearer now, on the edge of the pattern of pale light cast by his headlamps, a moving object, a figure, hunched, walking rapidly into Ellis's lane. A sudden sensation of hopeless drowning seized Ellis — he fumbled for the brake pedal, turned the wheel to the right, not too hard, aware of people on the sidewalk. He could see that he didn't have nearly enough distance to stop. But there remained a chance, if the shape in the street stepped back.

But the figure moved, head down, with deliberate speed. A tall, thick male figure in dark clothing.

' — light — ' Boggs said.

'Boggs!' Ellis screamed into his phone, as he at last was able to get his foot down on the brake pedal. The pace of the pedestrian in the

60

street faltered, his head turning, his mouth glinting. ABS kicked the brake pedal up against the pressure of Ellis's foot. He dropped his phone reaching to put both hands on the steering wheel and fought down against the ABS. The figure in the street leaned back the way he had come, but nothing could be done now. Ellis already could not see the man's feet, obscured by the hood of the car.

With a crack of breaking bone and plastic and a slight shudder of the car — amid the continuing ABS-driven stutter and squall of the tyres — the pedestrian swung sideways, pivoting unnaturally at knee height, and came down on the hood, striking sheet metal with hip, elbow, shoulder, a calamitous metallic noise, and he balanced there an instant that went long, one leg up in the air, ribs and shoulder on the hood, an arm thrown out, his head approaching the windshield. Then Ellis shut his eyes. He also began to scream. But over his own scream he heard the violent pop of the windshield, chased by the patter of glass on his hands and chest. A shard bounced off the closed lid of one eye. An impact sounded on the roof.

He looked. He could see ahead only through a vertical area of unbroken glass on the left and a small, sagging, jagged hole where the pedestrian's head had struck, and there the pedestrian pin-wheeled through the space lit by the headlamps, hair on end, pant legs and jacket aflutter, flinging dark blood from a wound in the knee. The legs came down against the road one after the other and crumpled, and then he was out of sight. Cool air streamed through the gap in the windshield, and Ellis felt a painful straining of his leg against the brake pedal and the shape of the pedal underfoot while it jerked with animal movements, then chattered a last time, and the car lurched and halted. Ellis sat gasping, hands still on the steering wheel, foot still hard on the brake pedal. Through the hole in the windshield he saw that he had stopped at an angle, with his right front wheel against the kerb. When he closed his mouth, he gagged. He coughed, worked a chip of glass forward, and spit it. 'Boggs?' he said.

He reached into his mouth to drag out another fragment and looked at the shape of it — a tiny shining cube on the end of his finger — with a sense of incomplete comprehension. He thought: Boggs Boggs Boggs.

A horn droned. He unbuckled his seat belt and stood out of the car. An SUV had struck the rear of the muddy pickup, and presumably the interminable horn was the SUV's.

The SUV had begun to turn in an attempt to avoid the pickup, and it sat at perhaps a thirty-five-degree angle to the lane lines. That collision didn't look very severe. Vehicles were stopping behind the SUV, while in the opposite lanes cars moved by slowly. Ellis saw all of this in a glance, as well as the many stark lights along the roadway, the shining jewels of tempered glass at his feet, and on the sidewalk an elderly man who gazed at him with an expression of curiosity. A stranger, who had just witnessed an accident. Ellis watched the man watch him, until he recalled again what had happened — the figure in the street, the sound of traffic behind Boggs's voice on the phone. He moved forward. At first he saw nothing, only open lane, and he had a surge of hope, that perhaps he had somehow imagined matters to be much worse than they actually were.

But then he looked further ahead. He hadn't understood how far the pedestrian had been propelled by the collision. The man lay beside the kerb, on his side, in a shadowy interval between the overhead lights, alone, his legs inhumanly twisted. Centrifugal effects had thrown his shoes from him and pulled his socks halfway off. Ellis approached at a staggering run. Looking now at the man and his clothes, he began for the first time to understand that this might not be Boggs. The dark made it difficult to be certain, but the man's hair appeared lighter than Boggs's, he looked thinner through the trunk of the body, and Ellis hoped, Let it not be Boggs. This was the only thing he wanted. The man's face pressed the street. Ellis fell to his knees. The man had a beard, but more trim and again of lighter colour than Boggs's. Greyed. This man was probably twenty or thirty years older than Boggs, and Ellis nearly laughed.

A woman crouched beside him. She had round spectacles and small fat hands. Ellis said to her, 'I think he's dead.'

'I'm a nurse,' she said and edged him aside.

He sat on the grass between the kerb and the sidewalk with his knees to his chest. He rocked forward and back, his sense of relief already gone. A broken body lay on the ground, and it seemed clear to him that in his impatience he had killed a man. He tried to recall the decision to pass the pickup on the right — it had hardly been a decision. He had seen the situation and responded. Watching the nurse as she touched and manipulated the man, he felt a great deal collapse on him until it seemed he should be blinded or deafened, or perhaps the world should cease altogether.

'He has a heartbeat.' The nurse glanced

64

over. 'Can you find a blanket? Something to cover him?'

Ellis stood and took a step backward. He turned to the sidewalk, where a number of people had gathered. One moved toward him, and Ellis looked at the approaching figure with a curious fractional delay between perception and understanding: Boggs, wearing a dark blue jacket and a white shirt open at the collar, reaching toward Ellis. 'I thought it was you,' Ellis said. 'I thought I hit you.'

'I'm fine.' Boggs touched him on the shoulder. 'Although I might be sick. That poor guy's legs. Are you OK?'

'I went to pass on the right, and when I got on the brakes it was too late. I hit him pretty hard. Probably thirty-five, forty miles an hour.'

Boggs nodded. 'I saw your car.'

'There's a nurse. She wants something to put over him.'

Boggs pulled off his jacket. 'Here,' he said. 'Take it. Excuse me. I'm really sorry, but I'm going to be sick.'

Ellis took the jacket and moved toward the fallen man, but several people now huddled and crouched there. 'Give us room,' the nurse said.

Ellis tapped a young man on the shoulder, and the jacket was handed down. Ellis stood peering, but because of the others he could see little. 'How is he?' he called. No one replied. He tried to press in, but an elbow nudged him away, and he lost resolve. Traffic moved in the opposite lanes, people walked by on the side-walks. The continued progression of time was surreal. Where had Boggs gone to be sick? He looked down at himself, at the clean, unmarked length of his clothes. The muscles of his right leg ached from pressing the brake pedal.

He returned to his car and stood next to it — a hole smashed into the windshield, a shallow dent in the hood. The windshield's shatterproof glass shaped itself around the hole like a stiff, glittering fabric. It seemed as if a kind of error had been made in putting him into the centre of this accident, if only he could work out the origin of the error and remedy it, he would now be in the theatre, a little anxious, a little bored.

The SUV's horn — which had continued to drone on and Ellis had forgotten — stopped. A police car sidled up beside the pedestrian, lights orbiting.

Peering into the glare thrown by the headlamps of waiting cars, he could make out small intermittent markings made by the pulsing of his ABS. He moved back along the street, counting paces. He estimated that he had braked for almost thirty feet before the approximate point of impact, and then for another eighty feet prior to coming to a stop. Using these distances and a standard friction factor, he mentally calculated that he had been travelling at about 50 mph when he began braking, and he had been travelling at around 40 mph when he hit the pedestrian, assuming that he had correctly estimated the location where his car met the pedestrian — no physical evidence of that impact showed on the roadway, and he could only make a guess from memory.

The measuring and calculating helped to calm and structure his thoughts. He stood at the open door of his car waiting for the police, examining a shallow dent on the roof, where the man's leg or arm or hip had struck before he was thrown forward. He heard a short shrill warbling, an alien sound difficult to connect with anything in the field of reality. It frightened him a little, and only after it had sung out several times did he realise: his cellphone. He found it on the floor of the car. 'Heather?'

'Ellis? Is Boggs there? Where are you?'

'Heather — ' he said. He felt a dread of speaking, as if doing so would make events irrevocable.

'It looks like there was an accident.'

'Yes.'

'Are you stuck in traffic?'

'Where are you?' Ellis said.

'There you are. Is that your car?'

He looked from face to face along the sidewalk and saw her as she stepped into the street toward him. She wore a long black skirt and a short black jacket, clutched a purse with one hand, held her phone to her ear with the other. 'Are you OK?' she asked.

Dark hair cut straight at the neck, teetering a bit on tall heels, she looked large-eyed, confused. Ellis examined her with an aching uncertainty. Where was Boggs? 'Wait there,' he said. He hung up the phone and put it in his pocket and hesitated, recalling how he had nearly laughed when he realised that the man he had hit was not Boggs. He thought, perhaps I am not sane. Then his muscles moved and carried him toward her.

'You're all right?' she said.

'I thought I'd hit Boggs. But it wasn't Boggs.'

Her mouth open, she peered up at him, and he was a little glad to see her stunned. At least he wasn't crazy to be stunned.

He asked, 'Have you seen Boggs?'

'No.'

He stepped back to look around. 'I hit a pedestrian,' he said. 'I was on the phone with

Boggs when it happened.'

She moved to put her arms around him and he felt off balance, then his legs lost strength altogether, he collapsed to the ground, and because she would not let go she came down with him. He sat on the street crying, the asphalt rough under him, a pair of headlamps pressing him with white light, and he and Heather were clinging to each other when a police officer gripped his shoulder.

The rear seat of the cop's Crown Vic smelled of soap, bleach and plastics. Heather bent at the window and gestured with her fingers, back and forth. Ellis attempted to smile, but on his face it felt mangled. 'I'm going to look for John,' she called and waved again and turned away and glanced back and turned away. The cop had already gone. A wire barricade blocked off the front seats, where a CB radio blurted numbered codes.

After a time he glanced out the window and saw, down the sidewalk, Heather running and — it seemed, faintly — Boggs's tall shape moving away in the distance. And Heather ran after her husband until she vanished. She must have taken her heels off, Ellis thought. He examined the door, but the handle was inoperative. He watched the place where they had gone, but saw only the night, and eventually set his elbows on his knees, closed his eyes, and waited, listening to the world's small unimportant sounds.

He could still smell the odour of tyres scrubbing against asphalt. Although he rarely thought of the accident that had killed Christopher — avoided the memory — the smell made that memory inevitable. He knew that Heather would also be thinking of it. Christopher, his half-brother, had lain ruined in the street, too. Here, however, there was not the smell of burned flesh.

4

After the accident, released by the police, Ellis went home. He tried to phone Heather, then Boggs, without success.

He lay awake all night, unable to move his thoughts past what had just happened.

'It's not illegal to pass on the right,' the cop had told him, without glancing up from his paperwork. 'On the other hand, jaywalking: illegal.' Ellis asked if he could ask the name of the man he had hit, and the cop looked at his notes and said, 'James Dell.'

The rooms in Ellis's duplex were haphazardly furnished with a thoughtless mix of antiques and items from Target — the long battered wood dining table had only two cheap plastic chairs, and in the living room an ornate grandfather clock and an imposing writing desk stood over otherwise modern furniture. While the sunlight in the windows gathered strength he sat in a stiff-backed armchair, listening to the clock ticking, ticking, and staggering him forward through time. That Heather failed to call worried him, but he couldn't bring his mind to focus and speculate on reasons, he could only think of the accident.

When the clock had struck noon, he finally stood. He needed to see what he had done, and he did not want to hesitate. The police had impounded his car, so he phoned for a taxi. He asked the driver to take him to the hospital.

Sweating, he went through sliding, quiet, automatic doors and between white walls to a desk where he asked for the room of James Dell. The clerk looked into her computer. 'Are you family?'

Ellis whispered yes, and she told him that Mr Dell was in critical care, room 312.

As the elevator ascended and Ellis leaned in the corner, two stout nurses in teal scrubs complained to each other about their shift schedules.

Three hundred twelve stood open, but a curtain suspended from a curved track on the ceiling obscured much of the room's interior. Ellis knocked at the door frame, and a woman with a flat, reddish face peered from behind the curtain. 'Are you here for lunch orders?'

He shook his head. 'I'm sorry.' He moved around the curtain. The woman sat on a stool on casters at the foot of a bed that held a man with a respirator on his face, an IV line in his arm, bandages on his head and arms. A white sheet concealed the rest.

'Are you a doctor?' the woman asked.

He still wore the clothes he had put on the day before — slacks, a belt, a pale blue dress shirt now badly wrinkled. 'I'm afraid not,' he said. The heart monitor beeped in slow rhythm. Where skin could be seen between the bandages it was dry, pale and darkly veined.

'You're crying,' the woman said.

'I'm sorry,' Ellis said again and raised his hands and pushed the tears off his face. 'I'm the driver.'

'The driver?' She looked at him out of her flat face, then swivelled — her stool creaking — to the bed. The heart monitor counted time and Ellis stood not moving, afraid of moving, of time, of the woman, of the man in the bed, of sound and smell, of air and light.

'I couldn't stop,' he said.

'No,' she said. 'I'm sure.' She looked at him. 'Please. Don't let it bother you very much. I'm sure it was an accident.'

Ellis, in his surprise, said nothing. The only sounds were of faint voices and clangour up and down the hall, of the heart monitor and slow breaths in the mask. The man's lidded eyes barely showed amid the bandages.

'Both legs were broken,' said the woman, 'with multiple fractures. And three ribs, punctured lung, cracked vertebrae, internal bleeding. They're not sure yet how hard he hit his head.'

Ellis recalled the pop of the man's head striking the windshield.

'There are more operations to do. But they hope he might show some alertness today.' Her gaze drifted. 'All there is to do is wait.'

He found more tears on his face and pushed them away. Suddenly, the woman caught Ellis's fingers in her own hot, soft hand. He had expected her to rage at him, expected her to curse him and send him away, and now he had to ask himself, What did he want here?

'Are you — ' he began. But the questions that came to mind were either empty or heartless.

After a minute he pulled away. 'I think I had better go.'

But he stood while the woman sat as if she had not heard, gaping at the bed. Eventually a nurse entered with a plastic apparatus in her hands. When she glanced at Ellis, he nodded and turned and stepped out of the room. For a minute he stood against the wall, letting it prop him, dizzy and gasping.

He summoned another taxi and watched the side window as it carried him home. Children with baseball bats stood on a corner. A handwritten sign taped to a street lamp advertised a weight-loss plan. They passed a series of wide paved fields populated with ranks of glittering vehicles — car dealerships. The cab driver said, 'Nice day.' It was. The land lay ablaze with sunlight, as if some power wanted to be sure that nothing would be left unrevealed.

But soon traffic slowed, and they halted for a time in the darkness beneath a thundering interstate overpass. Ellis's phone rang, Heather's name on the display. He answered, 'Love?'

'Ellis,' she said, and he heard a trace of fracture and guessed that, somehow, things had gotten worse. 'I'm sorry that I didn't call sooner. John and I were up late. Ignoring each other. Yelling at each other.'

'I went to the hospital to see the man I hit.'

'You did?'

'He's bad. He looks terrible. I broke his legs, his ribs, vertebrae, everything. He hasn't woken up. His wife said they weren't sure how hard he hit his head, but I remember. It hit the windshield. It hit hard.'

'It's not your fault.'

'If I had stayed in my lane. If I had had some patience.'

'If he hadn't been in the middle of a busy street in the dark.'

For some time neither of them spoke. Houses flashed by the window of the cab.

She sighed. 'Have you seen John?'

'What's he done?'

'He hasn't called you?' she asked.

'No. I tried to call him, but I didn't get an answer.'

'He was very emotional. He left here saying he was going to kill himself.'

In the window streamed a mall and a thousand empty parking spaces. Ellis closed his eyes against them, but only gained the impression that they would go on forever.

'He got a lot of papers from his desk and spread them on the dining table. All of our financial stuff. Insurance. The mortgage. Our wills. The papers for the cars. Then he labelled folders and filed everything into a neat stack. Then he wrote down a list of phone numbers, his lawyer, his financial adviser, people like that. Then he got on the computer and set up folders on the desktop for all of the financial files in there.'

'He did all this last night?'

'I'm hysterical, and he says, 'That should be everything you'll need.''

'Maybe it's one of his funny jokes.'

'He's upset about you and me.'

Ellis hunched forward and pressed his head into his knees. 'He knows? How? We didn't do anything last night.'

'I don't know.'

'Someone should talk to him.'

'He won't answer his phone for me.'

'I mean someone other than you or me.'

'Who?'

Ellis winced. 'I hoped you would know someone.' He suggested the names of a couple of men at the office that Boggs might be willing to talk to. Then, after an exchange of vague murmuring, they hung up.

He collapsed on the sofa, and there might have been a seepage of sleep. The grandfather clock ticked unvaryingly. Then it stopped — he had forgotten to wind it. He lay in the silence, watching the busy movements of the leaves of a locust tree in the window, sweat slipping sideways down his forehead.

When Heather phoned again the ring startled him badly.

'John called,' she said.

'OK.' He would have liked to leave it at that. But he went on, 'And?'

'He's — ' She laughed roughly. 'He talked about me, mostly.'

'He's trying to make you feel guilty,' Ellis said.

'Yes. That's what he said.'

'He's not serious.'

'I don't know. I don't know.'

'He's horrible. He's ridiculous,' Ellis said.

'He said something about the lake.'

'What something?'

'I don't know. I was crying, I was yelling at him, and in there, with the crying and the yelling, he said something, a lake, the lake.'

'We can't just drive around to every lake in the world.'

'There's a camping spot where we used to go, when we were first married. He went alone a couple of times more recently. He always liked it.'

It seemed to Ellis that he knew what she meant, that Boggs had mentioned to him something about a rocky beach there. Of course Boggs could have gone anywhere, but it might be like him to go to water, to the possibilities of drama offered by water.

Ellis said that he would look there. 'Yes,' she said. 'Should I come?'

'Both of us together is probably not a good idea, is it?'

She offered her car, but he said he would buy one.

5

Under an afternoon sky whitened by haze he walked past low houses, past square graceless apartment blocks, past gas stations, past a strip mall. An adult entertainment cabaret named Lavender. An Applebee's. A sallow office complex with tinted windows. After a mile and a half he came to a used-car lot. He walked among Fords and Pontiacs and Buicks and Chryslers and Jeeps, disliking all of them without particular reason, until he found a grey Dodge minivan — six years old, 87,349 miles. He looked at the interior, looked at the underbody, looked at the engine then started the engine and looked at it again. Light scratches marked the hood, a crack spanned vertically the passenger-side mirror, something orange had stained the carpet behind the driver's seat, but otherwise it appeared to be in good shape. A goateed salesman in a blue blazer with anchors stamped on its shining buttons watched. 'You have a family? Kids?' he asked.

'No.'

'Well, it's terrific for hauling cargo.'

'Minivans are pretty safe,' Ellis said. 'You

don't see a lot of fatal accidents involving minivans. Some, but not a lot.'

'Huh,' said the salesman. He thumbed and twisted his anchor buttons.

'At least I haven't,' Ellis said. When he had written a cheque and transacted the paperwork he sat unmoving in the driver's seat a minute, then started the engine, let it idle, did not touch the controls but stared at them. He took out his phone and called Boggs, but Boggs did not answer. He set his hands on the steering wheel to absorb the engine's trembling. He had not driven since coming to a stop as James Dell flew into the darkness of the street ahead. He thought about driving. In some gentler world devoid of cars and highways and stop lights and parking lots and accidents he would not need to drive. But in this world he needed to drive. When he lifted a hand it shook, but he put it to the gear shift. The minivan lurched from reverse into drive. But otherwise the process of crossing the parking lot and turning into the street was routine.

★ ★ ★

'Human error is to be expected,' Boggs had said, shortly after Ellis began working for him. 'You've got a lot of people hurling themselves around in machines weighing two tons plus, under the regulation of laws that the people driving these machines understand only poorly. And they're going to be making mistakes anyway because of limited attention spans, flawed perceptions, psychopharmaceutical use, poor decisions, haste and et cetera. So you really have to expect that from time to time someone will crash into someone else, and someone will be hurt. Which doesn't stop anyone from suing anyone else for their errors.'

Ellis bought a map at a gas station, and with the map and his phone lying on the passenger seat he drove to the interstate and joined the westward flow. The broken white line flickered beside him, the odometer wheels rolled, the sun moved down.

Boggs had claimed that the accidents didn't shock him. What shocked him was that there weren't more. He said, 'The ability to drive on a road with thousands of others and probably survive the experience gives me a little faith in the humanity of humanity.'

Ellis phoned Heather. He'd begun to doubt himself, he told her. Even if he found Boggs, what could he say?

'Tell him that he's — ' She stopped. 'A friend. Tell him that he's loved.'

'He'll laugh. I'll be lucky if he doesn't kill me.'

'You'll know what to say. You'll think of it.' But her voice was uncertain.

He passed a series of middle-size cities with big box stores by the interstate exits, then ramped off the interstate and passed white-clad homes and the dark vertical lines of telephone poles and reaching trees, the lowering sun flickering yellow in the leaves. He travelled north, slowing in the limits of little towns with a block or two of storefronts. Pizzeria. Barbershop. Bar. Pharmacy. Bank. Auto body shop. Between towns, small ranch houses squatted over flat, aggressively green lawns. He passed a bar with a painted sign, 'The Cloverleaf Lounge' — a vinyl-sided structure with a couple of high, small windows and a sagging banner: 'Bud Light $1.50'. He came down a gradual hill to an intersection where, off to the side, a swathe of raw earth lay levelled and heaped beside two enormous yellow machines. Ellis waited under a green light for a semi to clear the opposite lane, then turned left toward the lake.

He travelled a couple more miles before it struck him that he had been in that intersection before. With Boggs. They had done an accident-scene inspection there — an old motel had stood on the ground now scraped down by the yellow machines. The neon had been gone from the motel sign, its lawn had been untended and overgrown, but a handful of cars had stood in front of the rooms and a shirtless man had been loitering in the parking lot, scratching his thighs while Ellis and Boggs dodged in and out of the intersection with measuring tapes and cameras. Three years ago? More or less.

A sign pointed at the park entrance.

Narrow, high-crowned roads led to three different camping areas, and Ellis drove through the loops of each, past RVs, SUVs, pop-up campers, pup tents, fire pits, tiki torches, lawn chairs, and a few couples, children, solitary men. None were Boggs, and none of the vehicles were Boggs's convertible. He phoned Heather to be sure that he had come to the right place, to see if she had any ideas, and she directed him back to the most remote of the camping areas. He circled through it twice more. Then he drove by the others again, then turned at the sign for the boat ramp, followed a short road to the water, and found the area empty. He parked and walked down to the wavelets lapping and rattling small round stones. Above him, forest loomed and reached toward the water and the spectacle of the setting sun. Haphazard on the beach lay pale rounded driftwood, beer bottles, a tyre. Seagulls rose and fell. To the south a man and a couple of children were prancing at the water's edge. In the other direction, smeared by distance into anonymity, a single figure moved. Impossible to say that it wasn't Boggs.

Ellis started that way. The sun balanced on the horizon and cast a street of dazzle over the water, and the distant figure resolved into a woman in a bikini top stooping to collect stones. Past her the beach lay empty. Ellis turned back and a wind gusted from the lake and pulled his clothes out against his body. Inland, campfires glowed amid the trees, faint and skittish.

At the boat ramp he stood looking at the water, indigo under a cavernous twilight, listening as the waves moved and ticked stones against one another, thinking of what he had done to the stranger, James Dell, and to his friend, Boggs, and he felt that the condition of his soul, if he granted that such a thing existed, was wretched and very possibly beyond repair. That he would have been glad to trade places with James Dell in his hospital bed.

He drove away from the lake, out of the park, through the murk of the forest, between the open dark fields. At the intersection where the earth movers had rid the world of the motel that he remembered, a startled rabbit bolted and raced toward the piles of dirt.

He turned, but stopped on the shoulder. The night had absorbed the twilight and stars glowed. He attempted to phone Boggs, but there was no answer. He sat with a gnawing in his chest, and when he could not bear to be still any longer, he stood out of the minivan. A single overhead street light cast a thin, pinkish illumination on the intersection. He studied the asphalt, the painted lane lines, the timing of the stop light suspended overhead. Little traffic moved through. A black pickup. A silver SUV. The drivers glanced at him and went on.

The accident that had occurred here, three years ago or more, involved a Mercury Grand Marquis — a chromed, civilian version of the big Crown Vics that the police liked. The Mercury had crashed into a tiny Ford Fiesta. The Ford was stopped, waiting for the light, when the Mercury impacted it from behind and sent it careering diagonally through the intersection, hitting two other cars along the way, then sliding off the roadway where it stopped with a telephone pole enfolded in its driver's side and the driver — a young woman, a cosmetology student — dead in her seat.

Witnesses reported that the Ford had been

waiting at a red light. The timing of the stop light relative to the collision was impossible to verify, but even if the light had been green, the driver of the Mercury had an obligation to attempt to slow and stop, and there was no physical indication that the driver had touched his brakes. Also, the driver admitted fault. In fact, he told police that he had accelerated into the impact. He said that he had been *possessed by demons* — an assertion that the police recorded without comment in their report alongside licence numbers, scene information and vehicle descriptions.

At issue had been whether the Ford should have protected its occupant better, but through an evaluation of crush damage Ellis and Boggs had calculated that, at impact, the Mercury was travelling at about 70 mph, far exceeding any governmental test standard. The Ford had also deposited a set of tyre marks that swooped across the intersection and which he and Boggs had carefully documented, but were now long erased from the asphalt by weather and passing traffic. Ellis crossed the road to the telephone pole. At about waist height he found an impression of crushed and splintered wood where the Ford had struck. He remembered photographing it years before.

Scuffing at the base of the pole he found bits of glass — maybe from the Ford, maybe from some other collision. He watched several cars move by. None were Boggs's. Although the case had never gone very far, he and Boggs had referred to it often. The notion of demon possession came in handy when faced with inexplicable driver actions.

He drove up the road to the Cloverleaf Lounge. Inside, the dimness made it impossible to discern the colour of the walls or the tables or even the tie of the short, broad bartender who stood projecting an attitude of everlasting patience. Ellis ordered a beer. When it was set before him he asked if there had been anyone here who looked like Boggs — tall, big, with bright blue eyes and a brownish beard. The bartender, studying a point behind Ellis, shook his head.

Ellis hunched at the bar, sipping his beer, looking around whenever the door opened. He wished he had brought a photograph of Boggs. He felt tense with futility. He drank up and ordered another. The space was filling, mostly with men in blue jeans, boots and bas-relief belt buckles, slouching, laughing, turning from time to time to stare at the TV in the corner where a baseball game played.

'You lose something?'

Ellis discovered at his side a man with a

circular face and quarter-circle shoulders from which hung a sack-like T-shirt.

'Me?'

'Saw you standing around on the corner like you'd lost something.'

Ellis hesitated.

'Maybe you found it,' the circle-faced man offered. He smelled of armpit and deodorant.

'There was a bad accident there,' Ellis said. 'Years ago.'

'Sure, there's been plenty of accidents there.' The circle-faced man grinned — tiny, even teeth with gaps between. 'My girlfriend and I met in an accident there.'

Ellis stared.

'Love works in mysterious ways.'

'I guess so,' Ellis said.

The man introduced himself: Mike. He said he knew a guy who was deer hunting and accidentally shot some woman's dog, and that was how he met her and fell in love. He knew another guy who broke into an apartment to steal a stereo and was surprised by a woman coming out of the bath, so he ran his mouth like crazy to keep her calm, ended up marrying her.

Mike talked on like this and led Ellis to a table under the little TV, where a woman with heavy shoulders and breasts and gleaming wide eyes sat over a glass of cola. Mike said her name was Lucy, and she said hello. When Ellis glanced around everyone in the bar seemed to be watching him — but it was the TV overhead. He searched the faces, and when he began listening again Mike was saying that after four years he and Lucy still had not married, which was his own fault. 'I just can't seem to settle into the idea of being a claimed man.' Lucy sat sipping her cola. She peered at Ellis as if he were a figure atop a far hill and she was trying to decide whether she had anything worth saying considering the distance to be crossed.

A sheen of sweat flashed on Mike's forehead in time with the TV. He asked Ellis what he did, and Ellis explained — reciting his usual answer — that he analysed things like tyre marks and crush depth to determine the movements and velocities of vehicles involved in crashes, and that his analyses supported the work of his boss who testified as an expert witness in civil litigation. He described, for an example, the accident that had occurred just down the road, and as he spoke of it he recalled a police photo of the Ford at its point of rest, with the cosmetology student slouched over the steering wheel, eyes closed, skin pallid, blood seeping from her mouth and ears.

'Sure,' Mike said. 'That's the same one.

That's the crash where I met Lucy.'

Ellis looked at Mike, then Lucy, and she did an odd thing, curling herself, as if she hoped to fit into a crate.

'I was turning left,' Mike said, 'and Lucy was turning right and that first car was hit by a truck and came spinning through and whacked Lucy then me and she spun and I spun and we came together — ' He clapped his hands and held them. 'My door against hers. Our windows were broken, and I looked over and said, 'Are you all right?' and she said, 'I think so. Are you?' and I said, 'Except for my heart. My heart! I'm in love!'' He grinned at Lucy. 'Anyway, the truck turned turtle in the ditch. I knew the guy that was driving the truck, too, by the way, my step-uncle. When I was a kid he carried worms in his pockets to scare me.' Mike giggled and showed his teeth.

'It didn't roll into the ditch,' Ellis said. 'And the driver was demon-possessed.'

'What?'

'And it was a Mercury Grand Marquis, not a truck. I think we're talking about different accidents.'

'No, no,' Mike said, with the enunciation and patience of a gentle man speaking to a moron, 'the first car was stopped and hit from behind and came bang into her and me and then the first car went flying off the road. Killed a girl.'

'Well, that is similar.'

'Sure it is. What did you figure out about it?'

'We had the Mercury going seventy.'

'A truck all right, a GMC. I know that because it was my step-uncle's. Seventy? No. I don't believe that.'

Ellis shrugged. He wasn't sure if they were talking about the same accident or not, but it didn't seem to matter. 'Step-uncle?' he said.

'Banged the jeebus out of my old Monte Carlo. Never aligned right again. And my uncle's still getting his tighty-whities sued off by that dead girl's family. Some good came of it, though, since we met.' He flickered a smile toward Lucy.

Ellis shook his head. He said that he was looking for someone that might have been through that intersection recently, and he described Boggs and Boggs's convertible.

'Going to be tough to find the guy,' Mike said, 'if that's all you've got to go on.'

Which was right, Ellis knew. He wished everyone in the bar weren't looking toward him. He felt small and suspect, and the image of James Dell kept coming up before him. The air here smelled like urine. He had not eaten all day, and the beers were moving in him.

'Could be I saw him,' Lucy said.

'You did not,' Mike said.

'It was a blue convertible.'

'It's green,' Ellis said.

Mike laughed. But Lucy said, 'Sure. Green. He had the top down, and he was playing the radio loud.'

'Did you hear it?' Ellis asked.

'Someone talking,' she said. In the crowd noise and the noise of the television and the thud of a jukebox, they were now leaning close over the table, and Mike's little, bright teeth stood only inches from Ellis's face. 'I saw him pulling away from the corner there,' Lucy said. 'Went south.'

'Did you notice the licence-plate number?'

She only stared.

'Anyway,' Mike said. 'Another drink?' Ellis shook his head. Mike pressed his fat hands on the table so that they flattened and the table rocked as he stood and walked away.

Ellis, avoiding Lucy's saucer eyes, looked again through the crowd. 'What did you mean when you said he was pulling away?'

'He was pulling onto the road there.'

'From off the road shoulder? He had stopped? What was he doing on the shoulder?'

She shrugged.

'Went south?' Ellis said. She nodded, but her gaze was fixed over Ellis's shoulder. 'How did he look?' he asked. 'Happy? Sad?'

'When he hit my car, Mike didn't ask if I was all right,' she said. 'He just sat. He was crying pretty hard. The airbag broke his nose.' She aimed her glare at Ellis from atop her distant hill. She was drunk, he realised; her drink wasn't just Coke.

'That green convertible, was it dusty? Clean?'

'You worked for that awful attorney.'

'My boss and I worked for an attorney, but it wasn't the accident that you're talking about.'

'Mike's uncle's been sued broke, so he's living with Mike now. Mike would've married me if it weren't for what happened.'

'We just present a side of an argument, that's all. It's not personal. We operate in an argumentative, oppositional legal system.'

'Mike's said it himself, that he'd have married me by now, except for what's happened to his uncle and all that that's put onto him. How can he afford a wife, he says, when he's paying his uncle's debts? Since the accident his uncle can't hold a job, gets really bad headaches. But his uncle's the one who gets blamed, gets sued. It was an accident. He didn't want anything like that to happen. But you people come after him, and you take his guts out and throw them around the room while he watches.'

'I never worked a case like that.'

'It must be the same. How could it be so much the same but different? It was this kind of car or that, whatever. You weren't there. I was there.'

He had been certain, but now he admitted to himself that it had been years, and this would not have been the first time that he had misremembered or transposed details between cases. Yet, he kept referencing his memory, and the only vehicle he found there that had been driven in a demon-possessed state was a Mercury. 'You don't remember anything else?' Ellis asked. 'At all? About the convertible?'

'You can't help,' she said.

'No.'

'You could get them to drop it all. You could talk to the family.'

'With due respect, you ever wonder if Mike's just feeding you a line?'

She opened her eyes and gazed at him with liquid, hopeless hate. And then Ellis felt a meaty hand on his neck. 'What's that?' Mike said into his ear. 'Say that again?' He sounded sad.

'I'm sorry,' Ellis said.

'That's all right. I heard you.' Mike pulled out his chair and sat. 'I'm just doing the best I can, like you, right? Like anyone. Right? That's OK. It's all good.' He peered at Lucy. 'So you'll talk to him, but you won't talk to me?' He laughed. To Ellis he said, 'I'm in the doghouse.'

Lucy said, 'Mike's a good man.'

'Really, everything's beautiful,' Mike said.

Ellis sensed the edge of a vortex. 'I have to go,' he said, standing.

Lucy had her gaze fixed hard on him, but Mike said, 'See you round,' and then Lucy's expression suddenly turned melancholy. 'Luck finding your friend,' she said. Looking at Mike she said, 'If everything were beautiful, then it wouldn't be so hard, I don't think.'

Ellis started shouldering by people. In the parking lot he ran, and in the minivan he reversed and turned and accelerated. A mile down the road he stopped on the shoulder and sat in the dark. He watched the mirror as if Mike's white shirt might reappear.

Eventually he convinced himself that the important thing was that someone had seen Boggs. He switched on the dome light, spread the map over the steering wheel, and looked at the line of the road he was on and its route south, the branchings of that line, the branchings of those branchings. Occasionally a car came up with a whisper and a light that slowly filled the minivan, then flashed past, replaced by dwindling red tail lamps and the yammering of insects.

He felt his eyes with his fingers and weighed his exhaustion and his options. He was very tired and the beer had fogged him. He decided he had to try to sleep a little. He drove back through the intersection and into the park, turned into the boat-ramp area, eased into a swathe of tall grasses at one side. A wind thrashed the tops of the trees, the lake made a great open space where moonlight sparked on the waves. He reclined his seat and crossed his hands over his stomach.

The noises of the insects were apocalyptic. The day had been hot but now a chill settled into him. Despite exhaustion, he slept poorly. The figure in the road — James Dell — approached out of the darkness and made noises of impact as he broke at the knee and then came down on the hood with a leg up in the air, and he thought also of the sheet-obscured figure on the bed, the noise of the breath in the respirator, the wife's hand that had gripped his own.

★ ★ ★

He opened his eyes and watched the vague, irresolvable shapes of the trees, then stirred and looked at his watch. 3:11. He groped in his pocket, brought out his phone and called Boggs. Four rings, a click, and the quality of the quiet on the phone changed. Ellis waited.

'Hello?'

'Boggs.'

'Who is this?'

'You know who this is.'

'Well, to hell with you, too,' Boggs said. 'It is the middle of the night.'

For perhaps an entire minute neither of them said anything. Finally, Ellis said, 'Boggs, I'm really sorry.'

'Great apology. Good job.'

'Whatever you want me to say, I'll say.' Another silence, and in the darkness Ellis had a sensation of the minivan floating, as if the lake had risen to bear him away. 'Heather says you're talking about killing yourself.'

'Do you know,' Boggs asked, 'why I answered the phone when I saw that it was you calling?'

'No.'

'Me neither.'

'But here we are,' Ellis said.

'Do we have to talk about who is and who is not going to kill themselves?'

'No, we don't.'

'I don't think I want to talk at all.'

'But you answered the phone.'

'I can't explain it.'

'Where are you? Let me come see you.'

'I've got hold of some conclusions, Ellis. I won't say it was a lifting of a darkness, but more like reaching the end of a road and saying, 'Now I see, this road doesn't go through. It ends.''

'I don't know what you mean by that, but I'd like to.'

'Please, don't talk that way. Have some dignity. And maybe the road ran off the top of a cliff. Maybe it ran smack into the sea. Maybe it was a road done up in gold brick and candy and banners and whiskey bottles, and when I say it ended, maybe I mean that I woke up.'

Ellis smiled. 'Maybe you're talking nonsense.'

'Maybe. It's late. I can't seem to sleep. Here's what it is. I feel as if I'm trapped by the action of some huge machine, a complicated arrangement of motors, gears, shafts, all turning and grinding, and what's worse is that the machine is me, and its design is my own, which caused me to give you your job, to give you my wife, and finally to give you even my own job. To give you, basically, my life.'

'I'm not going to take your job, Boggs. I don't want your job — ' Ellis stopped. Having said this, he regretted how it implied the truth of the rest. He said, 'That guy I hit isn't doing well.'

'I'm surprised he's alive.'

And again neither spoke. It seemed a mutual feeling might begin to seep into these intervals, but Ellis detected none. 'I talked to this couple tonight,' he said. 'They met in a car accident.'

'That's lovely. You ever talk to Heather about your brother's accident?'

'Not really. Why?'

'That's what I thought. I thought it was a little curious.'

The comment made Ellis wary. He said, 'That accident with the driver who was possessed by demons — what was he driving?'

'Something big. I don't remember.'

'Come on.'

'Really, I don't,' Boggs said. 'Why?'

'Tell me where you are.'

'No.'

'I know that you drove to the lake. Then you turned south. Didn't you?'

Boggs said nothing.

'Possessed by demons?' Ellis asked.

'Righto,' Boggs said. 'They're everywhere.'

And the line died. Ellis looked at the phone until the screen's backlight went dark. He reclined in the seat. Heather had interpreted the comment about the lake through her frame of reference, but if Boggs's interest was actually the accident site, then the correct frame of reference was the one Ellis knew.

The feeling of sleep never came, but suddenly he woke to a sky stained crimson.

He unfolded his map again and contemplated it. He recalled an accident that they had worked on a couple hundred miles or so to the south of here. Another somewhat to the east of that. Another south of that. Touring accident sites. Over the years, once or twice, Boggs had mentioned the idea.

★ ★ ★

Waterfront cottages. A solitary and vast weeping willow. The cars on the road had their lights on, then one by one they switched off as the sky's first dark blush retreated before a more forceful blue. Ellis pulled over for gasoline, a bottle of orange soda and a package of Pop Tarts. The stop, although short, sparked an anxious guilt — if Boggs was on the road, he was gaining distance.

He skirted the lake southward, along a two-lane highway through dull, weathered towns like wrack along the shore. Marinas full of idle white boats. A gift shop advertising seashells far from the sea. Outspread water the colour of rolled iron. In the distance dark clouds dangled wraiths of rainfall. Moving away from the lake he crossed a terrain of flat reedy marshes where only the road seemed solid. At a light he waited behind an SUV and watched through its rear window a small screen that played a cartoon that involved many computer-animated insects. He merged onto an interstate and passed between broad ditches and lines of wire fencing while further out stretched cornfields and here and there a house and sometimes a road running parallel to the interstate, a car there moving in near synchronisation with himself. The mile markers fled by. A white pickup tailed him for thirty miles, then he glanced in the mirror, and it was gone. He watched for Boggs's car, not only among the vehicles around himself but also in the traffic across the median. But traffic went by constantly and fast, his thoughts wandered, and he caught himself staring at the lane ahead. A black tyre mark arced toward the median. Another extended straight ahead, stuttered, then stopped. Another showed the doubled wheels of a semi.

When the phone rang it startled him, and

the body of James Dell leapt onto the windshield — he answered breathlessly.

'Where are you?' Heather asked. 'Are you coming back?'

Ellis told her about his conversation with Boggs the night before. He told her that he was going to look at a couple of accident sites. 'I think I can find him.'

'I don't know,' Heather said. Her breath caught. He said her name softly a few times.

After hanging up he drove on.

When calls came from the office, he ignored them.

He exited the interstate and came to an empty road between flat fields of low soybean plants. He stood out of the minivan and walked the road's edge. He knew the place he wanted by the bent lip of a steel culvert that spanned under the road. A Thunderbird had veered off and hit the culvert, tearing open the gas tank. The occupants lived, but in the fire one boy lost thirty per cent of his skin, lost his eyelids, lost his ears. His deposition had been an interminable accounting of medical conditions and complications — a vision of the life that might have been Christopher's if he had lived. Or, at least, that had been the thought that had edged into Ellis's mind before he forced it away.

The state highway department had been

sued for leaving the sharp edge of the culvert exposed, but the case had settled out of court, and it appeared the state hadn't bothered to make any changes. Ellis stooped to peer inside: darkness, a trickle of water moving through. He walked the road shoulders looking for a sign that a car — Boggs's car — had stopped. Cumulus cluttered the sky. Sweat traced slow paths down his skin. When he'd begun working for Boggs he hadn't anticipated how very many of their cases would involve fires. But burn victims made juries sympathetic, so car fires attracted lawsuits.

It had been autumn when he and Boggs had inspected and documented the accident scene here. A lean mutt, white in the muzzle, had trotted across the harvested fields and stopped to watch. Then it wandered over to the hard-sided case in which they carried their equipment — camera, measuring tapes and rods, plumb bob, rolls of tape, orange safety vests — and lifted a leg. Boggs had shouted and sprinted toward the dog. When it ran, Boggs went after it, grabbing clods of dirt off the fields and throwing them while the dog trotted ahead. The chase was hopeless, but Boggs ran until he became a small figure far across the dark earth of the fields. He returned slowly, laughing, and asked Ellis if he knew the joke about the guy who took his dog to the vet. ''My dog is cross-eyed,' the guy says. 'Can you do anything?' The vet looks at the dog's eyes, then at the dog's ears, and then its teeth. After a minute the doctor says, 'We're going to have to put him down.' 'My God, because he's cross-eyed?' 'No,' says the doctor. 'Because he has cancer.'' When the dog circled around a few minutes later, Boggs tossed it a granola bar. Ellis had loved the joke, but when he repeated it a few days later to a woman beside him at the bar — he and Boggs were out for a drink after work — she only granted it a frown, and Boggs, shaking his head solemnly, said, 'I think that's maybe the worst joke I've ever heard.'

Ellis moved slowly, peering at the ground. Looking for what? He was unsure, but he had some experience in looking without knowing exactly what he was looking for. The knack for it lay in guessing where to look for what you didn't know. Was this, then, where to look? But it was impossible to say. A solitary vehicle, a large old Lincoln, passed by, rattling, the driver's grey sexless head hardly higher than the steering wheel, wavering in the lane. It startled a few sparrows from the weeds at the edge of the road, and then the car was gone, and Ellis stood alone again.

Nothing here, but a culvert and a memory of a dog joke. Nothing. Nothing, and what had he really expected? There were a lot of places like this. He decided to go on, but he felt as a chill the notion that he might now be compounding any number of mistakes.

A strange insect of stunning size met its end on his windshield, and over the miles its parts lifted away. He entered again the hurly-burly of the interstate. A little Toyota with glistening rims flashed by in the left lane — it had to be moving at near 100 mph, and Ellis expected to watch it oversteer and begin barrel-rolling down the lanes, bodies flying out the windows. Energy increased with the square of velocity. But the Toyota only dwindled into the distance and vanished.

That afternoon he walked back and forth over an intersection of two gravel roads. This was the place where he had found an unopened package of lime-green boxers abandoned in the weeds, and he and Boggs had spent a few minutes prancing around with underwear on their heads. It was also the place where a Honda had propelled itself deep into the side of a Jeep Wrangler and fractured the spine of the Jeep's driver. Now there were traces here of any number of vehicles, but the tyre patterns were disorganised by the gravel, and Ellis couldn't see a means of connecting any of it to Boggs. When he sat again in the minivan, he discovered that most of the day's hours had already been destroyed. He thought, Should I give this up? Was it absurd to be doing this? Why would Boggs be doing this? He thought, I need to give this up. But the idea of sitting still somewhere — his duplex, an office — seemed horrible, a hell. Driving again, he phoned Heather and talked once more about the idea that Boggs was driving between accident sites, as if to keep the idea warm by the chafing of repetition.

She was quiet. He heard a TV in the background. 'I keep thinking that this is my fault,' she said. 'I'm going to go to work tomorrow. I think it would be good to see the kids. What are you going to do about your work?' she asked. 'Your job?'

'I don't think I'm going back.'

'Oh.'

'If Boggs were there or if he weren't, either way, I would feel like shit.'

'I'm sorry,' she said. 'I know you liked it.' A couple of seconds passed. 'I've been looking at his things,' she said. 'I can't bear to touch them. These folders he set out. His shoes. His magazines. His skim milk in the fridge. His mug that says, 'You're OLD when gettin' lucky means finding your keys.' I hate that one. I've been trying his phone number every few hours. Since you got him at three in the morning, I'll be up all night trying him.'

'I'm not sure that's a good idea. You'll drive him crazy.'

'Crazier?'

'I don't know.'

'Well, he always wanted some magical life, not this one,' she said, 'like a child.'

Ellis said nothing. He passed a semi pulling a long tank with a polished surface that drew the world into shining horizontal lines. 'Enough about him,' Ellis said. 'Tell me how you feel.'

'I'll tell you what I feel.' Then she was silent for a long while before she said, in a rush of exasperation, 'I'm sad.'

He laughed. 'I'm sorry,' he said. But she laughed, too. 'We're a couple of clowns,' he said, 'crying on the inside.'

'I hate self-pity,' she said. 'I hate it. It's useless.'

'Go on.'

'But it's a cruel, cruel world. It's a darkness.'

'Last one out turned off the lights.'

'I was once in a bathroom stall,' she said, 'and someone turned out the lights as they left.'

'What did you do?'

'Nothing happened. I calmed down and felt around to find the wall and I followed it out. But it was terrifying! A dark restroom is the archetypal darkness.'

'Life is a dark restroom full of blind clowns crying on the inside.'

'Is it a crime if a blind clown shouts fire in dark restroom?'

'If a clown falls in a forest of deaf clowns in a dark restroom, does he cry on the inside?' He was laughing. 'What are we talking about?' he said. He tried to stop his laughing, but it only grew worse.

'Send in the clowns,' she said.

His diaphragm hurt.

'All right,' she said. 'It's all right.'

'The crying leading the crying,' he said.

They were silent a minute.

'It's going to be hard for us,' she said. 'To explain to friends. And, to live together, to be a couple together, when all that we've had until now were snatches of moments.'

'I've thought about that, too.'

'Is that why you've gone off?'

'No,' he said. 'No, no, of course not.'

'Listen, I need to be angry, and you won't give me any room to do it. I'm losing my mind. And you're out there. Why are you out there, when I'm so furious?'

He was silent.

'Say something.'

'Do you want me to say I'm sorry?'

'No, no. I don't know. Maybe, I want you to say you're angry, too.'

'I am. I'm very angry.'

'You don't sound like it.'

'I'm angry!' he shouted.

'I'm angry!'

'I'm fucking pissed!'

Heather laughed, chokingly. 'All right,' she said. 'We're both losing our minds. You will come back?' she said. 'I feel like everyone has left me.'

'Of course I'll come back.'

'I'll hold you to that. I can be ruthless.'

'You know,' he said, stopped, debated, went on, 'Boggs mentioned Christopher, and it made me wonder what you remember about when he died.'

'What do you mean?'

'What do you remember?'

'Let's not talk about that now, for God's sake.'

'We should've talked about it a long time ago.'

'Maybe, but we didn't. Now John says something, suddenly it's urgent?'

'You were at the Exxon station when it happened, right?'

'A Mobil station, or whatever it was. I

don't want to get into this.'

'Exxon, I think.'

'I remember a Mobil,' she said.

'A red sign. I remember it was red.'

'Yes, Mobil.'

'Exxon is the red one,' Ellis said.

'Really?'

'I drove past one a few miles ago.'

'I guess I could be mixed up.'

'But you were there, right? Were you actually looking directly at the intersection when the collision occurred?'

'Stop it,' she said.

'I'm wondering, what's Boggs getting at?'

'Nothing?' she said. 'You know him. We can talk about this, but I want to see your face.'

'You're putting me off.'

'I am.'

'Please, just talk.'

'Not about this.'

They said a few empty things. Gaps opened between phrases. She said goodbye.

He phoned the hospital and asked about James Dell. Dell was still in 312, the receptionist said, but no one answered the phone there.

He put the phone in his pocket and bit down on his tongue until it bled.

Later he caught the minivan drifting over the white line and into the rumble strip. He startled awake, but soon he was struggling again with his eyelids, and he had to defer to a staggering exhaustion. He took the next exit and followed a two-lane road until he came to an abandoned Gulf station, graffiti-tagged, windows boarded, pumps gone. He parked behind the building and reclined the seat to sleep.

His watch marked creeping minutes. A haze softened the moon. His back ached. He called Boggs a couple of times, without success.

Screaming, he woke from a dream that he could not remember. Nor did he want to; to prevent its return he kept his eyes open and sat feeling stunned and wishing the night over. But accidentally he slept again, this time in a deep oblivion.

He bought breakfast bars and orange juice and ate in the minivan, watching vehicles move between gas pumps, watching drivers talk on their cellphones with mirthless expressions. James Dell's pallid, desiccated skin suddenly hung before him, as if in a curtain, and with it the choking antiseptic odour of the hospital — he remembered that these had been elements of the dream that woke him the night before. He started the minivan and began to drive.

He drove another hour, road to interstate

to exit, parked, stood out of the minivan on a gravel shoulder, walked the acceleration lane to the point where it tapered out, then turned and strode into fallow land.

Milkweed, tall grasses and clusters of sumac patched the ground. In the middle distance stood a few maples, and past those the land rolled with hill-backs bristling with serried corn. The interstate exit provided access on and off a two-lane that extended straight out of sight to either direction. Beside it, near the interstate, stood a lonely rectangular brick structure covered with extravagantly flaking white paint. On one wall were three large blue block letters: VFW. A red Chevy pickup, at least twenty years old, rested beside the building. In front stood a vintage howitzer, also painted white, weeds brushing the bottom of its barrel.

Ellis moved slowly in the grasses and weeds, some of which offered clusters of small white flowers. When he turned, he could see the trail he had cut, pressing down the plants as he walked. He looked for a similar trail that Boggs might have left if he had been here, and studied for several minutes a couple of weeds he found broken, but he had no experience in this kind of tracking and could make no conclusions. An hour passed. He stopped after each step, examined the ground and its objects. The delicate pale bones of a bird. A pizza box collapsing into the earth. An oval sink basin. Then, half buried in the dirt, he discovered a wooden shingle.

It was from a Toyota Tacoma pickup that had carried on its bed a home-made camper sided with wooden shingles. In the midst of a snowstorm it had slid off the roadway and mired here in snow. A tow truck had come out to help. And the tow-truck driver was killed when a semi came off the roadway, slid through the snow and pulverised his upper torso against the back of the Toyota — like fingers in a stamping press. In the police photos that Ellis had studied, nothing could be seen of the man except for the blood smeared over the two surfaces that had killed him and a single booted foot extended from beneath the semi. When Boggs saw it he said, 'Like the witch in *Oz*.' Using photogrammetric techniques, Ellis had analysed a stack of police Polaroids of tyre marks in the snow to prove that the tow truck had been parked fully on the shoulder and not in the highway's right lane, as the semi driver claimed.

After the shingle, finding nothing more, Ellis drifted into abstraction, staring at a runnel-fed low place a short distance away, full of cattails and redwing blackbirds that

113

moved in bursts and called in trills. The humid atmosphere resonated with the yellow-white hammering of the sun.

Finally he walked up the acceleration ramp and down the road to the building with the howitzer.

It had a concrete parking lot with crabgrass flaring from the cracks. Here and there lay a few scattered cinder blocks. A plastic lawn chair tilted on a broken leg. The building's windows were glass block, and Ellis could see nothing in them. He knocked, and a stout, blue-eyed man of seventy or so opened the door immediately — as if he had been waiting — and said hello.

Ellis said hello and the man nodded and shook hands earnestly and said hello again. 'I'm sorry to bother you,' Ellis said.

'So you know,' the man said, 'this hadn't been a VFW post for the fifteen years since I bought it from the VFW. I never have gotten around to painting.' He scuffed a head of crabgrass with his foot. He wore a brown T-shirt marked with *Harvey Mudd College* and a pendant oblong of sweat. He said, 'My wife, now in heaven, always said a man living alone would forget how to live in the world. But I don't give a damn, I don't have anyone to impress.' He had his hands in the pockets of his jeans and held his elbows flared out.

'A while back,' Ellis said, 'I did some engineering work on an accident that occurred down there by the ramp. Do you know the one I mean?'

'You're an engineer? I used to design ball-peening systems. I designed ball-peening machines for GM and ball-peening machines for Ford and ball-peening machines for Boeing and ball-peening machines for the National Mint. Do you know about the famous eleventh-century swords of Toledo — not Ohio! — Spain? They could be bent almost double and they would spring right back, good as new. Guess how they did it?' The old man stood happy and flexing his hands.

'Ball-peening?'

'Ball-peening!' the old man exclaimed. 'The guys who knew how to do it took the secret of it to their graves and the idea was lost for a thousand years, until GM tried blasting their springs clean with steel shot instead of sand. They lasted longer! Ball-peening!' He bounced on his feet and leered. 'I saved the Feds millions of dollars when I showed them how to peen the money-printing dies. I told them that they could take it out of my taxes. Guess what happened to my taxes.'

Ellis felt his feet sweating in his shoes. 'What?'

'Nothing!'

'I'm looking for a friend of mine,' Ellis said.

'The gentleman in the green convertible?'

Ellis lifted his hands but stopped short of grabbing the man. 'When was he here?'

'Yesterday afternoon, stereo blasting some book at top volume.'

'Did you recognise the book? What did the driver look like?'

'Never took to books. Driver seemed like, I'd say, a man in a convertible — sunburned, wind-blown. He asked about this accident, the one that you mentioned. The guy, Chuck, who died there, was someone I'd seen a couple of times. At the Cracker Barrel at breakfast. He was a grits-and-gravy guy. Personally, I hate grits.' He sucked his lips and looked around as if he regretted this last comment. A single haggard willow stood behind the VFW building, its branches low and trailing in circles under the pawing of a breeze. Traffic ran steady and fast on the interstate lanes. 'I didn't know what had happened at first. From here all you could see was the flashing lights, the red and the blue, bouncing off the falling snow, colouring that part of the sky. The snow had been coming and going all morning. So I walked a little closer. It was a horrible mess. I stood above it, and I didn't know exactly what had happened, but an ambulance came, and I could see it was bad. I remember thinking it seemed strange, that mess, someone dead maybe, I didn't know yet, and all around it was a really beautiful morning. The air had that edge in it, that cleanness, like you should bottle some for later. A clear blue sky coming out of the clouds, sky the colour of those original powder-blue Ford T-birds, the ones with the porthole side windows. And these hills are pretty in winter, white, rolling. I never get tired of them. My footprints in the snow looked like the footprints of the last man on earth. I remember I thought, it's bad down there, but it's nothing to do with me. Nothing to do with me and I feel fine, just fine, I thought, by God, I'm happy. I hadn't had a clear feeling like that in a long time. Course it turned out it did have something to do with me, as I knew Chuck a little, and I felt pretty bad about it then.'

They stood looking at the traffic. A convoy of five semis. A Prius.

'Funny how you think things like that,' he added.

Ellis made himself speak and asked a few more questions about Boggs — had he seen which way Boggs had gone, or paid any attention to the condition of the convertible? — but learned nothing. 'I explained to your friend that ball-peening is badly neglected at most of the major engineering schools.'

Ellis excused himself and returned to the accident site. He'd not noticed anything beautiful about it, which made him think he might have missed something. He scuffed around until a thought came, and he went back up the ramp and knocked and asked where Boggs had parked the convertible.

'About there,' he said, pointing.

One tyre had made a light impression in the soil. With a pen, on the back of a receipt, Ellis sketched the pattern of the tyre print. He stared at it to try to brand it into his mind. Then he took out his map again, thinking, I'll never catch up by following him. I need to jump ahead.

PART THREE:
THE PAST

6

In France, late in the reign of Louis XV, a man named Nicolas-Joseph Cugnot devised the world's first automobile, a steam-powered wagon. Cugnot called it a *fardier à vapeur*. Equipped with wagon wheels, a kettle-shaped steam generator and a tiller — the driver steered as if piloting a boat — it could accelerate to speeds as high as 2.5 mph. Perhaps inevitably, having invented the *fardier à vapeur*, Cugnot also invented the car crash, when he drove the *fardier à vapeur* into a wall. Although no one was hurt, Cugnot lost his research funding.

So Ellis reported to Boggs during a plane flight. 'Thank God,' Boggs said, '*fardier à vapeur* isn't a term that's stuck.'

Ellis had started the research out of simple curiosity, but Boggs had encouraged him — a good anecdote might be useful in court some day. Ellis went on: more than one hundred years elapsed before the first fatal automotive accident occurred. In 1896 a woman named Bridget Driscoll was strolling with her daughter in the grounds of London's Crystal Palace when she was struck and killed by an

121

Anglo-French Motor Car Company vehicle. Witnesses reported the Anglo-French vehicle was travelling at a 'tremendous speed', later estimated to be 4 mph.

'No way,' Boggs said. 'Is that even possible? Four miles an hour is barely a fast walk.'

'It's a bit like letting yourself be trampled to death by a marching band.'

'I don't know if I can even use that in court. It might kill my credibility.'

Prosecutors alleged, Ellis went on, that the automobile had attained such an impressive velocity only because the driver had secretly modified the engine to provide more power. Nonetheless, a jury determined that the death of Mrs Driscoll was not the fault of the driver. Instead, the jury called the death *accidental* — the first application of that term to an automotive collision. Ellis quoted from the coroner who examined Mrs Driscoll: 'This must never happen again.'

Boggs chortled. 'And here we are.'

They had spent the morning inspecting the collision damage to a Mitsubishi SUV that had crashed into the back end of a trailered yacht at a closing speed of 75 mph. Stored in a field behind a gas station, the Mitsubishi was filled with rainwater, its contents were rotted, and a family of rats were living in the dashboard. Boggs cursed spectacularly while they worked, and Ellis held his breath until he nearly passed out.

Boggs bought two mini-bottles of Scotch from the flight attendant and drank the first neat from a transparent plastic cup, a dainty object in his large hand. They flew above a smooth white cloud surface like a perfected landscape.

'Christopher was your half-brother on which side?' Boggs asked. The question startled Ellis; it was the first time Boggs had ever asked about his brother. But, of course, Heather must have told him about Christopher.

'My father's,' Ellis said.

'What was his mother like?'

'Skinny, tight pants, too much make-up. Smoker. I never saw much of her. Whenever I heard about her, it seemed she was moving into a new place with a new guy in a new town. I couldn't figure out the understanding she had with my dad. But every so often he told Christopher to get ready to leave. Then she turned up and took Christopher away for a night, or a week, or whole summers. The longest was nearly two years. When Christopher came back from that one, he was fifteen. He had become much more withdrawn. He couldn't bear to look at us, to speak with us. It was as if our family made him physically ill.

He literally refused to speak to me.'

The plane banked. The clouds had broken, and in the window lay the miniature streets and buildings of an industrial city absent industry — houses lay gutted with constituent elements strewn into overgrown lawns, factories crouched amid empty parking lots. 'I was excited when Dad said Christopher was coming back. But then it might as well have been a stranger who moved into the house — ' Ellis lifted his hands. 'It was confusing.'

'Sounds like adolescence.'

'Actually, I think, fundamentally, he was just a jerk.'

Boggs looked over. 'Well,' he said, 'the dynamics of a family are pretty much the most inexplicable, anti-analytic thing on earth.'

As they descended, the city's empty apartment towers presented faces of glassless window openings, black voids repeated in ranks. Few cars moved on the street grid; traffic surged in large numbers only on the interstate, en route to other places.

7

Ellis did later observe that *the big streets* — Mill Street and Main Street — were really not very big. But they were the only through streets in Coil, a town stuck out among corn and sugar-beet fields, a town with a one-block brick-fronted downtown, several bars and churches, and one supermarket, one movie theatre, one pharmacy, one bowling alley, and more or less one of everything else people really needed. It served as a bedroom community for men and women who worked in automotive factories twenty miles away.

Although Ellis's father rarely held a job for long, he had for a few years managed to keep a position in sales for a concrete contractor. When business was slow, he drove around looking for gravel driveways and cold-calling at front doors, hoping to talk a homeowner into a beautiful, solid, maintenance-free concrete drive. Eventually he was fired, but at their own house the job had already been immortalised — the summer that Ellis turned eleven, the entire lawn had been laid with concrete. For the rest of his childhood, the house stood on a small hard plain of grey, graded for run-off, gridded by expansion joints, the driveway marked by two shallow gutters on either side. Sometimes his mother put a few flowerpots along there for colour.

To Ellis, the main consequence of the concrete was that in the summer the lawn grew so hot that he could hardly bear to be outside. The house itself was built sometime in the seventies and looked much like all the neighbouring houses — two storeys of white aluminum siding with faux shutters bracketing the windows, a TV antenna stuck up over the roof, every room carpeted, cottage-cheese texture on the ceilings, pink tile in the bathroom, green appliances in the kitchen, and an unfinished basement that was his father's refuge and hiding place. He liked it for the isolation, but probably also because it stayed cool in the summer. Upstairs, as the concrete gathered the sun's heat, they put box fans in the doorways and windows and ran them on high, so that loose papers and magazines lifted and fluttered and everyone yelled to be heard.

Ellis and Christopher had always been separated by a certain incomprehension, and Christopher had often treated Ellis with disdain, but he also usually showed enough blithe kindness to pull Ellis's guard down before eventually hitting him with something from his arsenal of understatement — the stare, the sneer, the too-childish compliment, the glance away, the unanswered question, the joke not laughed at. Even this treatment, at least, represented a kind of attention.

What changed in the two years that Christopher was away never became clear to Ellis, and he could hardly even mount a reasonable theory of an answer. His only evidence was a series of very long low-voiced telephone conversations that his father had held during that period, slumped, staring down at the kitchen table, careful of being overheard. Years later Ellis asked his mother, and she claimed to be unaware of any change in Christopher's manner. It surprised Ellis, and it took him some time to realise that her sense of permissible gossip was limited to the living.

When Christopher returned, he couldn't bear, it seemed, to talk to Ellis or his parents or even to look at them, as if to see their faces would give him hives. He made concessions for his father and, to a lesser degree, his stepmother, but he literally refused to speak to Ellis. Days passed before Christopher allowed Ellis so much as a chance meeting of eye contact. Ellis would have liked to return the disregard, but he wasn't as good at it, he couldn't entirely avoid, dismiss or forget his half-brother who, after all, lived under the same roof and ate at the same dinner table. He didn't know what to do about it, and so he lived with it, like a needle in his skin. It pained and pained.

One day he heard over the fans a lifted voice, his mother's, outside. From the window he saw his father, his mother and Christopher standing around a large black coupé. When he stepped outside his mother was yelling, ' — buy this?'

'For Christopher, darling.'

'You didn't buy Christopher a car!'

Dad's gaze didn't quite meet Mom's. He turned and paced back and forward along the length of the car. Tall and thin except for a bulge at the belly, he walked with an up-and-down bob, like a towering bird. He looked bewildered and said over and over, 'It's only an old Fairlane,' as if an old Fairlane weren't a car, exactly.

Then he added, excitedly, 'And the radio only gets AM.' Mom stared, then set her head back, held her arms straight and fisted at her sides, and made a long, thin wailing noise. Ellis and Christopher and Dad watched her, Dad grimacing. When she breathed he said, 'Gosh, Denise.'

She did it again.

Dad slouched, and when she stopped he

said, 'Christopher's sixteen.'

She took a breath, but then Christopher opened the car door and slid into the driver's seat. Mom said, 'You're not driving that.'

Christopher closed the door and stared at her. After a second Dad said quietly, 'Sure, you can go for a drive.'

Mom shook her head, but hopelessly. Then she moved, at a run, around the car to the passenger door and opened it, as if to get inside. But she turned to Ellis. 'Go with him.' She leaned to peer at Christopher. 'Take him.'

While Ellis climbed in Christopher started the car and adjusted the rear-view mirror. Cigarette burns scarred the dash and from somewhere flowed a nauseating odour of turned milk. Mom closed the passenger door, and Christopher glanced at Ellis, in the thinnest possible acknowledgement, then put the car into reverse and backed into the street, and they went away into the big streets.

They bore west. 'Where are we going?' Ellis asked. Christopher already had his left arm in the open window and his right hand draped at the bottom of the steering wheel, as if he had been driving this car for years. He said nothing.

'Do you like it?' Ellis asked.

Christopher frowned.

Ellis put a hand out the window to cup the invisible torrents of air, and after some minutes he reclined his seat a little. He said, 'Even with the windows open, it stinks.'

Christopher's eyes never left the road. His hair licked around in the wind. They travelled over two-lane roads past open fields, past barns and silos, past houses with lawns polka-dotted by dandelions. For miles they moved among trees, then broke suddenly into expanses of empty furrowed fields wafting the odour of manure. Christopher slowed entering the towns and accelerated out of them. Some of these towns had names that Ellis recognised although he was certain that he had never driven through them before. Then, eventually, they began to encounter towns with names that he had never even heard of. They only drove, not speaking, but Ellis felt happy. They spanned distance without any intention that Ellis could discern, and to drive without purpose struck him as original and exciting.

When they arrived home hours later the sky was a lavender field spread with small rough tatters of shining gold, as if something had been broken across the firmament and set afire. Christopher took the keys from the ignition and went into the house without looking back. Ellis stood a minute looking the car over. It was big for a two-door, painted black with pits of rust on the doors and fenders and a broken nameplate on the right side that said *airlane*. Soon everyone called it the *airlane*. Ellis never again rode in it.

★   ★   ★

During the course of their affair Ellis had agonised over it, had strained his memory, had lain sleepless, but he could not recall when he had first met her. Instead it seemed as if she had appeared among Christopher's vague and various friends from nowhere, had come into Ellis's life without entering and instead, like a ghost, had been revealed by slow degrees, in an accumulation of signs. Perhaps, inasmuch as he had initially seen her at all, he had only seen her through the distortions of his own relationship with Christopher.

He did recall one late evening when he had drifted downstairs to the living room where the television emitted the only light, a flickering greenish ambiance, and in this gloom he slowly discerned that Christopher was sitting on the sofa, that beside him an additional pair of eyes glinted, and that those eyes were female.

'Hey,' she said.

'Hi,' Ellis said. She gazed at him for a second before turning again to the television. She sat a small distance from Christopher, one hand interlinked with his. Ellis recognised her but didn't know her anymore than he knew any of Christopher's friends. Christopher had obtained a job that summer mowing lawns at the golf course just outside of town, so his arms were tanned brown and covered with fine shining brass hairs, and he exuded odours of cut grass and gasoline. Turning his attention just far enough to include Ellis, he puffed his lips — perhaps in a sort of snicker, perhaps as if to blow him away. For a minute no one said anything. But Ellis was excruciatingly aware that he was wearing his pyjamas. He made himself stand for a few seconds longer, as if casually, just checking out the TV show, then returned to his bedroom. His pyjamas were three years old, or more, and he had never really spent much thought on them, but he noticed now their deficiencies — too short for his arms and legs, and printed with cartoon cowboys wrangling cartoon giraffes. He didn't know why these facts had not struck him before. Giraffes!

His mother mentioned that Christopher's girlfriend's name was Heather Gibson. And even before he knew her name, Ellis knew — it seemed the kind of knowledge that simply hung in the air of a high school — that she was a favourite of the school's art teacher. Ellis also had the impression that she was a little aloof, but nearly every upperclassman seemed that way to him.

Everyone also knew that Heather's father was a cop. One evening he arrived at the house in his squad car and came inside to introduce himself, crushing fingers with his handshake. No, he did not want to sit. Yes, he would accept a glass of water. He drank, and under his heavy moustache his mouth clamped and winced as if he had a tack in his shoe. Grunted and waited until all of Ellis's parents' attempts at conversation had suffered and died, and then he turned and sauntered out again.

Heather hung out with Christopher on the sofa, or in his room, or rode with him in the *airlane*. To talk with her in Christopher's presence seemed impossible, and Ellis's internal default position held that he didn't want to anyway. He might have never known any more about her, except that every once in a while she walked to their house from school, and one evening as he was walking out of the subdivision he mĕt her alone in the early darkness. His mother had sent him to buy double-A batteries at the gas station. He saw her from a long way off, and watched, and watched.

Approaching, she said hello.

'Christopher isn't home,' he said.

'Oh,' she said. Then, 'My dad's working the night shift tonight.'

'That sucks.'

'I don't want to go home.'

He nodded.

'It's your neighbourhood,' she said. 'Let's not stand here.'

He stared at her until he realised what he was doing and grew embarrassed. He looked around — the park lay across the street. He said, 'The park.'

They crossed the street and passed under a row of poplars. They threaded through trees and picnic tables to a small playground — swings, a merry-go-round, a set of monkey bars. He hesitated here, and Heather stopped beside him. A little further on the land sloped downhill to the creek, and Ellis could hear its burble. 'That's a good swing set,' he said. Below the vertical parallel lines of the chains and the U's of the seats connecting the chains lay a series of scalloped holes where the earth had been eroded by the passing of feet. Growing up, it had been his favourite because the swings hung from an unusually tall frame and he could fling himself to alarming heights.

Heather sat in one and began twisting side to side. A minute passed in silence.

'Do you think that Christopher and I are a good match?' she asked.

'I don't know,' Ellis said.

She swayed forward and back. 'Guys never tell you what they really think.'

He spent some seconds considering this. He asked, 'Do girls?'

'I try.'

'Do you think that you and Christopher are a good match?'

She pulled her legs back, kicked forward. Soon Ellis had to step out of her way. She flew by, receded. At the furthest point of her motion, Ellis could hardly see her, then she appeared from nothing to rush up, passed upward, returned backward, slipped away, vanishing. 'I like him,' she said loudly, to be heard, and her voice changed pitch with her motion, and Ellis recalled a word: Doppler.

He edged forward and held himself as near to her path as he dared. Her hair collapsed around her face and hid her eyes as she receded. 'He doesn't talk to me any more,' he said.

'But he's pretty sensitive inside.'

'Maybe everyone is, I guess.'

She laughed. 'You two are a lot alike.'

'I don't think so.'

'It's true.'

'Like what?'

'For one, you both look that same way when I say something that you disagree with. You tighten your eyes like that. And your nostrils.'

He concentrated on relaxing his face.

'Do you think it's possible to think too much?' she asked.

'Sure,' Ellis said. 'Sometimes all I want is to be able to stop thinking.'

'Dad says I think too much about things like my mom did. My mom is dead, you know.'

'From thinking too much?'

'She had cancer. In her boob.'

He said, 'I'm sorry.'

'It's OK. I hardly remember her. How old are you?'

'Fourteen.'

She said nothing. A set of flashing lights moved down the street. The siren was off, so the lights passed silently. Ellis moved an inch or two nearer to Heather's path of motion.

Rising, she said, 'I don't want to kick you.'

He stepped back again. Then he circled and took the swing next to hers, pushed off, pumped his legs. He tried to swing side by side with her. The chains of his swing squealed where they were bolted to the crossbar, a noise that paused at the suspended zenith of the swing's motion. 'I haven't been on a swing in a long time,' he called.

Stars then trees then earth. Earth then trees then stars.

'Do you have a girlfriend?' she asked.

He swung to and fro once, before he admitted, 'No.'

'That's what I thought.'

She slowed, then hopped off her swing in mid-air. Her silhouette floated against the stars before dropping.

'Should get back,' she said.

He went backward and forward. He liked the cool of the air. He felt he did not want her to leave. He pulled hard and swung his legs.

'Are you coming?'

He pushed off at the top of the swing's motion. The atmosphere felt thick. Then he landed suddenly and tumbled forward onto his hands.

'Are you all right?'

'Yes.' But his hands and knees were scuffed, and remembering what she said about boys, he revised. 'Not hurt bad, anyway.'

She started toward the street. 'Smells like rain,' she said.

The air did offer up a faint mineral odour. As they passed under the poplars he watched the vague form of her back, the pendulum swings of her arms. They were nearly to the street, where they would be under the street lamps, out of the concealing darkness, and he felt a dread that caused him to reach to touch one of her swinging arms.

She stopped to peer at him. 'What?'

'Want to hear a joke?'

'I guess.'

'Knock knock.'

'Who's there?'

'Fuck.'

'I can see where this is going.'

'No, it's grammatical.'

'What?'

'Just say it, 'Fuck who?''

'All right.' She smirked a little. 'Fuck who?'

'No, it's fuck *whom*.'

She laughed. He plunged ahead. 'Do you really want to know what I think?'

He could not see the expression of her face clearly. They both stood as if waiting for the other, until finally she said, 'OK.'

'I like you a lot.'

He feared she would laugh again, but she did not. She did not move or say anything, and that perhaps was worse. The leaves above collided against one another with soft noises and a few cars moved by with throbs of sound.

'Thanks,' she finally said. 'But I have a boyfriend.'

'Yeah,' he said.

And now she laughed. She stepped close and pressed her face into his shoulder and turned her head from side to side, a warmth and movement so unexpected that it hardly seemed credible. Clumsily he reached to the back of her neck, but already she was stepping away.

When they reached the entrance to the subdivision she said goodbye as though she expected he would go in, and he did. He glanced back, and she was walking quickly away. Yet as he continued around the curve of the street toward home he had a slippery sense of accomplishment. He glanced up and saw clouds obscuring the stars in the west. In bed, he lay turning his thoughts and waiting to hear the rain. He lay awake until late, but he didn't hear any rain, and then he slept.

★ ★ ★

And after this, he still felt prevented by Christopher's presence from speaking to her. To go through him to Heather appeared as impossible as building a V-8 from the contents of his bedroom — the task made a mockery of his resources and his tools. He listened to them from his room, but he never could make out words. Their laughter made him upset and anxious; he could not think what they might be laughing over together, unless it was himself. He found a few doodles that she had done, on a corner of a magazine, on the back of a piece of junk mail. They were of random objects. A shoe. An egg. A hand. He stared long at these. At the places where he knew she had been — the living room sofa, a chair at the kitchen table — he put his face to the surfaces, and smelled for her.

Then one day he went up the antenna. He had no particular intention of spying: he didn't even know that anyone was home. His father had had cable TV installed a couple of years earlier, and the antenna hadn't been used since, but it still stood beside the house on a structure of steel tubes. The crossbars happened to form a kind of ladder, and Ellis liked to go up to see the horizon and watch the traffic in the street, to be alone and above things.

A rain had fallen earlier in the afternoon, leaving the bars of the antenna tower cool and moist. He paused at each rung to be sure of his grip. At the second floor, at Christopher's window, a narrow vertical gap remained between the shut curtains, and in this gap he saw a movement, the colour of flesh, perhaps an arm rising. He looked away, to the concrete below. A low chorus of engines muttered at idle in Main Street, on the other side of the fence. He listened for a few seconds. Then, leaning precariously, peering through the opening between the curtains, he saw Christopher, shirtless, facing him, and he feared that Christopher could see him, but Christopher made no sign of doing so. In front of Christopher stood a desk chair. His attitude and posture seemed odd. He twitched. Also, someone sat in the desk chair with a head of brown hair, Heather's, and she leaned toward Christopher. Briefly, Ellis thought they were talking, but then he saw that this was incorrect. Heather faced Christopher — who faced Ellis — with her head at the level of his hips, and he had his shirt off, and his pants were down. Heather moved slightly, put a hand on his naked hip, and he rolled his head. Ellis adjusted his hands, looked again down at the concrete. She was giving Christopher a blow job. Ellis felt a weird laugh rising but swallowed it. Christopher made a meaningless vowel sound, loud enough to be heard through the window, and Heather's head inclined. Christopher took a small step backward. Heather turned and moved and Ellis couldn't see her any longer. Then Christopher, too, moved and could no longer be seen. A soft muted sound of Heather's voice came through the window as Ellis pulled himself back to the frame of the antenna's tower, arms trembling.

He moved down, stood breathing, examining his fingers — they had set into claw-like hooks, and to make them move and straighten required peculiar concentration. After a minute he walked to the front of the house. He wandered down the driveway between the flowerpots — two rows of containers of empty dirt — and returned up the driveway. He went in through the door and closed it behind himself noisily, took up his algebra homework on the sofa, peered at the symbols without comprehension. Had he believed that Christopher's relationship with Heather was immaculate? No, and yet he had not imagined the other either. He had even, in fact, tried to imagine it, but he saw now that his imagination had failed him. He also felt aware that his announcement to Heather in the park — *I like you a lot* — had been rendered pathetic.

He heard Heather coming downstairs, her steps entering the kitchen. Water ran. Chair feet rubbed on floor tile.

Soon Christopher came down the stairs

and joined her. In a low voice she said something. Ellis left his algebra and went to the kitchen. The two of them sat on either side of the small kitchen table, Heather giggling. Ellis went to the cupboard and took down a bevelled glass for milk and observed them sidelong. Christopher cracked a knuckle. Heather traced shapes on the table with the tip of her finger. Christopher looked over. 'Ellis.'

After being ignored for so long, to be addressed by him was stunning, as if the refrigerator had started flipping cartwheels.

'Ellis!'

Ellis sipped his milk, watched the floor.

Christopher walked over and stood before him, so that when Ellis looked up he saw his half-brother grinning.

'What are you looking at?' Christopher said, his tone turning soft-hard with insinuation, then repeated himself. 'What *are* you *looking* at?' He had known — Ellis realised — that Ellis had been at the window, watching. He had known and allowed it to go on.

Christopher reached forward and pushed Ellis on the shoulder with force enough to snap his head back against the cupboard. His milk glass hit the edge of the counter, fell, and broke.

Ellis nearly cried out and took a wild swing, but with an effort he held still. He wanted to be cold, and he wanted to make a comment that would wither Christopher's superiority, but his mind failed to propose one.

'Jesus,' Heather said. 'Don't be a jerk.'

'Yeah,' Ellis said. This seemed insufficient, so he added, 'Back off.'

Christopher nodded. 'OK,' he said. He grabbed Ellis by the shoulder and swung him around and pushed him toward Heather. 'Go get her, champ.'

Ellis stumbled to a stop in the middle of the floor. He hoped she might come to comfort him, but there was only an awkward — nothing. Silence. 'Hey,' he said. She didn't look at him. 'Here's a joke,' he said. 'Do you know the difference between a cheeseburger and a blow job?'

She stood and walked past Ellis to the door. 'Come on,' she said to Christopher. Christopher grinned at Ellis, and left.

In the empty room, Ellis said, 'I hate you.'

★   ★   ★

Ellis bitterly avoided them then, and hid himself in books and earphones.

Several days had passed when he heard,

144

even through his earphones, a collision in the intersection behind the house. Bored, he left his room and passed through the living room where Father and Mother were watching TV. Without looking up, his father had said, 'Don't be out late.'

Early autumn, late in the day, and the overhead lamps flickered into feeble luminescence as Ellis walked out the curve of the street and then between the collapsing brick posts that marked the entrance of the subdivision, into a stench of burning rubber, plastics and other petroleum products.

The traffic idling in the street included two semis that obstructed his view of the accident vehicles until he moved up to the corner: a rear-ended station wagon on the kerb had burned black from the rear bumper to halfway along the hood, and at the far side of the intersection lay a black coupé wrecked aslant over the front. Policemen and firemen stood around the burned station wagon, and several prone figures, evidently injured, lay here and there in the street. The scene looked familiar, like other accidents here, though somewhat worse than average. Ellis regarded it without focus, almost in a state of daydream, until one of the people on the ground sat and screamed, a woman's scream. A cop held a bandage to her face and urged

145

her gently back down. 'Calm, honey, please, please — ' Ellis knew the cop: Heather's father.

And then, with that element of familiarity established, his sense of what he saw flickered and surged. He ran forward. He had not imagined that the black coupé might be the *airlane*. But it was. The person screaming was — Ellis saw — Heather. And the figure beside her lay under a grey blanket and did not move, and Ellis dreaded everything ahead.

He called Christopher's name, feeling the syllables in his mouth, their rhythm slow and clumsy, tasting of smoke and chemicals. One of the firemen caught him across the chest, but with a sudden fierce motion he slid under it and lunged forward. He pulled away the blanket: a hardly recognisable face, a horror — a mass of blisters, blood and blackening, lips burned off white teeth, eyes and nose bloody holes — a blackened shirt, and the jeans on the unmoving body might have been anyone's, but he knew Christopher's white-and-blue leather sneakers. Someone drew the blanket over again, and a hand grabbed Ellis's arm, restraining him. Heather screamed, and the bandage fell and exposed the left side of her face, blistered and bleeding. Awkwardly she swung herself so that her face landed against Ellis's chest, and he felt moisture on the skin. Terrified, he closed his eyes, but he filled with the smell of sweat and blood and burn and the sound of Heather's incoherent voice.

Her father pulled her away, and someone else dragged Ellis back. He wanted to run away, but he could barely breathe and the grip on him was too strong. He closed his eyes, and let time pass. Yet when he looked around again little seemed to have changed. Christopher's car was not the one that burned, because his car was not a station wagon, and the burned car was plainly a station wagon. He looked at the vehicles and verified this.

Then he saw that the sky had fallen off and revealed the dark and the stars. He was seated on a kerb. The form of his brother lay still under the grey blanket, alone, but Heather was gone. Heather's father crouched down, hat gone, hair smeared. 'What happened?' Ellis asked. He shook thinking of how his parents would react.

'Breathe, OK? Concentrate on breathing.'

'That's not his car,' Ellis said and gestured at the burned station wagon.

Heather's father shook his head. 'He blew through a red and hit the wagon, and it exploded. Then he went in to help them. Heather wasn't in the car, thank God.' He glanced around in agitation. 'She was at the gas station buying a Coke, but she saw the fire, and she ran over. She tried to help your brother. I'm sorry. Breathe, that's all you need to think about now. Breathe. I need to go be with my girl.'

She hadn't been in the car. She had been at the gas station. Ellis worked to understand this. And then his mind, exhausted, gave up.

Later, with a feeling of waking, he startled upright in his bed. From another room came a series of small strange sounds. Ellis listened for several minutes before he realised that these were the whimpers of his father's weeping.

★ ★ ★

After Christopher's accident, Ellis scarcely left the house for several days. In the autumn cool the box fans still stood around the house, but they were quiet. Ellis came to hate the quiet; the time would have passed more easily in the summer, when the noise and wind filled the air.

He did wonder at the chances of it, because they knew of many accidents in the intersection, and yet he had never thought of it as a particularly dangerous place, never heard his parents or anyone else describe it

148

that way. No one advised special caution there. Maybe — he thought — if one actually worked out the statistics, it would have appeared no more dangerous than an average intersection with the same traffic load. Maybe he had seen so many accidents there only because it happened to be near home. If accidents tended to occur in intersections, and that was the intersection he saw most often, he would often see accidents in that intersection. And if Christopher drove most often through that intersection, then it would be the intersection where he would be most likely to have an accident.

His mother cried unpredictably in sobs that took her like a seizure, up to and through Christopher's funeral. But the next day she said to Ellis, 'We have to move on,' and she resumed old routines and sent Ellis back to school. She carried boxes into Christopher's room and began packing the things there. Dad, however, looked ten years older, and his sense of focus — never a strength — seemed to vanish entirely. At dinner he looked at his food until it lay cold. At night, Ellis found him standing in the living room, staring at the wall. He slept until noon or later. Often, at all times of day, he wandered into Christopher's room, looked around, then wandered out.

One day a ruined car appeared in the

backyard, a thing crushed and bent across the front by enormous forces. Ellis stared at it from the kitchen window and again it took him some seconds to recognise the *airlane*.

He went down into the basement. His father was working sandpaper over a cylinder of wood. Ellis scuffed his foot, and his father stopped sanding but sat there considering his hand — as if it were a little machine that he was unsure about operating — before he looked at Ellis and asked, 'What do you think?'

'Mom won't like it,' Ellis said, and then he went back upstairs. Despite the collision, the broken *airlane* nameplate was still on the side of the car. He tried the driver's door, but it wouldn't open. The passenger door, however, opened. He crawled in and slid over to the driver's side. The damage to the car had pushed the dash and steering wheel close to the seat, so that he had to squeeze in. Setting his hands on the steering wheel, he imagined the traffic, the stop light ahead, nearing, a car crossing there, the dusk sky beyond.

When his mother came home and discovered it, she went into the basement and began yelling.

She argued and pleaded for days, but his father would not allow the *airlane* to be moved. It was critical to him in some way that

150

he could not articulate. 'Christopher died in there,' he said, as if to explain. This was not true, Mom pointed out: Christopher died in the other car. Dad shook his head. He offered to build a shed around it.

In the next weeks Ellis's father wandered around the house moving the furniture — never far, only a few inches in one direction or another, in a way that made entering a room vaguely disorienting. He began to go through several shirts a day and running laundry for shirts he had worn only a couple of hours. For a while Ellis's mother complained about this behaviour, and then, eventually, she began to ignore it.

When Ellis and his mother moved out, a little more than six months after the accident, the *airlane* still lay in the backyard. His last night in the house, Ellis sat at a window, studying it — under a moon the concrete of the lawn glowed a little, and in the middle of that space the black car sat absorbing light, perfectly dark.

His father was out of the house, no one knew where, when Ellis and his mother departed in an orange-and-white U-Haul. The latch of the small hinged vent window on the passenger side was broken, and the wind pushed in with a giggling noise. His mother made a three-mile detour to avoid the intersection where Christopher died. Winter had dragged to a muddy end, and they passed stubbled brown-grey fields, stands of leafless trees, an occasional barn and silo. The truck's engine rumbled and rattled and grunted, as if straining to the limits of its power, as if the things they were leaving behind exerted a gravity that could be escaped only by great physical effort.

PART FOUR: MOVEMENT

8

The State highway tracked an east-west line sagging and rising through a series of gentle hill slopes, then slumping into a lowland where bright signs and flat buildings latched to one side like suckling creatures — a pair of strip malls, a Costco, an Olive Garden, a McDonald's, gas stations, and various others, including a two-storey motel, of 1960s vintage, which appeared to be the oldest structure here, remnant of a previous age. These were all accessed by a road with a lane in either direction and a centre turn lane — a three-lane. The motel faced the three-lane with a discordant ensemble of pastel yellow, aquamarine and, on the second-floor balconies, salmon pink.

Ellis parked under a semicircular scalloproofed canopy in front of the lobby and walked to the backside of the motel to check the view — the rooms here gazed without obstruction at the highway. He went inside and asked for a second-floor room, in back.

He stepped into the room and frigid air gripped him; mounted into the opposite wall was a roaring air-conditioner unit. Next to it stood a sliding glass door onto the balcony. A green-and-blue watery wallpaper flowed from the ceiling to a plum-coloured carpet bearing a history of spills and heels. A bed covered by a polyester blanket, two wooden side tables, a dresser, a desk and two hardback desk chairs crowded against one another. On the dresser stood a TV, and over the bed hung a little framed picture of a jumping swordfish — it looked as if it had been cut from a magazine. Ellis turned down the air conditioner, then stepped onto the balcony. He stood for some minutes, watching the traffic on the highway, then went back into the room, retrieved one of the desk chairs and set it on the balcony. He sat and watched the road.

To the motel's immediate left Ellis could see a Jiffy Lube and on the right was a drive-through bank. Ahead, across the highway, lay a golf course where people in twosomes and foursomes took practice swings, hit balls, watched them fly, settled into golf carts to drive a hundred yards then got out again, searched for balls, took practice swings, hit little spurting chip shots, stood around on the green talking, took practice putts, putted, all of this at a leisurely pace that contrasted oddly with the traffic's incessant flurrying. The highway had two lanes in either direction, separated by a shallow grassy ditch. Once, a Suzuki Samurai had been stopped in that ditch with a driver who happened to look in his rear-view mirror just in time to see a semi sliding sideways, off the lanes, toward him.

As the afternoon passed the traffic in the westbound lanes clotted and dragged into a low-speed crawl, which didn't begin to clear until a couple of hours later. Ellis phoned Heather and told her where he was, what he was doing, described the motel. 'Do you think it will work?' she asked.

'Driving, I could miss him by a minute, I could pass him in the night. Statistically, my chances are probably better in one place.'

'It sounds more healthy. Give yourself some downtime.'

'I guess.'

Soon the sky was hung with a scatter of white stars, and the traffic had thinned to a swift motion of lights pressing the speed limit.

He wondered if Boggs might come here at night. He thought it unlikely. No one visited old battlefields in the dark.

Hungry, he stepped back into the room and then stood looking around, a little dazed, after so much driving, with the shock of still being in the same place. He went out the front of the motel to the three-lane and walked on the shoulder. At the Target he bought a bag of new clothes, then crossed the parking lot to the Olive Garden and consumed portions of penne and chicken. When he finished his stomach complained against the quantities, and he sat watching his glass of beer, the tiny bright sparks there that rose straight upward. His waitress stopped to comment on his sunburn, and when he told her he'd had his arm hung out of the window of his car for a couple of days, she talked about her car, a Buick that smoked when she started it.

He returned to the motel, slept, woke, dressed and set himself on the balcony as the sky, still sunless, began to brighten. Boggs will come, he assured himself.

On the morning of the accident the highway had been glazed by a light rain. When the man in the Suzuki in the ditch looked at his mirror and saw the jackknifed, overturning semi — the assets of the hauling companies were, like fires, beacons for hopeful litigants, so Ellis and Boggs had often been involved in cases with semi-trailer trucks — coming broadside toward him, he ducked. The roof of the Suzuki was crushed flat, and the driver had to be cut out with a Jaws of Life, but he walked away. The semi, however, continued into the opposing lanes, flipping. Even more fortunate than the man who walked away from the Suzuki were the occupants of a Ford Taurus that passed under the trailer at the apex of its flight — police photos showed the Taurus parked beside the road, undamaged, except for the radio antenna, which had been hit by the flying semi and bent to a right angle, like a crooked finger.

Then the semi flopped onto the roadway behind the Ford and a fifteen-year-old Dodge pickup pulling a pop-up camper trailer crashed into the trailer's roof. Several seconds passed before a Toyota Highlander, travelling at approximately 64 mph, struck the pickup from behind, smashing the pop-up camper to pieces and forcing the trailer hitch into the Dodge's gas tank, igniting a hot fire that spread rapidly forward and backward. The pickup burned, the Toyota burned, the semi and its load of discount brand furniture burned. Two fatalities in the pickup and three in the Toyota. Only the driver of the semi, who extracted himself from the overturned cab with broken arms, survived.

Boggs was contacted just days after the accident by an attorney associated with the manufacturer of the pickup. After landing at the airport, Boggs and Ellis had driven first to look at the Toyota, which was held in a vehicle storage yard of a kind that Ellis — still early in his career — had never seen before, a collecting place for vehicles involved in ongoing disputes. Towering racks held vehicles atop one another, three-high, like shelved pieces in a gigantic museum. A rack ran five hundred feet or so, ended at an aisle, and then began another set of racks, and these rows of racked vehicles ran out to a distance of a half-mile or more. Big trucks with long lifting forks hurtled between the rows and spun at speed around the corners.

They found the Toyota, and Boggs hailed a forklift to pull it from its second-level rack and set it on the ground. The forklift then went away, diesel engine gnashing. Through the stacked vehicles, more of the lifting trucks were sometimes visible, charging around like beasts with great horns. Ellis looked at the vehicles to either side of himself — a Yukon with the front end flattened as if a slab of concrete had landed on it; a Dodge Ram with the circular imprint of a wheel in the damage of its grille; a Mini with the sheet metal ripped off one side as if it had run into a big planing saw.

'Ellis, hello?' Boggs said. 'Still with us? What's going on in your noggin?' He was unwinding a plumb bob. He had already laid four tape measures around the Toyota.

'Just looking.'

'And thinking?'

'Not really.'

Boggs grinned. 'Now that's a talent.' Boggs shuffled and kicked his feet, still grinning. 'As for me,' he said, 'my dancing frightens children and makes adults nauseous.'

When they came to the scene — here, the place that Ellis now sat watching — the tyre marks had been still visible on the road, only a little faded. And as they worked at documenting them, Ellis glanced at their photos of the vehicles' tyre treads and noticed that the police had confused the tyre marks of the pickup and the Toyota. Which was bad for their client, the defendant's attorney, because it meant that the Toyota had braked longer than the police had assumed, and hit the pickup at a lower speed, which made the breakout of a fire seem less reasonable.

'Of course,' Ellis said, when he showed the error to Boggs, 'we could pretend we didn't notice.'

Boggs cocked his head. 'That would be a little unscrupulous, wouldn't it?' He held Ellis's gaze a second, then shrugged. 'Anyway, when you start doing stuff like that in this business, it catches up. The other guys are smart, too, and we end up looking stupid.'

Much later, Ellis described that conversation to Heather, and the shame he'd felt. She had, slowly, smiled, and asked, 'But you still love me more than him, don't you?'

Watching the traffic and the golf course, sorting his moods, he passed the day. A membrane of tension that had been stretched through his mind seemed to be weakening. He'd never understood the use of idle vacations, of endless sitting under the sun, but maybe this was it.

Immediately behind this thought, however, regret flipped itself back into view, and with a sense of compulsion he called the hospital and asked for room 312. The fifth ring cut off as the phone picked up. 'Hello?' Mrs Dell said, tentative.

Ellis hesitated.

'Hello?'

'I'm Ellis Barstow. I stopped in a couple of days ago.'

'Yes?'

'I was wondering if there's any change in your husband's condition.'

'They cut him open and did some things, to alleviate pressure, I think. And tests. Scans. He looks — ' She was silent. 'Not good.' She breathed. 'They say wait. Wait and see. They try to be kind, but they make me feel like a child.'

'I'm sure they're doing their best.'

'Sometimes when I ask a question there's a strange look. I wonder if maybe they just don't like to say, 'I don't know.' Sometimes I wonder if they know anything, really.'

'They're doing what they can,' he said, without conviction.

'Fifty per cent,' she said. 'I asked if he would live. Thirty said another. Per cent.'

'I'm sorry.' A pickup glided over the highway before him, pulling a camper trailer sheathed in aluminum, the sun dancing on it.

'As if we were talking about the humidity.'

'It is meaningless,' he said.

'I can't even think about it.' She added, in a odd tone of complaint, 'He loves me.'

'Of course.'

'He loves music. He's an excellent dancer. I doubt if he'll be able to dance any more.'

'I hope so.'

'I should ask what per cent they have on dancing.'

Ellis laughed but caught himself and said again, 'I'm sorry.'

'No, no. You're kind to listen to me.'

Some seconds passed.

'Are you still there?' she asked.

'I am.'

'I'll let you go.'

That night he returned to the Olive Garden. He had the Buick-driving waitress again. She was heavy from the waist down, her face sagging with fatigued skin, but her smile was broad and earnest. She interpreted his return as a compliment to the food. She said the cooks here took greater care than at the Red Lobster where she used to work, and she attempted to talk him into a dessert. He said no but ordered another drink.

The restaurant emptied, he sat contemplating his beer, thinking his work with Boggs had made him strange. No one except Boggs saw the road and the world as he did, so that they seemed to live in a world of the same stuff as everyone else, but terribly rearranged. No wonder Boggs had become his friend. No wonder he didn't know what to do now except to look for Boggs. His waitress brought him a piece of chocolate cherry cake, whispering, 'Free free free!' It would just be thrown away, she said. He began eating only to placate her, but the stuff tasted marvellous. He forked through it slowly, then worked the crumbs up one by one, thinking to himself that it might be as good as anything that he had ever eaten. This idea made him teary-eyed. The waitress stopped to pat his wrist. 'It does that to me, too.'

Late the next morning he was sitting on the balcony again when his phone rang. He answered, and Heather said, 'I'm here.'

'You're where?'

'The guy at the desk won't tell me which room you're in.'

'How can you be here?'

'By the miracle of the Dwight D. Eisenhower Interstate Highway System. Will you tell me your room number?'

'I'm just surprised!' He told her the room number and sat waiting. Giddy. Anxious. She seemed to take a long time. And then yet longer, so that he began to worry that he had hallucinated her call, that he had been alone for too long with his own brain, and now some of the synapses were firing up delusional echoes and distortions.

When a knock sounded at the door, he flung it open. Heather stood there — small in the dim hallway, wearing a snug black T-shirt, jeans, flip-flops, hair pulled back, eyes red, tired, intent on him.

'Please — ' he said, reaching. They clung to each other and soon were talking energetically, nonsensically. Suddenly Ellis lifted her and dropped her on the bed.

They made love with the clumsiness of

delirium, then lay cupped together until Ellis stood and dressed. They talked and joked about her drive, about the weather. She talked to the ceiling and Ellis drifted around the room. He came to the balcony door — now, although it was a Saturday, the traffic had begun again thickening and slowing in the westbound lanes. He hoped that Boggs hadn't come and gone.

'I was a little afraid you'd send me away,' Heather said. She laughed. Without leaving the bed she was pulling on clothes.

'That's why you didn't you tell me you were coming?' he asked. 'I'm glad you're here.'

'Everyone loves a surprise?' she said.

He laughed. 'I don't care.'

She went into the bathroom, and he heard the water running. He opened the balcony door and stepped out. A couple of crows hopped in the grass between the highway and the motel. He heard her emerge from the bathroom. 'Is John out there?' she called.

'Nope.'

A few seconds passed. 'Hey,' she said.

He turned from the highway to look at her. She sat on the foot of the bed, and she seemed to be looking at the highway behind him. He glanced over to see if something were happening there.

She said, 'I'll go if you want.'

'No, no.' He hesitated, then moved into the room to stand in front of her. He knew enough to wait for her to go on.

'What are we doing?' she asked.

'What do you mean?' It had been a mistake, apparently, to go onto the balcony. But she knew why he was here. 'We're in a motel room, talking.'

'Really?'

'Yes.'

Her gaze collapsed to the floor. 'Could you possibly stop calculating what you say to the decimal place?' She gripped the edge of the bed with her hands, then straightened and stood and moved and touched the bed, the wallpaper, the TV.

He said, 'I'm sorry — '

'Don't,' she said. Her face blushed, splotching white in the scars. 'I just sometimes keep wondering,' she said, 'if there's anything more between us than shared disasters. What are we doing? What kind of fucked-up catastrophe of circumstance are we?' She laughed, not happily.

His breath shook. 'We're just two people in a room.'

'You're the brother of my dead boyfriend. You work for my husband, and you're his friend, and he's gone insane. It's not a good situation. It's a very complicated, very awkward and very bad situation.'

By now a liquid and opaque dread had filled him. His glance strayed between the tension in her neck, the highway, the sword-fish. 'You drove out here to break up with me?'

'We're just bonded by trauma,' she said.

'I didn't even like Christopher,' he said. 'If you think that's all I have invested in this — '

A diesel went by with jake brakes thundering. He glanced toward it, and she said, 'OK, go. Go. Go look for your buddy.'

'I'm here to watch for Boggs.'

'OK,' she said. 'Go ahead.'

He went onto the balcony and sat. He locked his gaze onto the roadway.

Some minutes passed.

In the room, something crashed.

He went back in as she pulled over the two bedside tables, then the desk. She pushed over a desk chair and then yanked the bedclothes to the floor. She turned and stood before him, gasping, her face strained.

'Calm down,' he said.

'Stop that! I haven't slept in days. I don't know what's happened to my life. I can't stop crying. I don't know what anyone wants. And you say calm down.'

'I'm sorry,' he said.

'Don't say that.'

Then he didn't know what to say.

In the silence, she reached up with curious gentleness, as if grasping at a butterfly. He braced for her to strike him. But she brought her hand to her own face, gripped her cheek, and pulled down, clawing, nails trailing blood.

In surprise he shouted and lunged, and they fell together onto the bed. 'I hate you,' she said, while he fumbled to restrain her arms. A small woman, but strong. Finally he pinned her, and she said, 'I hate everything.'

He panted. Blood trickled from her face. 'Stop this,' he said. 'Stop this.' She only stared at him, and he cried, 'Stop this! I didn't ask you to come here.'

'No, you didn't.' But the resistance had gone from her arms.

He discovered he was squeezing her harder than he needed. He rolled away, stood flexing his hands. She lay unmoving except to breathe irregularly, staring at the ceiling, eyes streaming. His body shook, bright and hot. He sat on the floor. 'You're OK?'

She said nothing, went into the bathroom. When she came out, holding a washcloth to her face, his adrenalin had drained off, leaving him sagging. She sat beside him.

His heartbeat slowed.

She touched his hand. 'I'm sorry,' she said. 'Let's not use that word.'

She giggled a little, weakly, or nervously. He shook his head. Then, in a loss of control, he, too, laughed.

'Go watch for John,' she said. 'I'll join you in a minute.' He sat moving his fingers experimentally before he stood and went onto the balcony. Time passed, and when he looked back into the room, all the furniture had been set upright again, and she was gone.

To find a clear thought was difficult. He'd never seen her do anything like this before, and he couldn't guess what she might do now.

He sat, then stood again, and tried to analyse, to review the variables of the problem. Now, particularly, when everything and everyone had turned strange, it seemed important to be exact. Heather had been his half-brother's girlfriend. She had liked his half-brother. Ellis, however, had not liked his half-brother. This difference had been shrouded behind the fact of his half-brother's death. Then, she had led Ellis to his job, and thus to his boss and friend Boggs. He liked Boggs. Heather, who was married to Boggs, did not like Boggs; or, at least, she did not love him. Not any more. And now, having learned of the affair between his subordinate and his wife, Boggs threatened suicide. The shape of the relationships was not a triangle but a square bisected along a diagonal:

Ellis   Boggs

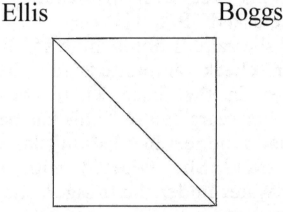

Christopher   Heather

But this failed to adequately capture the problem, because it also had a temporal aspect, which extended along a third dimension. He tried to visualise a graphical shape for the events on that axis, but it eluded him.

But the situation was not a technical problem. Perhaps to try to understand it as such would only lead to insanity. How then to understand? To see each other clearly? How to prevent everything from being contaminated with guilt, doubt, resentment, anger? Was that why she was gone? Was she gone?

A half-hour later, she knocked on the door and came into the room with two cold bottles of Chardonnay and a package of plastic cups. She offered one to him.

He took the cup, but set it aside and rubbed his face with his hands. 'Was that you?' he asked. 'Before?'

'No,' she said. 'I don't think so.' The marks on her cheek amounted to three small scratches, in the place where the fire had scarred her years before. 'This has been hard.'

'It made me feel like I didn't know you.'

'It's over.' She fidgeted with the wine bottle. 'Water under the bridge?' she said. 'Or did I burn it?'

'No, you didn't burn it,' he said. 'But you really scared it.' He held out his plastic cup. They sat with their wine, watching the road. After some minutes he said, 'I figure he won't come here after dark, when he can't see anything.'

She refilled his cup.

They drank the two bottles of wine.

Into the evening they talked about inconsequentials and trivia, and he found himself laughing hysterically as the day's end came with the sun cutting under clouds boiling in from the west, so that the fading light and the arriving cumulus appeared like a massive collapse, an avalanche of glory pounding down. When the sun had gone from sight he suggested the Olive Garden, but she wanted to walk farther, to a family-owned Mexican restaurant in one of the strip malls. The piñatas nailed to the wall were dusty, the carpet filthy. A pudgy girl of five or six wandered in and out of the kitchen gripping a naked Barbie doll. But the margaritas tasted strong; the salty, greasy food filled him.

'How long will you stay here?' Heather asked.

'How long will you?'

'Why can't you answer a question?'

'A week.' He said it and felt strings and cords all through him jerk tight. Why a week? He had no idea. And what would he do then? But he had announced it, and he let it stand.

'Today is Saturday. You got here on Thursday? At sunset Wednesday, we go home?'

He said yes.

★ ★ ★

The next day he sat on the balcony, and Heather sat with him, or she went back into the room and turned on the TV, or she slipped out of the room without notice. She returned once with a change of clothes, a magazine, chewing gum, and then a second time with food and wine. With the TV on, she called out comments on a home-decorating show. On the room's desk she had already accumulated a little pile of things she'd found along the road and in parking lots — buttons and dimes, several bluish pebbles, a few coffee stirrers, a pocket-sized calendar.

He watched the wind striking the eighth-hole flag. A man stood on the balcony two rooms over and shouted into his cellphone about estate planning. 'No, no! There are springing and *non*-springing powers of attorney!' For a long while in the mid-afternoon Ellis heard nothing from the room behind him except for the grunts and subdued voices of a tennis match on the TV and the fainter noise of ice crunching between Heather's teeth.

He asked, 'You play tennis?'

'I've made things out of tennis balls. You?'

'No.'

'It's kind of sad.'

'Tennis is sad? Tennis is love and matches.'

'That we don't know these things about each other.'

She sat on the balcony with him, and through the remainder of the afternoon they talked in a lazy, intermittent, negligible way. It resonated in him differently than their conversations in the past, and it struck him that they'd never before had time like this. The sun might track over the sky, from its first appearance to its end, and the two of them remained together, not hiding, not racing the hour. The traffic always looked the same, more or less.

'Maybe we should stay here forever,' he said.

She smiled.

The sun hung a couple of fingers above the horizon, and a fine layer of dust, or pollen, or pollution, had settled over his skin. 'When we leave here,' Heather asked, 'what'll we do?'

'Live together,' he said. 'Get married?'

'If John just runs away and we never hear from him again, I'm not sure how difficult it'll be to get a divorce.'

He wasn't sure either. 'Should've done it a long time ago,' he said.

She stood and went into the room.

The horizon line began to eat into the sun. When he went back into the room, she was lying on the bed, watching him. 'Why didn't you say something?'

'What?'

'If you'd said something, I would have divorced him a year ago,' she said. 'You pursued me, you found me. You knew what you wanted. I liked that. And me, I should make that jump alone? Me? I've never succeeded at anything. Never. And now I'm supposed to leave everything, with no word from you. When I've failed at my marriage. I've failed as an artist. I try to teach art to little kids, and the kids hate me.' The left side of her lip twitched. She looked toward the room's door. 'I couldn't pull your brother out of that car.'

He crossed and uncrossed his arms. He lowered himself to the bed. He said, 'I'm sorry.' She groaned. 'I am,' he said.

★ ★ ★

They lay in opposite directions on the bed, his head at her feet, with a hand gripping her ankle. They were naked. Street lights threw pale slants through the half-drawn windows. A yellow light cast on the ceiling advanced, strained to reach to the ceiling's middle point, held there, then collapsed back in a rush, only to return and work to reach the middle of the ceiling again. He watched this cycle several times, with empty fascination, like the action of waves on a beach, until eventually he became aware, too, of the traffic noise and realised that the light on the ceiling was caused by the passing of vehicles' headlamps. He turned from it and moved his other hand to her other ankle, so that he held both.

'Your kids don't hate you,' he said.

'A few do.'

'You're not a failure.'

She said nothing.

'I didn't know,' he tried, 'that you felt your art was a disappointment.'

'Well,' she said, shifting a little, 'I don't take it seriously, which is the problem. I don't have the confidence to take it seriously.'

'You should.'

'It doesn't matter. I'm not very creative or interesting. I'm not very smart. I don't have confidence. I don't know what I want.' She laughed. 'Should I go on?'

'You don't believe any of that, I hope.'

He heard the sheets shift as she shrugged. 'I'm just telling you how I feel. I think some of my problems are just a part of growing up without a mother. No one taught me how to live as a woman in the world. I hate this kind of talk. Let's talk about something else.'

'I'm sure you can be a great artist if you want. I'll insist. I'll lock you in a dungeon and bring you pieces of trash to work with.'

'Maybe I just want to paint kittens and rainbows. Flags and eagles.'

'Eagles and kittens?'

'Kitten-eating eagle flags,' she said.

'Sounds more like your style.'

He clung to her ankles and felt her settle a hand between his thighs. Eventually they slept that way.

The next day she came and went again, returning with food, with sunscreen. He waited for the times when she was out before he used the bathroom. He didn't like to admit that he had to abandon his post even for that. On the room's desk lay a considerable pile of cigarette butts that she had collected and a cellophane-wrapped 100 count box of matchbooks that she had found beside the road. They were bright red, with Ziggy's Smokehouse written on them in a white script, and an address several states over. Later she came out onto the balcony with a motel pen and pad of paper. She drew a delicate scene in miniature of the highway, and the eighth fairway and flag, in blue ballpoint, cross-hatched for texture. Looming over the scene and looking down were giant flower heads with elaborately realistic, human, pinched faces, as if they'd just smelled something terrible. One smoked a cigar. Heather rolled the sleeves of her T-shirt to her shoulders, and turned her face to the sun. 'I always wanted to live on a beach.'

'We can do that,' he said.

That night people on the golf course played with flashlights, hitting green-glowing balls. Ellis and Heather left the room and walked for dinner. The waitress who had given him cake sat in the booth with them to tell an incoherent story about her husband's hair plugs. Back at the motel room, they joked of Detroit and Los Angeles, of how one might find a Little Detroit in Los Angeles. The next morning he arose before her and sat in the early cool outside, thinking pleasantly of sleeping in the same bed with her through a night and rising and not leaving, of talking lazily with her, of watching her step from the shower towel-wrapped and hair wet, of detecting the scent of her in the bed and in her towel, of watching her stretch in the morning, up on her toes. Of listening to the noise of her urinating, of the sharp odour of her shit in the bathroom, domestic intimacies that he seized and understood without complication. Much seemed unmanageably complicated, but these things were simple and granted him a knowledge of her that he had lacked.

She sat on the balcony toying with the matchbooks, folding and fitting their flaps together in various schemes of assembly. 'What are you trying to make?' he asked.

She shrugged. 'I don't know.' She pulled them apart and began again and again, sometimes working in a couple of Marlboro cigarette packs she had also found. She created something like a spiral staircase. Then took it apart and worked out a swanlike creature. She had a few pieces of broken mirror as well, which she tucked into the crevices of the matchbook sculpture, so that here and there it shone. She hunched over the matchbooks for a long while, making tiny adjustments with small, sure fingers, and she looked absolutely capable, as if the making of small new curiosities signified the skills to do anything, to move the world.

Small dark scabs had formed where she had scratched herself. Eventually he took her feet onto his lap and massaged them, and she slouched in her chair and fell asleep. Watching her, he recalled the airport, years before, his misery and awe. And now? Now he was moved to happiness.

Later that afternoon she went into the room. Two golf carts in the seventh fairway had collided in a way that bent a rear wheel, and several men in shorts and polo shirts gathered around it. Then, one by one, they wandered off, abandoning the damaged golf cart in the middle of the fairway.

'For some reason I keep thinking,' Ellis called, 'maybe a circus will come down the highway, on parade. A couple of elephants marching down the highway would make me very happy.'

Heather didn't reply. He peered into the room, but she had gone.

He watched the highway for a few more minutes, then went in to use the toilet. A pair of red panties that Heather had laundered in the sink were hanging over the shower curtain rod. He ran a finger over the seams, then washed his hands, splashed water on his face, dried it away, and his phone rang. 'Chinese?' Heather said.

'Where are you?'

'I'm just wandering around. I found a bag of water balloons.'

He returned to the balcony. An iron shot rose off the seventh fairway and fell and dribbled onto the green, still far short of the pin. 'I'll walk over to that Chinese place for takeout,' Heather said. 'All right with you?'

Ellis said OK. He leaned on the rail and looked over the traffic. On the edge of the highway away to the right something snagged his attention, a tall figure. Ellis knew as soon as he focused on it that it was Boggs — Boggs bending to look at the ground, Boggs striding along a few paces, Boggs bending to the ground again. Ellis's breath caught, and Heather said, 'What?'

'He's here.'

'John?'

Boggs straightened, turned his face to the

sky and raised his arms outward. Ellis still held the phone to his ear but had forgotten it when Heather clicked off. He was watching Boggs, and he didn't see her until she was already running across the lanes of the highway.

The traffic gapped and she crossed quickly. Boggs didn't appear surprised to see her. She stopped maybe ten feet from him, her mouth moving. Boggs lifted a foot and looked down at it. His lips hardly moved as he spoke. Heather advanced, and she shouted.

Ellis crashed through the room, downstairs, past the reception desk, around the building. By the time he reached the side of the highway, Heather and Boggs seemed calmed. They were talking. Ellis rushed through a break in the traffic. 'Hey!' he called from the median. It looked almost like a conspiracy, and as he waited for an opening to cross the remaining two lanes, he burned. And at the same time he was aware that he stood in the same ditch where a man had barely ducked a semi.

When traffic opened and he could move forward his frustration grew confused. Heather stood downcast. Boggs studied the sky. He looked well tanned, rested and sad, like a man in the midst of a disappointing vacation. Heather didn't look at Ellis, but instead toward the golf course, perhaps at a rattling flag there, perhaps at nothing.

'You're all right?' Ellis said. But having said it, he was unsure who he meant or what *all right* could possibly indicate.

'Say something,' Boggs said. He seemed to be ignoring Ellis's question, to be talking to Heather. She didn't move or respond. The three of them stood in silence. This wasn't what Ellis had expected; his strongest temptation was to run down the roadside, away from it.

Boggs said, 'OK then.' He smiled at Ellis. 'We were just rehashing some history.' He glanced at Heather, but she stood silent. Ellis circled in order to see her face — but she wasn't looking at anything: her eyes were shut. She seemed pale, and when Ellis touched her she was trembling.

'Did you hit her?' he asked Boggs, furiously.

Boggs set his hands in his pockets. 'Of course not.' He started away, into the golf course.

Ellis took a step after him, but stopped and went back to Heather. 'What did he do?'

She shook her head.

'Let's go back to the motel,' he said.

'Are you going to go after him?' she asked.

'Do you want me to?'

'Don't ask me that!'

He stared at her. 'I couldn't see as I came down from the room — '

'You didn't miss anything.'

'Then what — '

'Go,' she said. 'He's going to kill himself, isn't he?' She motioned as if she would shove him, but she did not touch him.

Boggs now was at the far end of the seventh fairway. Ellis looked from him to Heather. 'Are you sending me away?'

'No,' she said.

Ellis cursed. He studied her gaze a second, but she was now steady and opaque. He turned, ran.

Boggs had nearly reached the golf course parking lot. Ellis sprinted through the rough along the seventh. He remembered that Heather had been married to Boggs for years; in comparison he hardly knew her.

By the time he reached the parking lot, Boggs, in his convertible, was pulling away. Ellis ran behind, with little hope.

Boggs, however, had to pause for an SUV backing into a parking space, and then as he came to the street entrance, the traffic there was heavy and seeping. Ellis thought he might actually catch up. And then — what? Vault into the passenger seat?

Boggs approached the street at speed and

made a screeching turn into traffic that terrified Ellis — vehicles from both directions braked loudly, swerved, blew horns. But Boggs, with apparent calm, had locked himself into the crawling traffic. Ellis, running hard, managed to come up beside him. He could hear Boggs's car stereo. It sounded like *Notes from the Underground* — a favourite of Boggs's, though Ellis had found it unreadable. He yelled, 'Boggs!'

'You all right?' Boggs asked, slowing a little.

'Yes.' Ellis had to fight for breath.

'Are you sure? I mean, in a bigger sense?'

'I'm fine.'

'You don't have to follow me, you know.'

'Let me help you!'

Boggs shrugged. His jaw had set hard, and he studied the windshield. Traffic opened before him, and he accelerated a bit. 'What do you want?'

'To talk!' Ellis shouted.

'Just say it!'

'What?!'

'What you have to say!'

'Let's sit somewhere!' Ellis gasped; he couldn't run like this much longer.

'What?!'

'This is stupid!'

'What is?!'

Ellis cried hoarsely, 'This isn't a joke!'

'No joke!'

'No!'

'OK!' Boggs was accelerating. 'Havalek thirty twelve!' he called, then pulled ahead.

Soon he had vanished. Ellis stopped and gasped for a minute with his hands on his knees. Then he turned and walked back along the road and through the golf course. He dodged across the highway lanes. When he reached the motel parking lot, Heather's car was gone. This made him feel guilty. Then, aggrieved. He didn't bother to go up to the room. He climbed into the minivan, started it and turned it onto the road. Every job had been filed under a designation based on the last name of the job's client — like Jim Havalek, a plaintiff's attorney — followed by a sequential number. Ellis recalled Havalek 3012 pretty clearly: a single-vehicle accident that had occurred about two hundred miles away. He pulled into the flow of traffic and phoned Heather. She said she was driving home. 'It's all right,' she said. 'Go on. You're doing the right thing.' Her voice sounded mechanical, maybe even rehearsed. 'You know,' she said, fading, 'you — ' She began again. 'You know why I called him John, not Boggs, don't you? Because he hates it.'

'Sure,' he said. He was surprised by the sympathy he felt for Boggs.

186

9

The sun had begun to set when he turned onto a road that followed along the edge of a lush ravine. A stream of water ran at its bottom and it turned and oxbowed and from out of it rose cottonwoods, willows and brush. Ellis drove slowly. He remembered that the place he was looking for came just after the road curved a long left then sharply right. The driver of the accident vehicle, travelling at 60 despite the 45 mph speed limit, had felt the back end break free in the transition between curves, began to swerve, fishtailed with increasing violence and launched into the ravine.

But as the road curved back and forth, back and forth, and the trees and brush of the ravine all looked much the same, Ellis began to doubt whether he could identify the right curve.

But then it was easy. A white-painted cross stood beside the road.

He parked. He had driven here as hard and fast as he dared, hoping that he might have a chance to arrive before Boggs — unless the way Boggs had pulled into traffic from the golf course indicated a recklessness that he could not match. He stood looking around. What had happened here? An idiot had killed his best friend. Was that the reason that Boggs had chosen it?

A photo of a smiling young man clung to the centre of the cross while at its foot lay a scatter of sun-faded plastic flowers. A beaded plastic necklace. Some broken crockery. A Yankees baseball cap slowly interring into the roadside.

A single-vehicle accident involving two occupants, young men, not yet old enough to vote, friends since kindergarten. During the driver's deposition, an attorney asked how far the steering wheel was turned when the car went off the road.

'I had let go.'

The attorney said, 'Excuse me?'

'I let go of the wheel. And I closed my eyes.'

The car, a little Dodge Neon, helixed into space over the ravine, smashed into the rocky stream bed, overturned and came to rest on the wheels. The driver said he kept his eyes closed — waiting, waiting, waiting, to be sure that the car had stopped and he was alive. Then he opened his eyes and turned to the passenger seat, and it was empty.

The passenger-side window had smashed open.

His friend stood a few feet away.

The two looked at each other. The one standing in the water said, 'I don't feel good.' He sat.

The driver dragged him over to the bank. When the ambulance arrived the EMTs put his friend onto a board and hauled him up to the road. He had no exposed wounds, but he had suffered a laceration of the liver, and twelve hours later, during surgery, he died.

Half of a year passed before Ellis and Boggs were hired and arrived to inspect the vehicle — a dozen energy-drink cans rolling in the rear-seat footwells, worn tyres, no load markings on the seat belts — and then came here to inspect the scene, plodding through the water to find and document bits of broken glass among the rocks, clambering up and down the slope to identify broken branches in the brush, using a machete to hack open view planes for their surveying equipment. Later they built an analytical simulation of the motion of the Dodge as it fishtailed, its subsequent leap, its initial impact with the ground, its crashing rollover. Painstakingly, they accounted for each dent in the sheet metal and the vehicle-to-ground contacts that had deposited window glass as well as the passenger-seat occupant, which allowed them to calculate forces to pass along

189

to biomechanics experts so that those experts could say whether the vehicle's seat-belt design was likely responsible for the damage to the liver of the passenger seat occupant.

Whose name Ellis would not have remembered except that it was printed on a sticker affixed to the cross:

Rick Elwin
1987–2005
We love you, Foxy!!

A photo showed Rick Elwin with big teeth, a droopy right eyelid, not much chin, and it was not obvious in what sense he might be considered foxy. He smiled but looked a little desolate, as if something in him already anticipated how the photo would be used.

Ellis picked up the baseball cap and beat the dirt off and set it atop the cross. He looked at the road for tracks or markings, but there were only the faint tyre marks his minivan had made in the dirt. He peered into the brush, wondering if Boggs had been down there. He didn't want to go down. It was muddy and the water was cold, he remembered.

He walked the road, through the S-curve where the driver had lost control. The road had been dry, the tyres worn but not bald, the vehicle otherwise in fine condition. Drug test negative. Just dumb. Not that anyone could say that in court. One could say, too much speed and an inexperienced driver. Possibly the two friends had been screwing around, but if so the driver never let it slip, and he seemed to have been honest otherwise, stricken and bewildered by the death of his friend. And as Ellis walked the curves suddenly, briefly, James Dell's horrible broken body lay on the ground in front of him.

He turned from it and watched as a Honda went by; it took the turns without difficulty. He crossed the road and stood under high old pines on a broad floor of needles and listened to the trees creak. The sky was darkening. He returned to the cross, and then, cursing, plunged down the side of the ravine to the water's edge. He took off his shoes, rolled his pants. The water was as cold as he remembered. He lurched through the water until he stood at approximately the location where the Dodge had come to rest.

In the mud was a shoeprint.

Ellis compared it to the size of his own shoe — the print was a bit larger, as Boggs's would be. He examined the tread, but he could not remember looking closely at Boggs's shoes recently. He moved upstream and down, looking for more prints, without success. He worked up the ravine slope above the print, but saw nothing, and he went back down and crossed the water and looked along the opposite bank. A heavy gloom gathered. He ended standing in the water where the Dodge had been, his feet numb with cold.

He closed his eyes and tried to think. If Boggs had been here and left, what now? Where next? Was it possible that this was a ploy to pull him away from Heather?

A wind stirred the cottonwood leaves into faint slapping noises.

The driver of the Dodge, too, had been here, with eyes closed. Ellis imagined the terrifying crash and the jarring halt. Eyes closed. No motion. No noise except a gurgle of water around the car. Waiting. Wishing it could all be reversed. Hoping to find it was OK. Then, opening his eyes, looking to his right, and there his friend stood in the water like an apparition.

Ellis opened his eyes and looked to his right: mud and rocks and weeds.

Except, of course, he was the one standing in the water. Like a man standing and breathing though already killed, already killed but not yet dead, an apparition.

The water chuckled. A tree creaked. A car approached on the road above — cars had passed there periodically, but this one slowed.

Right above him, it halted.

Then it honked.

Ellis scrambled up the slope as quickly as he could, but as he came out of the brush, the car had already accelerated away. He heard its tyres shrieking a little around a curve.

He ran to the minivan. The road wound beside the stream for five miles before it came to an intersection, a four-way stop, and in the distance, left, right and ahead, he saw no one. A honk! It must have been Boggs. He hit the steering wheel.

Then his phone rang. From it Boggs said, 'Right.' And hung up.

'Fuck you!' Ellis shouted. But with a sensation of internal flailing, he turned right and drove as fast as he could.

A couple of dozen miles passed with no sight of Boggs. He called Boggs and listened to it ring several times. Then, to his surprise, it clicked and he heard Boggs say, 'This jerk in front of me keeps tapping his brakes. Going uphill for God's sake.'

'Uphill?'

'It's a little hill.'

'Are you tailgating?

'I am now, because he keeps tapping the brakes.'

'I guess anyone who wants to gets to be a jerk.'

'That's right. It's an equal-opportunity society.'

'Where are you?'

'Just drive and drive and maybe I'll hit something.'

'You're crazy. You'll kill someone.'

'People out here know the risks,' Boggs said. 'If you've put yourself out on the road, then by implication you've accepted the associated risks.'

'I doubt that most people think of it that way.'

'People do all kinds of shit without thinking.'

'You're not an asshole. Stop it.'

'The problem,' Boggs said, 'is that you still want to think that we're friends. Look at what's happened. Look at where we are. What does friendship mean? This isn't it.'

'We don't have to be friends. We don't have to be anything. If you'll just get some help. Just go home.'

'You don't really want me to go home and inject myself into Heather's life again, go in and stir things and make a mess of the situation you've got.'

'Whatever you need to do to work it all out.'

'It would be a mess. I'm just thinking of your interests, Ellis.'

'Sarcasm is the lowest form of humour.'

'No, really you have to agree that puns are lower. I'll take bad sarcasm over a good pun any day.'

'If you have your humour, Boggs, then life's OK, don't you think?'

'Not really. What's the one got to do with the other?'

Ellis said, 'You said *right*, right? But where are you going?'

'Right, wrong. Left, right.'

'What?'

'With a W.'

'Oh. Oh.' Jacob Wright had been one of their clients. Ellis pulled to the shoulder and stopped the car.

'Now we're getting somewhere, huh? Get it? We're driving, getting somewhere. It's a pun, pretty low.'

'We're not getting anywhere.' He wasn't. He was stopped on the shoulder.

'Now, that's what makes it funny, because it's sarcasm, too.'

'Boggs,' Ellis said.

'Boggs. Boggs, Boggs, Boggs. *Boggs, can I have a job? Boggs, can I have your wife? Boggs, can I have your sympathy? Boggs, can I save your life? Boggs, can I feel good about myself?*'

'I'm — '

'*Boggs, will you accept my apology?*'

'Shut up, Boggs.'

'Am I bothering you?'

'You can talk a circle right around me. Good for you.'

'OK. Talk to the Dostoevsky.' Ellis heard an audiobook playing. '*That I should cast a dark cloud over your serene, untroubled happiness; that by my bitter reproaches I should cause distress to your heart, should poison it with secret remorse and should force it to throb with anguish at the moment of bliss. Oh, never, never!*'

Then the silence of the dead phone line.

Jacob Wright had been a major defence client, a fat, affable attorney representing a manufacturer. Including everything, including even the jobs on which he and Boggs had only spent a few hours before everyone concluded that the case looked bad and should be settled, they must have worked for Wright on more than a dozen different jobs. Maybe twenty. Maybe more.

Ellis took out the map. The nearest Wright job that he could recollect lay — like a confirmation — 180 degrees off his current course.

He turned around.

Night had now taken the world completely. He passed an array of towering antennas with

196

blinking red and white lights. An enormous solitary ghostly lit church. Fields where large numbers of fireflies were lighting, pale green sparks in great numbers all across the landscape — they glowed only as they flew upward so that they appeared to be always rising. Some rose over the road, and the ones that struck the windshield flashed brightly into green smears of phosphorescence that slowly, slowly faded. They began to mass in swarms that pelted the minivan — three, four on the glass before him, startling him with every impact, dead and luminous and beautiful. Then the fields ended with an eruption of residential housing developments; the fireflies vanished.

10

The road, the road: it came at him and spun out behind, varying without changing. Ellis knew — Boggs had taught him — that only four patches of rubber, each the size of the palm of a hand, touched the minivan to the road. They bore up its two tons of metal, glass, plastics and fluids, which in turn bore up himself and contained him and moved him in great comfort: climate-controlled, cushioned, radio and CD player at ready, cellphone charging, cup holders awaiting cups to cradle, visors set to block harsh sun glare, windows and mirrors powered at the touch of a button, cruise control to mind the accelerator.

His headlamps ghosted an interstate with a narrow median; a flavour of metal gathered in his mouth; cars came down the opposite lanes like fists. He drove until late, then slept in the minivan off a side road in a rutted open space. During the night he woke only once, with a raccoon crouched on the hood, staring with bandit eyes. Ellis pressed the horn, and the creature reared, smirked, loped away. Ellis watched a hanging half-moon and slept again until the sky was bluing. He woke cold but sweating. He turned the ignition for heat, but shut it off again and stood out to jog up the road a half-mile or so and back again. Swinging his legs and pushing himself forward without a gas pedal felt strange, and he returned to the minivan trembling and heaving, and rushed onward.

Like anyone, he could drive, he could hate it, and he could do it forever.

Sunflowers glowed in the window, endless bright heads peering upward. Black-and-white cows trundled over rolling terrain, drank at the foot of a madly spinning windmill. A haze filled the sky with the colour of weathered aluminum, and a monstrous Wal-Mart swam up out of the distance and flashed into the rear-view. Anything could be put rapidly behind; nothing could.

He felt very tired.

He spent much of the day at the place where a woman driving her daughter home from choir practice had stopped as a goose and four goslings crossed the road. While she waited on the geese, a pickup hit her from behind, and her daughter in the back seat died. Ellis spent more than two hours scrutinising the ground, moving up and down the road, but he could find nothing, so went on. Boggs wouldn't answer his phone, and

Ellis put off calling Heather. He despised himself a little for this, but he was angry with her, too. She owed an explanation for what had passed between her and Boggs on the golf course.

He drove amid squat glass ten- and twelve-storey office towers. A movie complex the size of a stadium. A row of car dealers, Nissans, Volkswagens, Audis, Fords, Chryslers, Suzukis, Saturns, Saabs, Hummers, closely parked, colourful and shining as jelly beans on a plate. Supermarkets and Starbucks and cheque cashing in little strip malls with names like Silver Water Square, Walden Center, Maple Grove Plaza. His stomach felt walnut-hard. His hands moved restlessly on the steering wheel. He examined the place amid alfalfa fields where two SUVs had met head-on, at a combined speed of 115 mph, and burned. One of the drivers died with his head — per the police photos — resting on the windowsill, his eyes rolled and exposed like a pair of eggs. Ellis stood on the road shoulder and scrutinised its gravel. After a time he moved forward a half-step. He tried to give attention to each individual stone. Moved forward another half-step. For this accident he and Boggs had developed an elaborate analysis involving Conservation of Momentum, Conservation of Energy and

Taylor Series expansions, but he could remember none of it, only the photos of the dead. Limbs burned to stumps.

That night clouds on the south horizon shone auburn with the reflected light of a city. Boggs did not answer his phone. He tried Heather, but she didn't answer. He felt sent away from her. Was that true? Was that why he went on? No. He was Boggs's friend, so he went on. Was that why he went on? Yes. Yes? Exhaustion came abruptly, like a blow to the head, and sleeping in the minivan now felt habitual and natural, so it seemed foolish to push to look for motels. He stopped in an abandoned construction site — holes had been dug, dirt lay in heaps, but the earth movers had departed and the weeds had grown tall. He was obscured from the road by sections of six-foot-diameter concrete pipe.

Despite his exhaustion he could not sleep, and he listened with eyes closed to the nearby hysterical repetitive call of a cricket until he felt ready to try to find the creature and kill it.

Instead he moved the minivan and turned on the radio and listened to how the love and blessings of the Lord might make one wealthy.

He woke in the dawn light and silence, and when he turned the key the silence remained.

He flagged a Chevy Silverado with a bearded young man and jumper cables. The bearded man gave him a look when the minivan came to life with the booming of a preacher's preaching on St John. Ellis turned it off. He'd had no idea that he'd turned it to such a volume.

The morning grew hot. Heat lightning glinted in the distance, and the road ahead shivered. He traversed rivers and skirted lakes, cut straight through low hills between walls of blasted rock, then stopped outside a Howard Johnson's, at the site of another Wright job, where a police officer in a trench for laying sewer lines had been killed when a Lexus landed atop him, studied the place for hours, then went on.

He sensed the danger of wafting away on a kind of easier, emptier slant life. When he was out of the minivan and he didn't have the flow of the road before him, his thoughts seemed especially disorganised. He stood too long staring. He handed the gas station attendant his keys instead of his credit card. He took a bag of mini-pretzels and a bottle of water, and the pretzels became a day's meal. While he was driving he had little sensation of hunger. He thought of James Dell in the hospital bed, his stomach empty, eating only the fluids dripped into his veins.

When he phoned the hospital Mrs Dell's voice was hoarse with emotion. 'He's worse,' she said. 'A lot of — worse. I believe he's going to die. They won't say it, won't tell me, but I can see it. His heart stopped this morning. They used the paddles. He looks bad.'

'I'm so sorry,' Ellis said. 'I can't even begin to say.'

'Can I tell you something? His heart stopped — ' She clucked her tongue. 'And something had finally happened. A part of me was glad for the excitement. They had to pay attention again. And it's been so dull, and I get bored. I don't know what to do. Sit, wait. Patience. Look at him, don't look at him. Think about him, then don't think about him. Talk to him, or don't talk to him. I don't know if he can hear me. They say it's possible he can hear, so I feel that I should talk. But it's hard. It's not like talking to him.'

'Tell me about him.'

'He's not well.'

'I mean, tell me how he was when he was — ' Ellis stuttered; he'd nearly said *alive*. ' — he was well. What did he like to do? What kind of person was he?'

'He loves dogs,' she said, 'but he never allowed himself a dog. He isn't allergic. He just didn't allow it. He's that kind of person.

He denies himself things. He can be difficult. He never is who he wants to be, I don't think. None of us are, I guess, but it bothers him especially. He loves sweets and never eats sweets. He hates the theatre, but he went. Maybe I sound bitter.'

'He loves you, though.'

'Oh, yes, yes. But, well, we fought terribly.' She laughed. 'We've never really had the life we should have. He denies that, too. He always thinks things should be finer, or rougher, colder or warmer. More difficult, unless they should be easier.' She coughed. 'I don't mean to talk about this. I don't want to.'

'It's all right,' Ellis said.

He stopped for lunch in a Subway decorated with a yellow that worked in his eyes like needles and paid for a sandwich served up by smiling young people. He felt like wreckage before them, unshaven and unwashed. He sat at a corner table obscured from sight and only swallowed two bites of sandwich before he left.

* * *

For two more days he drove between sites where they had done work for Wright. A Lamborghini that broke in half. A woman run down by a trash truck. A shuttle bus with faulty brakes. At each Ellis examined the ground minutely. If there were houses or businesses nearby, he went to ask questions.

The time in the motel with Heather already seemed a vague dream, one that he suspected he would never recover. When Heather finally called back, he didn't ask about what passed between herself and Boggs by the side of the highway, and she didn't raise it. They talked about other things, passionlessly. Maybe, Ellis thought, with the force of need, phone conversations always, by their nature, contain a cold, disembodied feeling.

He could see no sign of Boggs, could not get him on the phone. But he kept driving, even as he feared that he was getting further from Boggs, not closer, and he might be indulging a fantasy or an insanity. He couldn't think of a thing to do except to continue onward and hope for a stroke of luck, although the course of recent events made him appear to himself entirely luckless.

* * *

He was watching for an Outback Steakhouse, but he saw no Outbacks for miles, only T.G.I. Friday's, Olive Garden, Red Lobster, Lone Star, Black-eyed Pea, Chili's. Years had passed since he and Boggs were here, nothing on the roadside synced with the images in his mind, and he began to mistrust his memory. He had nearly decided to turn back when he saw the Outback's red neon.

He pulled up the exit ramp. A few drops of rain marked the windshield, but the wipers chased them off, and no more fell. The interstate beside him cut a trough in the earth, and he drove beside it on a two-lane access road, passing a hot-tub store with a blue hot tub mounted on end on the roof, an upholstery shop with barred windows, an office-furniture supplier in a converted warehouse. Unmarked buildings with rust stains down the walls. Deteriorating parking lots. All of it seemed like he might have seen it before, and he could remember none of it specifically.

In front of the upholstery shop he parked the minivan and crossed the access road to gaze down. The embankment's slope looked steeper from here than it had seemed from below. At his feet grew dandelions and weeds. A Camel pack. A crushed water bottle. In the south-west stood a swathe of near-black clouds while the traffic below ran bellowing. He took a breath and went down clutching the weeds.

The passing vehicles moved in long streams

and flows, sucking a wind that fluttered against him. He studied the shape of the embankment, the location of the acceleration and deceleration lanes, the proximity of the overpasses at the exits ahead and behind. Here, on an early morning in winter, after a night-time snowfall, a Dodge Durango had parked on the shoulder, occupied by a family of five Pakistani immigrants who had abandoned a rental apartment two days earlier and begun driving west. Ten minutes before the accident a police officer drove by and did not note any stopped vehicles — implying that the Dodge had not been here long.

The driver of the semi that destroyed the Dodge and killed everyone inside began to lose control after passing the previous exit. Perhaps he encountered a patch of ice. Perhaps his attention wandered. A standard black box in the semi recorded speeds of a few miles an hour over the speed limit, and conditions were poor — heavy snow and ice on the roadway, more snow sifting down. For a distance of several hundred feet the semi swerved back and forth — a little, then more and more as the driver struggled to regain control of the trailer swinging out behind him. Ellis had modelled the dynamics. When the driver got on the brakes, it caused the trailer to fully jackknife. The entire semi slid broadside. It was travelling at — Ellis had calculated — 46 mph when the rear corner ripped open the Dodge and hurled it down the shoulder, spinning in a complicated trajectory that Ellis laboriously reconstructed by an analysis of a stack of police photos of tyre marks in the snow.

When the Dodge came to a stop it stood empty, and the five occupants lay in little heaps here and there on the road. Scattered around them were suitcases, duffels, Fritos, a pair of flip-flops and a small charcoal grill.

No one alive knew why the family had left their apartment and started west, and the available evidence also didn't indicate why they had stopped on the shoulder — the same shoulder Ellis now trudged along. The Dodge still had gas in the tank. Maybe it had some mechanical problem. Maybe the driver wanted to look at a map. Maybe there was an argument. Ellis and Boggs had identified the accident location by walking the shoulder with a book of police photos, watching for the shape of the embankment and a bit of fencing that showed at the top. Or had it been a guard rail? Irritated, Ellis returned to the place where he had come down the embankment and continued on in the other direction. Maybe he had the wrong Outback, the wrong exit, the wrong interstate, the wrong city.

When he noticed a sudden quiet he ran across the lanes, to the centre median.

Cars roared into the lanes behind him. The median, about thirty feet wide, shallowed in a grassy ditch. At the bottom a seagull stabbed at a candy bar wrapper.

After throwing the Dodge aside the semi had continued to slide and swing around until its wheels scooped into the earth of the median. Ellis looked for furrows in the grass. He remembered photographing the tracks of still raw earth with Boggs, and it didn't seem likely that the highway department would have made any attempt to fill them. But he didn't see them.

He walked with the flow of traffic, then against it. A drop of water struck his face, then another. Soon a drizzle sketched visible lines in the air. The noise of the wheels on the road began to shift tone. He stood watching the moving columns of vehicles while his hair plastered down, his shirt grew soaked, his pants. A plume thrown by a semi landed against his ankles. Eventually the traffic must break. It passed through his mind that if he waited here long enough, inevitably he would see an accident occur.

When next he looked down the median, a

figure was coming.

It wobbled a little side to side, stopping now and again to peer at the ground, and eventually emerged from the rain in a baggy yellow-and-black Steelers jacket with the hood up, a girl, maybe thirteen or fourteen. Under one arm she held an object — a headlamp assembly, wires springing from it. She stopped about ten feet away and regarded him with a frown, as if he were a post in the ground in the wrong place. When he said hello, she nodded slightly and asked, 'What are you doing here?'

He looked at the traffic. His hands trembled in his armpits. The rain ran off the girl's jacket, the sleeves hung past her hands, the hood shadowed her eyes.

'I'm trying to get back across,' Ellis said.

The girl didn't answer. She turned to face the roadway as if she were at a bus stop and examined the headlamp in her hands. Ellis, confounded, wandered up the median a short distance, then returned and waited. Eventually he bowed his head. Eventually he shut his eyes.

Then the sound of the traffic changed. A course of rear lights brightened, cars slowed. Ellis had lost his expectation that the traffic would ever stop; to see it now seemed a flouting of nature.

They crossed the lanes between stopped cars and climbed the embankment and when he reached the minivan the girl was still with him. The rain had become extraordinary, a collapsing wave. 'Well, get in,' he yelled.

They watched the water move on the windshield. Except for the rattling on the roof, the minivan seemed a calm and hushed place. He started the engine to run the heater. 'That came out of a Ford Probe,' he said, gesturing at her headlamp.

She glanced at him. 'I know.'

'I can drive you home,' he said. 'But you have to tell me how to get there. I don't know this place.'

'You don't have to do anything for me,' she said. But she didn't move either, just sat in his minivan. She had some pimples around her lips and watched the rain with peculiar intensity.

'All right,' he said. 'I'm hungry. You hungry?'

He eased down the access road to a Wendy's. Inside he ordered hamburgers, fries, sodas. They sat in a booth with red seats, and she ate with a slow and precise method, one fry at a time until they were gone, the burger in small bites.

He picked the headlamp off the table and put his eye to the glass. 'You find this along the road somewhere?'

She said nothing.

'This was in a collision,' he said. 'At night.'

He set it aside, and he watched her look at it, then up at him, then at the headlamp again, her jaw flexing. 'How do you know that?'

'Bulb filaments are hot and soft when they're lit. When a crash suddenly accelerates or decelerates the car, if the filament is on, it's so soft that it gets thrown out of shape. It's like cracking a whip.'

She lifted the headlamp and peered at the bulb filament. Then she looked at him, with one eye a little squinted.

'Are you homeless?' he asked.

'No.'

His phone rang. He saw that it was the office and let it ring.

'Do you spend much time down there along the interstate?' he asked. 'Did you happen to see an accident that happened there, a semi hit a Durango, about a year, year and a half ago, in the winter, in the snow?'

She stared at him.

'I'm looking for a friend of mine,' Ellis said. 'He might have been down there recently, looking around. Did you see him?'

'Did you know people in that accident?' she asked.

'I think the people who knew the people in the accident all live in Pakistan.'

She nodded. 'I think the unknown dead are important.'

'What?'

'The unknown dead.'

He watched her. He didn't know what to do with her. 'Are you sure you don't want to go home?'

She folded a napkin edge against edge. 'OK.'

Under her guidance they crossed the city by side streets. 'My mom might know that accident,' she said. 'She might know about your friend.'

'Really?'

'I think so.' The rain faded. They entered an industrial district. A cement plant fronted by barrel-backed trucks. A rail yard. Rows of grey warehouses. They drove beside a junkyard where piled broken vehicles rose over a fence of corrugated metal. The girl pointed down a run of gravel and said, 'Here.' A double-wide trailer stood surrounded by several vehicles in various levels of dismantlement.

The girl started out of the minivan, stopped, waved. 'Come on. Mom's here.'

A fibreglass storm door on a spring clapped loudly behind him. The mother, a lank and weathered woman in a denim shirt, said to the girl, 'There you are,' and ignoring Ellis she rattled through a speech of reprimand — *How can you wander off without telling me? Don't you know I worry?* — in a tone of saying a thing that had been said before and would be said again without expectation of effect. Then she looked at the headlamp assembly. 'Four bucks. Maybe.' She turned to Ellis. 'Thanks for bringing her back. You want coffee?'

Ellis refused. The accident that he described, between the semi and the Dodge, sounded familiar, she said, but there were a lot of accidents, they ran together. He asked about Boggs, but she only shrugged and smiled, the headlamp still in her hands. 'I don't know where she finds these things,' she said.

She had unnaturally white teeth, hollow cheeks. She smiled and smiled, and when Ellis looked around, the girl had vanished. He thought of Boggs out there alone, and he wrenched around on one heel, toward the door, calling out apologies and goodbye.

No rain. The puddles showed fragments of sky in the gravel. As he crossed to the minivan, the girl wandered out from behind a Subaru Brat rusting along the door sills. A boy who appeared to be a couple of years younger trailed her, wearing a bandanna around his neck like a cowboy.

'I bet I know how you can find your friend,' the girl said.

'Your mom didn't know anything.'

'I have a technique,' she said.

'Really.' He looked for her to smirk, but she only nodded. He felt tired and drained of resistance and ideas. He shrugged.

They passed between rough rows of vehicles lying side by side, spaced just far enough apart to allow the doors to swing a few inches, cars and trucks caved, twisted, pierced, burned, or freed of doors, hood, wheels, trunk lid, roof or fenders. Like bodies gathered after battle. Like a sorting of things before the rendering of final judgement. Drops of rainwater clung to the sheet metal, puddled in the dents. The girl and the boy walked ahead, and the boy's steps clicked oddly — he was wearing tap shoes. And Ellis heard occasional shrill voices calling in other parts of the junkyard, words he could not make out.

A pile of rusting wheels. A pile of drive shafts. Somewhere a train moved, pushing vibrations that caused the entire field of vehicles to shimmer. Ellis lagged behind. It was easy to imagine that in any slightly different life he would never have come here.

The girl slowed and spoke without looking: the back of her head speaking to him. 'The thing is, dead people don't just go away. Things don't just disappear. Things leave an effect. Souls leave an effect. And here we have a bunch of things that have the traces of souls. They're not *obvious*. Maybe they're only the effects of effects or the traces of traces, you know? But it's not *that* hard to bring them out.'

Ellis hardly knew where to begin with this.

'Anyway,' she added, 'it can't hurt.'

Ellis asked, 'Are you talking about ghosts?'

She glanced back. 'Boo!' Then she turned into a cul-de-sac and stopped before a Monte Carlo — crimson paint, gold trim, the interior upholstered in beige. The paint gleamed, the tyres held air. But the passenger door had been forced deep into the vehicle, as if staved in by a battering ram. The girl opened the driver's door. She looked at Ellis.

'What?' Ellis said.

'You'll have to sit here.'

Ellis looked at his watch. The day had advanced into mid-afternoon. Overhead, clouds still dominated. 'Are you sure you haven't seen a big guy with a beard?' Ellis asked. 'Whatever he paid you, I'll pay double.'

'Don't you want to find your friend?'

He peered inside. Colourful paraphernalia

216

covered the dashboard and the pale seat fabric was spattered with stains. He tried to remember — he seemed to have no instinctive sense of himself any more — if in the past this was the sort of situation he would have extracted himself from. The stains appeared to be blood. An enormous blotching covered the passenger seat, which was distorted by the impacted door. He waited for the girl to say something ridiculous that would spur him away. But she said nothing.

The driver's seat held him as softly as a plush sofa. Gold braid and tassels ran around the windshield glass; cards printed with the images of saints hung from the ceiling; figurines of crudely painted plastic stood on the dash holding swords, sceptres or birds; faux leopard skin wrapped the steering wheel; a bust of a weeping Virgin dangled from the rear-view mirror. The sun had faded the colours of the cards and figurines. The leopard skin was soiled at three and nine o'clock. A small stain of, again, blood marked the chin of the Virgin.

'What now?' he asked.

She closed the door. 'Put your hands on the wheel.' She circled to the front and she looked at him down the length of the hood. 'Ask your question.'

'What?'

'The one you want answered.'

'Who's going to answer it?'

'That's a stupid question. That's not the question you want answered.'

He looked around the car once more.

'Ask your question,' she said.

'Where is Boggs?' he said. 'How do I find him?'

'One question. Repeat it one hundred and eleven times.'

He laughed. But she waited with a dark gaze. 'How do I find Boggs?' he said. He began to repeat it.

The boy with the bandanna had disappeared. The girl bent and came up with a rubber mallet. She swung it at the hood, and it bounced away with a crash that sent the entire steel body of the car into a short, resonating shriek. 'Keep going!' she yelled and lifted and swung, lifted and swung, in rhythm with the repeated question. Then, with a bang, an answering percussion began — in the mirror Ellis saw a boy, not the boy with the bandanna but a sleepy-eyed blond boy, swinging a pair of croquet mallets at the trunk. The noise was painfully loud. Then the boy with the bandanna reappeared, running up the hood, scrambling onto the roof, and the tap shoes began striking there like falling ball bearings. Ellis cringed. But the noise had begun to generate a rhythm of patterns within patterns, and the hanging cards jiggled and turned, the tinsel and the gold braid shimmered and sparked, the Virgin bobbled and the noise beat a rhythm in Ellis's core. He could no longer hear himself chanting the question — *How do I find Boggs?* — so that it seemed to sound only in his mind. The boy on the roof began to rock the car on its springs — saints swayed, the fur-wrapped steering wheel shook in Ellis's hands.

He had no idea how many times he had repeated his question when the girl yelled, 'Shut your eyes!' He did. Effects echoed and buzzed, waves of pressure moved in him. At some point he had stopped mumbling his question. The terrible splitting havoc went on and on. He had to admit, if anything could shift the substance of the world off its rational foundation, this might be it.

Then it stopped.

Silence.

'Listen for it!' the girl shouted.

He wondered, For?

For the voice of the person or persons who had been in this car? The voices from all the accidents he had studied and reconstructed? The voices from all the accidents everywhere, ever, from Bridget Driscoll at the Crystal Palace and onward? The accidents in this way became a mathematical progression past counting. Meanwhile a noise skimmed the edge of his awareness, a modulating of frequencies and a havoc of tempo, imagined, a fire in the ears. Before him hung shining pinwheels, depthless drifting auroras. He trembled. If time could fall away, if he could look in all directions, where would he look? But he could not even keep his thoughts focused on Boggs. Instead, he thought of Heather, with an aching.

Then he realised, with a dull internal settling, that he could not believe in this business of the traces of spirits and souls. Even after allowing himself to be brought this far, his mind shaken and emotional, some crucial part of him knew that this was nonsense. He experienced this knowledge as a flaw in himself. He seemed empty, lacking belief in a soul and therefore almost certainly without the possession of one.

A breeze hissed on the sharp edges of the car. There seemed a rhythm in it, too. Whisperings. A warble of metal ripping in the faint distance.

★ ★ ★

'Human factors analysis.'
'What?'

'People don't assess speed, it's hard to assess speed. We assess the gap. The gap between vehicles, the gap available to cross or turn.'

Darkness. 'Boggs?'

'Are you happy?'

'No. No, I'm not happy.'

'Are you depressed, Ellis?'

'I'm not happy.'

'Are you sad?'

'What is this?'

'Do you have feelings of guilt?'

Just before, the pallid, wrecked face of James Dell had been declaiming on the perversity of fortune with respect to the allocation of individual appearances, and as he spoke his left eye swivelled strangely with a cheerful ringing noise, then popped from the socket and hung on its nerve bundle. Behind James Dell, guffawing, stood Christopher, freshly burned. But that had been a dream. 'Boggs,' Ellis said.

'Are you proud?'

'Boggs. Stop.'

'Are you self-conscious? Self-doubting?'

Ellis said yes. He had fumbled and answered the phone still half asleep, confused as to place and time, responding automatically to the noise of the ring. He began to register how complete the darkness around

221

him was. He put a hand forward and felt a fur-wrapped steering wheel.

'Self-loathing? Have you had thoughts of killing yourself?'

Ellis waited.

'It's been interesting to drive and think.'

Ellis waited, but Boggs said nothing more, and Ellis finally said, 'All right. What are you thinking?'

'The road is a place where you know you might die at any instant. Right? It's a part of the nature of driving. On some level we're always aware of death as we drive. It's actually a part of why we like to be on the road. The possibility of an accident, of drama, of death, which is absent from our lives otherwise. Modern life is deathless, we expect that we will grow old and shuffle away to an assisted living facility where we can expire in obscurity. Is that really what we want, deep in our brains? Maybe something will happen on the road, now, or now, or now. You see? It provides an element of ultimate risk, and we desire risk. How many thousands die each year? I'll tell you: more than forty thousand, just in America. How many of them might be saved if only the speed limit were reduced ten miles an hour? It's less interesting that we slow to rubberneck the car crash on the side of the road than that we speed up again as soon as we're past it. That's what I've been thinking about.' He hummed a few notes of the theme from *CHiPs*. 'Seventy-two in a sixty-five zone,' he said.

'That's what you're doing now?'

'Let's allow a perception-reaction time of, say, two point five seconds, to get on the brake. And then braking. I'll be a full football field and more down the road before I can stop this thing. Where are you?'

'In a junkyard. What time is it?' Ellis asked.

'It's almost four.'

'A.m.?'

'No — '

'In the afternoon?' Ellis pulled the door handle, pushed the door. It swung partly open. A heavy tarpaulin lay over the car. He allowed the door to click shut.

'Is something wrong?'

Ellis let the question float. Then he said again, 'Boggs.'

'Witnesses are unreliable. The car flipped six times, went fifty feet in the air, did a triple lutz! Always prefer the physical evidence over testimony, Ellis.'

'Right. Right. Sure. Why are we talking about this?'

'You're wondering, does a suicide actually talk about death? Wouldn't someone intent on taking his life talk around death, the way

223

we talk around whatever is nearest to heart? I wonder, too. It's refreshing. I'm used to knowing what I'll do. Does this sound insincere? Is it getting under your skin. God, I hope so. You're still on the road? Still following me?'

'I'm trying to,' Ellis said, staring at the darkness.

'You do love your subtle distinctions.'

'Tell me where you are. Wright? Wright twenty-nine eighty-two? Wright thirty thirty-five? The one with the hood ornament in the eye?'

'Give up.'

'I'm going to find you.'

'This isn't about you,' Boggs said. 'I've known about you and Heather for a long while. She always had the sheets from that RV in the laundry. It isn't about that. What I'm doing is about me.'

'How long have you known?'

Boggs said nothing. Ellis knew he was unlikely to get from Boggs anything that Boggs didn't want to give. He tried to listen for background noise, but he heard only a faint high whine that seemed a lingering effect of the hammering on the car. Ellis said, 'If this isn't about me and Heather, what is it?'

'Well, maybe that was a lie. Maybe I was just trying to puncture your self-importance.'

'You really knew?'

'Come on, any asshole would have known. I *should* have known the minute you sat for your interview and you didn't dare mention my wife's name, even though she was the only reason you were there. But I thought you were too shy to try anything.'

'You let it go on, after you knew?' Ellis said.

Then Boggs hung up.

When he stood out of the car he was alone in long aisles of devastated vehicles. The grey sky lay close. The gate had been locked. He moved along the fence until he came to a Ford Excursion, climbed onto the roof, dropped over the fence. He would not have been surprised to find his minivan gutted, its parts spreading across the city. But it stood as he had left it. He eased slowly along the driveway to the road, then pushed fast, as if he were stealing it.

He returned to the access road beside the interstate where he had parked before, and he parked again and listened for some minutes to the bluster of the traffic. Then he went from business to business, enquiring if anyone had seen a man of Boggs's description. None had. He walked the top of the embankment, looking again for the accident's specific location, without success. It came to him that the girl was wrong: all things did not necessarily leave a trace, and even traces were not immortal; eventually the dead were absolutely forgotten, eventually the places where they died became merely places.

Sliding in the mud he went down and searched along the shoulder once more. The clouds had cleared and as he walked with the traffic he squinted into the sun. He recalled that the driver of the semi that had struck the Dodge had talked to the police about the sun in his face before he jackknifed.

But the accident had occurred in the a.m.

And therefore he was on the wrong side of the interstate.

He scrambled up the embankment, drove to the access road on the interstate's opposite side, parked in front of a Shell station. He remembered this Shell — when he and Boggs were here, they had parked in the same place. Boggs had gone inside and bought a hot dog from the rotating rack. Ellis had laughed at it, and Boggs had said gravely as he ate, 'Sweet porcine flesh.'

He crossed the access road and studied the ground. A pen cap. A black plastic garbage bag. A dirt-crusted wine bottle. Items cleansed of histories. And, here, the same tyre mark from the VFW parking lot.

He examined it a minute, then ground his heel into it and went back to the minivan.

On a map he put down Xs on Wright jobs. He was stunned to see how many there had been, and he feared he was forgetting more. Minutes passed, his mind wandered, another memory appeared, and he marked an X. Xs lay in all directions from here, and where to go next was unclear. He couldn't think of anything to do but pick one.

He stopped for the night in an empty corner of a Wal-Mart parking lot. He phoned Heather. 'Love,' he said.

'Stop saying that,' she said.

'What?'

'I don't think you know if you love me.'

'Why are you saying this?'

She was crying. He was glad that at least she was crying.

'You're cold,' he said.

Somehow, it sounded like a joke, and she laughed. 'Then I wonder, what do I want?' she said. 'Is it that I can't even have love without questioning it until it becomes something else?'

'Questioning,' he said. 'Yes.'

'You know.'

He said, 'Are you sure you can't talk about Christopher?'

'I'm going to hang up now,' she said, 'but

you understand that you deserve it, right?'

'Please, I don't — '

'Let's talk later. I can't now.' She hung up.

He called her again, but she did not answer, and he smashed the cellphone against the steering wheel, repeatedly, until it had broken into several pieces. Then he looked at the pieces and regretted it. He gathered the pieces and put them in a cup holder.

When he closed his eyes his thoughts clawed at one another in a kind of terrible dreaming. A tap on the window woke him. A security guard told him to go on. Ellis asked about the RVs parked nearby, and the guard said, 'RVs allowed, cars not allowed.' Ellis stared at the young man, but the absurdity did not seem to penetrate.

'This is a minivan,' Ellis said.

'Minivans not allowed.'

He drove on, down an unknown road, into darkness, trees flickering at the periphery. He saw no good prospect for stopping. His eyelids trembled.

The asphalt ended and he continued into the darkness on gravel and jarring washboard ruts. A glow appeared in the distance. A hand-painted sign, illuminated with flood-lights, said 'The Cricket Bar'. A bar seemed like a good place to rest — if he were questioned he could claim to be sleeping off his drinks. The bar itself appeared to be little more than a hut of weathered wood. He stopped in a far corner of the rutted parking lot, nosed into some brush, away from the handful of cars and trucks clustered around the building, where a couple of windows showed small, dim light. He could faintly hear voices. Cicadas screaming. No music. No one came or went from the building.

⋆　⋆　⋆

Sleep was a swift fall through perfect darkness. He woke remembering nothing, under clouds like a flight of giant apricots. The parking lot lay empty.

As he began manoeuvring the minivan it felt and sounded strange, but he gassed it out of the parking lot and into the road before he understood what was wrong. He stopped. The left rear tyre was flat. The right rear tyre was also flat. He studied them and found that both had small punctures in the sidewall. Perhaps from a pocketknife. The entire vehicle slouched back on the flat tyres, and he wondered how he had failed to notice the flats sooner. He stood looking at the tyres as if with sufficient attention he might discern that they were not flat after all. The minivan had a spare tyre, but it was not helpful because he needed two tyres.

He walked over to the Cricket Bar, knocked, and when no one answered, tried to open the door. Locked. He circled to the back and found another door, which gave the same result.

He returned to the minivan, locked it and began walking.

In the night all that he had been able to see from the road were the trees along either side, but now he saw that the trees on his left fronted a vast field of goldenrod, the flowers dim at first but soon blazing as the sun elevated. Then the goldenrod ended at a wood of birch, and the boles made stripes of vertical white that crowded behind one another into an obscure distance while ferns spread underneath. Dust rose from the road as he walked and powdered his pant legs and clung to the sweat on his neck. He'd been walking for perhaps twenty minutes when he heard a vehicle approaching from behind, and he walked on the grassy edge of the road to let it pass, but it slowed and idled at his back. A red Jeep Cherokee. Ellis did not glance at it again. He moved faster, and it stayed with him. He looked over toward the birch wood, and behind him gravel spurted. The Jeep roared up and drew even. A young man in the passenger window — pale hair shaved to stubble, face long and freckled under the eyes, eyes wrinkled with smiling — said, 'Your minivan back there?'

'Two flats.'

'That's some bad luck. Need a ride?'

'No, thanks.'

The young man grinned with big white teeth, straight as bricks. 'It sure looks as if you could use some assistance.'

'I figure it's a nice morning.'

'Just trying to be helpful.'

'Thanks anyway.'

'We're just trying to help a guy out. You don't have to be an asshole.'

Ellis said nothing.

The Jeep accelerated ahead, then skidded to a stop. The passenger stepped out, then the driver — a heavier young man with a ball cap down almost over his eyes. Ellis looked again at the birch woods, but he felt tired and slow and it seemed likely that they could run him down easily, and then it would only be worse. The young man with the white brick teeth kept smiling — an earnest, likeable smile, a smile difficult to doubt. But the driver scowled with fat arms hanging, and the two arrayed themselves so that Ellis could only face one of them at a time. The licence plate on the Jeep was mudded over. 'Two flats. That is some bad luck. How does that happen?' the smiling one asked.

'A statistical fluke.' Ellis felt adrenalin and a fearfulness that annoyed him. 'It could happen to anyone.' He expected a blow from behind, but expecting it did not help when it came: an exquisite pain at the upper rear of the head. The world chunked with black. He fell to his knees. His vision slowly cleared, and he watched the smiling man shape his lips around incomprehensible syllables. Beside him, the fat one held a short length of pipe. Then a flashing movement, and nothing remained but a monumental pain and darkness and the impossibility of movement.

Shades of white. These gradually tinted blue, then green.

Rough objects pressed — the gravelled earth. Dry, toothy weeds.

A faint shallow rasping noise intruded. He understood this to be his own breath. For minutes he focused on it.

Then, sitting up, he gasped and the black returned, but he strained and kept himself up. He felt a long soft welt near the top of his head and alongside it an open shallow wound, with blood clotting in his hair. His wallet, his watch and his keys were gone. His cellphone was gone. No, he remembered, he had broken that. When he shifted his gaze to the birch woods, the white trees trailed rainbow images. He looked at the road's narrowing empty distance, and he felt like sitting down and abandoning the difficulties of the world and waiting, waiting a long time, until his body merged into the rough earth, until he was consumed into something larger, something without self-awareness or memory.

Instead he walked, stumbling with confused balance, back toward the Cricket Bar. The minivan stood at the side of the road, doors open. The keys lay on the driver's seat. A hole gaped in the dash where the radio had been. But in the armrest console between the seats, under a clutter of receipts, he found his credit card where he had left it. He locked the doors, took up the keys and began walking again. He was paced by phantoms at the edge of vision, white things and red things and black things. They scrambled forward only to retreat as he turned to see them better. The sun stood high and felt hot on the wound in his scalp. Its heat there grew as he walked, until it pressed like a blade.

A vehicle approached from behind, and he held himself from turning to look at it. A pickup, it went by scattering gravel from the tyres, not slowing.

He did not see another vehicle until miles later when he staggered into an intersection. More cars went by without stopping, and he kept on beside buzzing high-voltage lines held aloft by enormous steel armatures. He came to a gas station with a garage attached. A mechanic, sitting at a large accounts ledger on a grease-blacked tabletop, looked at him for some seconds before asking, 'What happened?'

Ellis looked at himself, his clothes soiled and bloody. He said, 'I'm not sure.'

The mechanic laughed.

11

He found —

The rural stretch of interstate alongside a pasture full of roan Arabians where a Nissan Armada swerved into the median, over-turned, rolled into a Toyota Corolla in the oncoming lanes and bounced onward, killing three in the Nissan and two in the Toyota, and later a piece of human flesh was discovered in a windshield wiper of the Toyota, torn from one of the occupants as he was flung through the window opening.

The two-lane in front of yellow spiralling water park slides where a semi struck a Honda Pilot, which struck an Oldsmobile, sending it into the opposing lane to meet a Firebird head-on and everyone walked away except the driver of the Firebird, who was dead by the time anyone thought to check on him.

The highway between slouching hills where a Toyota Land Cruiser caught a wheel rim and rolled and the woman driving was decapitated as centrifugal forces pulled her through a window opening. Police photo-graphed her head sitting upright on the earth, as if she had been buried to her neck by children.

And while he stopped at the places of accidents that he knew, he passed others all the time: he saw tyre marks on the asphalt and rutted into roadside gravel and earth, paint transfers on the Jersey barriers, dents in the guard rails, broken glass and plastic glittering.

He spent an hour, two hours, with his map spread on the steering wheel, gazing at the Xs, trying to see a pattern or approach that would bring him to Boggs. He could see no pattern, however, and the way the Wright jobs scattered around left no obvious candidates for a stakeout. Although in his work he often examined a photograph or a scene repeatedly in hope that some new evidence would present itself, here the field was too large, the map gave him nothing, and he couldn't examine every accident scene repeatedly. He needed an intuition. He needed a way to shift his perceptions and see something new. Perhaps in this sense the girl in the junkyard had been right. But even though his situation appeared strange, even though memories and emotions shook and reeled inside him — still he failed to lose his sanity if that was what it was, failed to lose his mind even though his mind provided only this disorganised and apparently useless search.

He could not find an intuition, and along the way he also neglected his appearance. He grew embarrassed when he had to face people — gas station attendants, people passing an accident site. The minivan, too, looked bad. He wiped the windshield from time to time with a gas station squeegee, but the bodies of insects lay across the leading edge of the minivan in a continuous crust. He shoved receipts into the toothless mouth where the radio had been.

He slept one night in a field listening to the sound of cicadas like the cutting of a lathe. He slept another night in the open empty parking lot of a half-abandoned mall. The overhead lights pushed a glow that woke him repeatedly, thinking that he saw the sun, so that the night seemed to contain days that did not end, and when the sun did rise it had a taint of falsity. In the morning he circled the parking lot in the minivan and discovered a six-lane interstate below him where a thin mist had settled and commuters moved slowly. He went on, pressed by a logic grown inaccessible. As he fingered the stitches in his scalp, he wondered, how long had they been in? He was aware of losing a grip on time, of losing a grip on what he was doing, as if all that he could do was go on relenting to the movement of the road. Images of James Dell still occasionally startled him. He recalled Heather and a swirl of intense feeling came. 'Heather,' he cried aloud. Perhaps he had not even heard his own voice for a couple of days. Here on the road, he thought, it does not matter what I say. 'Heather Heather Heather,' he repeated until, over a score of miles, it became gibberish.

He stood before a dusty payphone in a mouldering 7-Eleven parking lot, thinking of her, but then, with shame scrabbling against the walls of his mind, he turned away. He looked at his hand and saw it shaking.

★ ★ ★

The day was beautiful. For miles uncountable wheat spanned everything not the road, a wind roiling it like water. A flock of starlings dove and wheeled. Then an odd, solitary half-timbered building was set off from the world by a rectangle of picket fence. A man worked over a fallen tree with a chainsaw. A retailer of farm equipment offered machines, green and yellow and shining. On the interstate he had the pleasure of accelerating again and moving among semis like a fish in a pod of whales. Bright billboards hove up out of the distance.

The trembling in his hand had spread — he looked at his legs trembling and felt muscles twitching in his face and in his hard, empty stomach. His grip on the steering wheel seemed to flutter. He set the cruise control so that he wouldn't have to feel his foot shaking against the pedal.

He passed an enormous truck stop, semis crowding and nuzzling. He turned off the interstate and went through a little clapboard town and then twenty miles later another town that looked so much like the first that he spent a while trying to reason out whether he could have inadvertently circled. He turned onto a side road. One gentle hill after another curved him up and down. In his head his teeth chattered.

A side road teed out on the left, and Ellis stopped with his turn signal flashing, checked his mirror, then turned, in the same place where a Pontiac Grand Am had slowed to do the same thing and was struck from behind by a semi pulling a load of soybeans. An oncoming Chevy Lumina had swerved to avoid the collision, went off-road, and began overturning, killing its occupants, a family of four that had travelled six hundred miles to visit grandparents who lived two miles from the accident site. In the police photographs toys in primary colours lay scattered along the path of the rolling Chevy. Ellis got out and a wind pulled at his clothes. He recalled a photograph of the driver of the semi standing by his rig, bowed. And another photo, of the body of an obese child, face down on the earth, an enormous plastic soda cup inches from an outstretched hand.

After a time, scuffing in the grass, Ellis found a green pacifier, half buried. He had forgotten that the youngest was so young. Earth clung to the plastic and it trembled in his shaking hand. He felt cold at his core although the sun gaped bright and hot.

He sat by the edge of the road, huddled. A mouse skittered through the grass. A grasshopper stood a minute on his thigh, then leapt away. He picked a piece of asphalt from the crumbling edge of the roadway and let it rest heavy and warm in his hand. He set both hands on the road surface, to feel its absorbed heat. Then he lay down in the lanes, on their warmth, and watched the sky.

Bright low clouds scudded from the west and away beyond the eastern hillbacks. There was no traffic, none at all, and he wondered at the terrible chance that three vehicles had met here. He heard the wind sifting through the grasses beside the road, but he could not feel it. The wind in the grass made a simmering, gorgeous sound. He thought, I

240

am learning something important. But if so he could not describe it to himself with any clarity, and then he thought, Perhaps I am not really learning anything at all. Perhaps I am only following deeper and deeper into a vacant delusion.

A vehicle approached — he felt it in the road before he heard it, a low vibration that gathered to itself the whisper of tyres turning.

He rolled out of the road just as the car, a Chrysler Sebring, barked its tyres, swerving and pushing a wind that flapped his pant legs. The Sebring didn't stop. Ellis lay in the gravel and here, pressed into the dirt beside him, was the shape of Boggs's tyre mark.

He walked over the site again, starting at the tyre mark and moving in widening circles, and eventually discovered a small piece of white paper hung in the weeds. A receipt for gasoline with a name at the bottom: *John Boggs*.

A ball of snakes writhed in his stomach. Now, after all, here was a new point of data. The gas station address named a town that he found on the map. The date was yesterday. The town lay in the east, and east was the direction he would have gone next, but apparently Boggs had been there, so he turned west.

He made two brief stops — one at the

scene of a collision between a street sweeper and a scooter, the other at the place where a garbage truck had crashed into a pickup with two kids in the bed playing with a set of magnetic chequers — before he came to a curve of roadway under a high hill. He and Boggs had spent most of a day working here, surveying, photographing. Not far away, perhaps a half-hour by foot, stood a mate to the hill, a little taller, with three windmills rising off it. Eight months after working below the first hill, they had been brought out to work on a second accident that occurred at the foot of the second hill, with the windmills.

The air here blew hot and dry, despite a lake that lay not far away. From the road he could not see the water; he remembered it from looking at aerial photos of the site. He had a bottle of soda that he sipped from but could not rid his mouth of a parched sensation. His chest ached vaguely. Tremors moved through his hands and arms, into his jaw and eyelids. His eyes, too, felt dry. Near the road the soil was sandy with tufts of grass, and he scuffed around with his foot until he found a swathe of broken glass. He picked up a piece the size of a housefly and felt its edges, watched it catch the sunlight. By examining the thickness and laminated qualities of a piece of glass it was possible to determine whether it had come from a windshield or a rear window or a side window. This appeared to be windshield glass, and he likely stood where the front of the van had come to rest. How many years ago now? Four? Six? The van, a rental, had burned, killing five of fourteen inside. They were grandparents, aunts, uncles, cousins, children, out on a weekend holiday. With so many dead and burned, some of them children, large amounts of money had been at stake. He and Boggs had worked a long time on this case and came to know it in great detail. They had never uncovered anything unexpected — after the first day's work, they probably could have predicted their ultimate findings to within a couple of mph. But they had produced reports and diagrams and animations, and Boggs had prepped for weeks to provide several hours of deposition testimony.

Traffic now moved on the two-lane road at about sixty, rattling the brush around Ellis. A double yellow line indicated a no-passing zone on the curve around the hill, but a small silver Plymouth had nonetheless been passing, and so came head-on toward the rented van. Both drivers swerved, so that the front left corner of the Plymouth struck the front left corner of the van and the left side of the van pushed upward, as if it had hit a ramp. It fell onto its right side and slid into the sand and grass. The deformation of a frame cross-member under the van punctured the fuel tank, and the gasoline ran down, pooled under the van and began to burn.

Ellis sat sifting sand and shards of glass. He picked out the shards and examined them one by one and set them aside in a little pile. He kept thinking that he needed to call someone, then losing track of the thought.

On the hill across the road a sign advertised Texaco gasoline, which contained useful additives.

He looked at the sand he held with thoughts of examining the grains individually. Boggs claimed that there was so much information in photographs that if you studied a job's book of photos long enough, you would always eventually see something new and useful. In Ellis's experience that was sometimes true and sometimes not, but there was always the possibility that in those cases where he had failed to find anything new it was because he had failed to study long enough. He turned the sand a little one way and then another to see how the sun played on it. Certain grains were black, others red or orange or white, their size inconsistent, with some nearly pebbles.

244

He walked down the road to a fading two-track trail that disappeared into a wire fence. At the time of the accident, there had been a gate. Two men had been sitting in a truck in front of the gate, talking about a possible cellphone tower, to be placed on the hill — Ellis saw now that it had never been built. One of the men in the truck, an ex-marine, had run to the burning van, found a window broken out of the rear doors, and reached in. Fighting through the smoke and flames thickening in the van, unable to see, grabbing hands or legs or shirts or belts, he dragged out seven people. He was a hero, but in his deposition he was taciturn and grim and spoke at length only of the screams of those he had had to abandon.

Two more occupants kicked through the windshield and crawled out on their own. The rest died.

A wind hummed in the fence, and Ellis put his hands on it to feel for the vibrations, but his hands only shook the wire. He walked back to where the van had come to rest and scoured again for caught pieces of paper or fabric, a thread, a hair. He worked his way through the weeds until he came again to the fence. From here he could see a few bright glimmers of the lake surface.

He climbed the fence and pushed through

brush. The water lay further away than it appeared, and the brush caught him as if to drag him back. His legs began to shake. He had to stand waiting until it passed.

Nearer the water, he bulled through tall sharp-edged grasses and came at last to an open place along the shore. He crouched. The water was clear, faintly rippling, shallow. He cupped a handful and smeared it onto his face. The opposite shore was also enclosed in reeds and grasses, and the narrow lake stretched away to uninhabited distances right and left. A few ducks loitered on the water.

A short squeal of tyres startled him, but no noise of impact followed. He stood to look at the road, and as he did he glimpsed a human shape to his right, near the water. He stepped through some weeds, wetting his shoes in mud. Someone face down at the water's edge — someone drinking from the lake or washing in it, as he had just done. But the figure did not move.

'Boggs?' Ellis called.

He stood watching, waiting for Boggs to raise himself, and the trembling took him so absolutely that he could hardly move for fear of toppling. After a minute he shuffled forward a few steps, and then he saw that it was not Boggs — too short, too thin, wearing clothes that Boggs would never wear. He stepped from one thatch of grass to another, until he stood over the body of a small, thin man, perfectly dead. Waves came across the lake to jostle it.

After a time Ellis crouched. Then he sat. The splayed feet wore white tennis shoes scuffed and greyed by use. The legs wore khaki slacks. A bit of exposed flesh could be seen at the ankle, vaguely obscene. A dark blue sweatshirt, soaked with water. Thick dark brown hair, wet and plastered to the head. The arms extended loosely, hands dangling in the water. Because the hair had no grey in it, the dead man did not seem to have been very old, but otherwise it would have been hard to say how young or old he was. A few hairs on his neck bristled out of the water. The noise of the road gathered volume for a time, then diminished.

The air of the day slowly cooled.

A pair of coots swam the shoreline and shied from the body and moved along. A magpie landed in the brush nearby, then startled away. Ellis looked up and watched, in a leafless dead tree some distance down the shore, several large black cormorants standing motionless.

He fell asleep — knees drawn up, head on knees — and woke in the night. In the distance, when vehicles rounded the curve of the hill, their headlamp beams revolved spasmodically forward and back. The sky glowed magnificently with stars. He was cold. A breeze touched him and jostled the grasses, and he became aware of someone seated a few feet away. The dead risen — this was his first thought — from the lake water to sit there and ruminate on him. But the stars made light enough to see that the body still lay where he had found it, face in the water, feet on the sand. And as Ellis studied the form of the person seated beside him, a car arced past and he saw the eyes gleam. He moved a dry tongue in his mouth and felt an eyelid twitch. 'I suppose,' he said, 'you think you're stealthy and clever as a ninja or a Comanche or something.'

'You look awful, Ellis.'

Even in the dark Ellis could see that Boggs did not look well, either — his eyes watery, his clothes rumpled, his posture poor. But his hair was trim, and he appeared to have been eating more than Ellis. Ellis turned, in a sensation of daze, uncertain of import, toward the body. 'I thought he might be you.'

'You keep doing that. Who is he?'

'I have no idea. Do you?'

'Have you looked in his pockets?'

'I don't want to touch him.'

'There might be an ID.' Boggs looked at the sky as he talked. 'There might be a medical-alert bracelet or a bottle of pills.'

The water slapped against the body.

'Anyway, now you found me,' Boggs said. 'You found me.'

Boggs shifted and the sand under him made little mouse squeaks. 'It comes to the same thing. What do you want to say?'

'I want to say that I'm sorry.'

The waves came in like the intermittent clapping of a child.

'That's it?'

'I betrayed you,' Ellis said.

'It's what's happened.'

Ellis let that wander out over the water into the night. He didn't feel capable of the enquiry that it implied. He hardly felt capable of breathing. The twitch in his eyelid grew worse. He asked, 'Did you slash my tyres?'

'I noticed that your rear tyres looked fresh. Nice deep tread.'

'Middle of nowhere. And as I walked out, I was jumped by a couple of thugs in a jeep.'

'That's terrible. Makes you wonder why anyone even leaves the house any more.'

'Did you do the tyres?'

Boggs's brow contracted. 'No. I have no idea what you're talking about. I have to say, this is a disappointment.' He stood. He grabbed the body by an ankle. 'Come on. Help me.'

Ellis stared.

'Let's get him out of the water. I can't stand looking at him like that.'

'The police won't want him disturbed,' Ellis said.

'I don't care.' Boggs lifted the other ankle, stood between the two and heaved.

'You're nuts,' Ellis said, but with a sense of obligation he stood, shaking, and clasped a leg — thin and clammy cold, making him glad his stomach was empty — and together they dragged the man onto shore.

'He sure is dead,' Boggs said.

Ellis very gently put down the leg that he'd been pulling. 'Someone might be looking for him,' he said. 'He could have kids.'

'We should roll him and get a look at his face.'

'Don't do that. Let him be.' Ellis felt near to weeping.

Boggs did not reply, but neither did he move toward the body. 'Might be that no one even knows he's gone,' he said. 'A solitary guy, wanders out here, dies, and no one notices. The universe as he understood it is extinguished, and it's the passing of a mite.'

'You really don't know anything about him?' Ellis asked.

'How would I?'

'It just seems strange that I'd stumble onto him here. And then you turn up.'

Boggs laughed. 'You think I planted a dead guy here?'

'What's your explanation?'

'It is what it is.'

'You have to admit it's unlikely.'

'That never stopped anything from happening.'

'That's not true.'

Boggs scoffed. With the point of his shoe he prodded the dead man's foot. It was difficult to look away from the body. The man's shoelaces were still tied.

'If you did set this up, I don't expect you would admit it.'

'No. That's true. I'm too smart for that.'

Ellis laughed. 'All right. Fate put him here.'

'Absolutely not. I'm not sure why you think it's so strange. People die all the time.'

Ellis laughed again. 'You know, it's good to see you, Boggs.'

The shirt had ridden up as they pulled the body from the water, showing a thin, pasty waist.

'Maybe he fell from an airplane,' Boggs said, scowling.

'What are you going to do now?' Ellis asked.

'Maybe he'd hitched a ride in the bed of a pickup truck, and he flew out on that curve and crawled here to die of internal haemorrhage.'

Ellis was silent.

'Maybe this is just a place that had some meaning to him and he walked over here and ate a handful of pills and waited for an end. Some connection here. You remember that guy who climbed through the windshield? Maybe this is him. The passenger seat occupant. The one who said the hero guy was a liar.'

'Really?' Though he had forgotten it, it did seem that Boggs might have told him this before, years ago.

'He said that the ex-marine hero man actually didn't do much. A number of people were helping, and this guy said that he pulled several people out himself, and it pissed him off that this other guy was made out to be the hero with the help of some cop buddies.'

'His saying that doesn't prove anything.'

'That's true.'

'I read that marine's depo. Dragging people out and dragging people out. The screaming. His hand was burned, he went to the hospital, there's documentation.'

'No one said that he didn't burn his hand. No one said that he didn't hear screaming but felt that the fire was too intense.'

Then with — to Ellis — unexpected finality, as if on a signal, the conversation stopped, and time ran a murky passage through the dark. Boggs sat still and Ellis felt as if to disturb him might initiate terrible consequences. Then he slept for a spell and woke feeling no less tired. When he searched the sky he saw that any number of stars had winked away, as if the universe itself were dying. The lake water lay quiet. A few redwing blackbirds lurched around, reeds rattling in their wake. The sun cracked bright over the horizon. He forgot the body and then saw it again and then he did not want to look, but neither could he move his gaze away. The man's sweatshirt held a peculiar and slowly changing pattern of dark and light where it was wet and dry. It seemed difficult to believe that the dead man might not move now, while the hair bristled from his naked ankles and the pores there appeared as if they might at any instant begin to sweat.

'Don't you think,' Boggs said, 'that if you weren't in love with my wife, you could come up with something a little more compelling to say? There must be a part of you that would be happy to see me gone. Maybe only subconscious. Your brain throws up some ideas, not others. What are the constraints on their formation?'

'You're trying to guilt-trip me.'

'Yes.' Boggs stood, and he seemed to tower in the new light. 'Let's go.'

'Leave him?'

'Yes.'

'We can't do that.'

'Actually, we can.'

The body's flesh was bone pale. The skin of the neck held two creases, an imprint of years of life.

'You're welcome to stay,' Boggs added.

One of the body's hands still extended to the lake, and the waves teased the fingers like a cat.

'How can we leave him?'

'We don't know anything about him. Later we'll probably wonder if he even really existed.'

Ellis didn't know which was more terrible, that he didn't know anything about the man, or that this meant that he might leave him. But Boggs started away and Ellis moved in his trail.

The world appeared to unsettle and shift as if composed of tiny swarming insects, and although he followed as best as he could, his foot caught in a hole, he fell and he lost sight of Boggs. When he reached the road Boggs had gone, and even the road lay empty. He clambered into the minivan and accelerated, tyres scrambling.

He drove south a mile, then turned onto a divided highway with entry and exit ramps and a grass median — it was a state highway, but looked like an interstate. He stopped below the windmills. Boggs was not to be seen. Ellis stood out of the minivan, but after a minute he climbed back inside. He felt at a loss. He doubted whether he had the energy to pursue Boggs further, and he didn't know what he should have said to him, but felt that he hadn't said it. Perhaps Boggs was right about his subconscious. Perhaps he really only wanted Boggs's spontaneous and unjustified forgiveness.

Eventually he stood out again and with aimless impatience he walked a little distance uphill. Wind ghosted the grasses. To his right grew a patch of waist-high milkweed and moving across the weeds were the long-limbed shadows of a turning windmill, shadows that came toward him and passed over him, and he had to fend off a sudden vertigo, and turned to the traffic below, coruscating in the sun. The accident had occurred in a fog bank and involved three semis, five cars, two SUVs, a minivan and a pickup towing a pontoon boat. Witnesses described an aftermath of smashed and overturned vehicles haphazard on the road, two of them burning, the pontoon boat on its side, injured people wandering and shouting, the sirens and lights of police, fire and ambulance vehicles drifting in the fog, and the bodies of dead pigs — one of the semis had been pulling a trailerload of hogs — scattered over asphalt and into ditches and fields, and all of this overlaid with the awful screams of uncomprehending, writhing wounded pigs, and the occasional report of a police pistol silencing one.

But what Ellis recalled vividly was that when he and Boggs came here to conduct their scene inspection a year later, a stray black-and-brown mutt with white in the muzzle had sat a short distance away from them and barked mournfully while Boggs had left the rental running, announcing Tolstoy's 'Master and Man' through open windows, the sound of certain words floating in the air like wallowing balloons, ' ... *cob* ... *sledge* ... *drift* ... *ravine* ... *mittens* ... ', while the two of them worked up and down the road, dodging in and out of traffic. No sign of the pigs remained, but there were long dark stripes where the vehicles' tyres had skidded and yawed, and a series of indentations on a guard rail where one of the semis had bumped and slid. They documented everything with cameras and surveying equipment, sweating and shouting to each other down the open distance of the roadway and over the roar of passing trucks. For most of the afternoon the black-and-brown mutt sat scratching itself and contemplating them from the edge of the ditch, occasionally sniffing and doddering around, and then this one, too, came to their specially outfitted hard-sided equipment case and lifted a leg. Boggs looked at the dog, looked at Ellis, then shrugged, yelled, threw a measuring tape and chased the dog down the road shoulder, arms upraised, yipping, shrieking. He had appeared absolutely happy.

And now on the opposite side of the highway Boggs's green convertible slowed and parked.

Boggs stood out gripping a white paper bag, and without hesitation he stepped into the lanes — a car swerved violently around him, honking. Others braked hard.

Ellis shouted and started down the hill toward him.

Boggs walked across the lanes and into the median, while traffic beside him came to a standstill, a chorus of horns blaring. He moved into the other set of lanes the same way, but there happened to be a gap in traffic and the effect was less dramatic. As Ellis came up, Boggs frowned at the minivan. He said, 'Don't they make some kind of a man's version of that?'

'Boggs — ' Ellis said.

'I brought doughnuts.' Boggs held out the white paper bag. Ellis pushed it away. Scenting the sweetness, he felt sick.

Boggs began up the hill, and after a second Ellis followed. Now and again he stopped to gasp and to yank burrs from the cuffs of his slacks. He caught up with Boggs at the base of a cyclone fence that surrounded the windmills, and they sat. The windmills swished and squeaked faintly, and the noise of the highway rose in a susurration. In the distance they could see the other hill and the Texaco sign about additives and the road that curved at its foot and the lake where the dead man lay. With the sun behind them, the lake waters appeared black. It was part of a chain of lakes stretching out behind a reservoir in the far distance. Nearer, a hawk floated round on a thermal.

'In the fog, you couldn't have seen anything from here,' Boggs said. 'All there would have been were pig screams and shots.' A semi, entering the fog, had slowed. A second semi, following the first, had not slowed as quickly as the first and hit it. Other vehicles coming into the fog piled up behind. A man in a pickup had survived a collision with an SUV and climbed out and, as he stood in the roadway, a semi ran him over. To explain how he ended up where he did — seventy feet down the roadway — was tricky, and Ellis and Boggs had concluded that a flange in the undercarriage of the semi had dragged him along until the semi jackknifed and overturned. It was the same semi that had hauled the doomed swine.

'What are you going to do?' Ellis asked.

'I'm thinking maybe a little hut near a beach in California, maybe sell juice and smoothies to girls in bikinis, and I'll have a small apartment upstairs, and I'll learn to surf.'

'Are you serious?'

Boggs grinned and shrugged. 'I'd like to see these windmills at sunset. Something about windmills has always reminded me of the end of things. Sunsets and windmills and Ragnarok. Nothing so large should be moving like that. It's as if we're trying to engineer the world into a freakish final image before we destroy ourselves.'

'Yeah. I'm tired, Boggs. Are you going to kill yourself or not?'

'I like you, Ellis, but I wish you had more sense. I like your melancholy air, your talent for writing a technical report and your skill at calculating crush energy, but you're kind of an asshole, too.'

'Talk to me about your decision process.'

'Jesus,' Boggs said. 'There's no process. I'm devoid of process.'

'No process. OK. You're just doing nothing.'

'I suspect that on some level in my poor brain I was giving it all to you. I never felt I was good at anything except work. She was my only other success, and I'd screwed that up. I didn't know what to do, and I didn't know what to do, and it became doing nothing, and it became a gift. I was giving her an out. And giving myself one, waiting for you two to take it from my hands. But you know what got into me and twisted? The way you dragged it out. How long have you been fucking her? A year and a half? Longer? You couldn't just run away with her? Bled me all that time. I thought I had decided to wait it out. But I broke, I guess.'

Ellis shook himself. Leaning forward, not looking at Boggs, he said, 'I can't have all of this on myself. You have your own volition.'

Boggs laughed. 'Sure. Volition. Awareness of my own volition has been eating me alive. Terrible stuff. On the other hand, let me tell you about an accident: one day I get out of a

260

depo sooner than expected, go to the airport, put myself on standby for an early flight, catch a tailwind and land on the ground almost five hours early. I get in the car and start driving back to the house. And along the way I happen to see, at the edge of the Home Depot parking lot, a familiar-looking RV. Did you really think, by the way, that that thing was inconspicuous? Why not go around fucking my wife in a lime-green school bus? So I stopped and watched the RV, and when it started up, I followed. It went to your place, you got out and you went inside. Jaunty, I thought, very jaunty. I hadn't seen you walk like that before. And then — then all the options sucked. Usually I know what I want to do, but with this thing, trying to decide what to do felt like trying to reach my hand down my throat to grab my liver. I gave up. I figured I'd let you guys figure it out. You seemed to have ideas. Why should I step into it?'

'Is this what you talked to her about, at the golf course?' Ellis asked. 'That I didn't tell her to get a divorce?'

'No,' Boggs said. 'I talked to her about your brother.'

'Half-brother,' Ellis said mechanically.

'Right.' Boggs said. 'And driving around. I don't know. I guess I figured we have to do something with our time. We might as well look at these places. When you're in a darkness and you see a few points of light out there, of course you tend to go toward them. And if you've lost something, you go back to the last places you can remember having it. Maybe it was a mistake, though. Too much.'

'If you're depressed, we can — '

'Stop that. I'm not depressed. Do I seem depressed? I'm just tired of thinking.' He glowered at the highway. 'Wounded pigs screaming. Something about the screaming pigs. People screamed in other accidents, but I started to think about the pigs. What does a screaming pig sound like? I imagine it sounds almost human, only a little different, in some unidentifiable way, to make you think, *What in the name of God?* And fog does weird things to sound. The cops wouldn't have been able to see through the fog, they would have tracked the sound of the screams, stumbling around to find screaming wounded pigs, and occasionally you hear your partner blasting away, and a scream somewhere stops. Not to mention the fires, the smells of burned vehicles and ham, the body of a man lying still to be discovered after being dragged under a semi. What are you to think? What's even the right question to ask? Is it: Who's to blame? Who can be sued? Probably not. 'It

262

changes life forever,' they say. So, it's like an inflection point, where the curve of a life changes direction.' Boggs joined his hands in an inverted V. 'The change of direction is important, but life is what happens before and after. That's the implication. But what if that's wrong? What if what's actually essential is the point of change, the instant when everything is altered: the accident, the collision, the rollover? What if that's life? Where everything changes. And if the accident is the essential point, then by travelling and gathering them together in my mind, I could see something new. Right? That was one thought I had. I guess it was stupid.'

They sat in silence. They ate doughnuts. Ellis tremored. The sky was cloudless and depthless and difficult to look at. Over time the wind gathered, and the windmills whirred and made whomp-whomp sounds. Sometimes one windmill or another boomed with a noise of aching steel. He worried hopelessly about abandoning the body by the lake. He felt an obligation to it, felt that he should have done something differently, although he could not think what exactly. Much of the past now felt this way. He had abandoned Heather and James Dell, too. Below moved the traffic, always moving. Red car. Black semi-tractor and shining refrigerated trailer. Green car. Silver SUV.

Purple pickup. Green car. He recalled that when he had been growing up, it had been next to impossible to find a new car in green; now they were everywhere.

'I saw the two of you embracing,' Boggs said. 'I knew she was only trying to console you. I knew you were probably only thinking about the man you had hit. But it only made it worse, to see you need her so much. And that was it. Nothing had changed in the facts of my life, but I saw them clearly. I couldn't go back to Heather, to you, to work.'

Silence again and Ellis sat huge with guilt, as if too obese to move himself, and time passed and perhaps he slept — was it possible to sleep with eyes open? The scene remained before him, but its meaning changed with the purity of dream. All of it lay under a great bell jar. All of it peered at him and waited. All of it was held in a fog with the noises of the end of world. All of it fell slowly away.

Suddenly Boggs looked up, startled. And Ellis followed him down the slope of the hill.

As they reached the edge of the road, wind galed off the passing semis, the sun strobed between the blades of a windmill, and Boggs began talking about putting up little windmills along the interstates to catch the wind thrown off by passing traffic. He said he wasn't sure if the energy captured this way would be

264

negated by an additional wind resistance experienced by the passing vehicles. He raised a hand to shield the sun and talked about the worst gas station bathroom that he had ever seen. He said something about water, most of his words lost in the traffic noise. Then he turned and stepped into the road. Ellis, surprised, hesitated, and the air pulsed with the passage of the SUV that struck Boggs and carried him away.

Boggs flipped over the hood, bounced off the windshield and roof, and turned heels over head, limbs outstretched, as the SUV passed below. He came down on his shoulder with his head bent strangely while the SUV continued ahead a hundred feet before the brakes locked the tyres and they began to cry and the SUV spun in the roadway. A semi travelling behind it had time and space to slow and stop. Traffic began to back up. Ellis stared, waiting for something more to happen — it seemed something more must happen. Time passed, and he thought, I should understand this now. Someone was shouting. Nothing happened except that people shouted and traffic accumulated in a long idling column behind the stopped semi. He went slowly toward Boggs, already sure that Boggs was dead.

PART FIVE:
THE RECONSTRUCTION

12

The room — small, oddly shaped, poorly lit — lay at the end of a cul-de-sac hallway, at the place where an older hospital building had been mated to a newer addition, the room itself a structural afterthought formed by opening some space off the side of a storage closet. It had several corners, one narrow window, and provided barely sufficient floor space for a few pieces of equipment, two chairs and a single bed. On the ceiling a fluorescent light box flickered. 'They brought me back to life and then what? Then they put me into a tomb,' complained James Dell, his voice a croak. He sipped from a plastic cup and water overspilled his lips and flowed onto his green hospital gown, where he batted at it. Pale and brightly scarred, he lay in collapse, a pair of eyeglasses with thick black frames owling his eyes.

Ellis had come here in a state of exhaustion that left him stumbling and half blind, fearful that James would despise him, that James would refuse him. But James seemed hardly aware of him. Instead he worried aloud about money, and because of money he wanted to leave the hospital. His wife said he couldn't leave. He said it was a free country. Mrs Dell said the doctors said he shouldn't leave. He tried to get out of bed but fell back with a shriek and moaned. He said she should help him. She glowered and said she would not help him to act like an idiot. He said he would soon be broke. She said he had no choice. He said he would be broke and would soon live under a bridge and cook rats for dinner over a barrel fire. She said he had never cooked a thing in his life. He said she should have let him die rather than be bankrupted into a life of homelessness and rat-eating and could she move the pillow under his leg nearer to the knee? Which she did. But on and on they argued, with loud indifference to anyone who might be listening.

Their volume rose and fell; James's strength was inconsistent. Ellis sat in the corner in one of the plastic chairs. Now that he was here, he had little sense of reason or purpose. He recalled the collapse of James Dell onto the hood and the patter of glass against his own face — and now he sat beside James Dell's bed and James Dell complained that there were too many commercials on and changed the channel and Mrs Dell hounded him to change it back and leave it, please.

Meanwhile the light in the little window over the bed brightened and faded with the passage of unseen clouds.

Eventually Ellis excused himself to go to the bathroom. When he'd finished he considered walking out of the hospital and driving away. But he wanted to watch one more time the opening and closing of James's eyes, the life of his thin limbs, the sneering of his lips.

James lay alone in the room, holding up a hand and staring at it.

Ellis said, 'I wish I could do more than say I'm sorry.'

'Sir.' James grimaced. 'If you apologise again, I'll have them throw you out.'

Ellis sat. The overhead light flashed. A passing bed rattled in the hallway.

'I shouldn't have crossed there,' James said.

'I shouldn't have tried to pass on the right.'

'I've passed on the right a thousand times.' James's voice guttered with self-disgust. 'Nothing wrong with it.'

Ellis hesitated, feeling he should apologise, afraid to apologise.

'She went out for some lunch,' James said. 'The bitch.'

'She was here all the time that you were in the coma.'

'I don't doubt it.'

'It was very hard for her, her husband — '

'I'm not her husband. She's not my wife.'

'She isn't?'

'Ex. We were unmarried eight and a half years ago. She can go any time she wants. I don't love her.' He wound his sheet on his finger. 'I wish I did. It would be something.'

Then he sat forward with a jerk and looked around. He complained that she had been away too long and she was spending money on lunch when she could have just as easily eaten off the tray of food that the hospital gave him.

A short, cushiony nurse came in to fret over the machines.

Ellis rose and excused himself.

He drove to Heather's house. In the street before it he slowed the minivan to a crawl and remembered years before, passing by here in naivety and embarrassment, while Boggs waved from the garage, and it roused a sensation that he could not name but it was excruciating. A car came close behind him, and he accelerated away. Then through a route of miles he turned and turned back, slowed, turned into the drive, let the minivan idle down its length. He stood a minute in the driveway. The garage was closed, the windows dark. The grass of the lawn had grown long. Black clouds were heaving up out of the west.

He reached for the doorbell, but then tried the knob instead, and at his touch the door opened. He stood looking in at the darkened living room. 'Heather?' he called, softly. The walls were worked with innumerable bright colours — images in crayon, watercolour, construction paper, cellophane, papier mâché, stickers, marker, glued buttons, seashells, bottle caps — pieces of art that her students had given her or had simply abandoned. Some of it she had framed and some of it was stuck up with thumbtacks, so that they filled the walls from floor to ceiling with stick figures, mountains, houses, flowers, monster trucks, rainbows and various abstractions and images so crude as to be effectively abstract. Their initial effect could be overwhelming, but he had seen them a couple of times before when he picked up Boggs for work trips, and he looked at them now only to try to detect whether anything had changed. All over the floor lay many objects, scattered or assembled in piles — pens, coffee mugs, silverware, magazines, drink coasters, a tube of Crest, sheets, a bar of soap, telephone books, wire hangers, a TV remote. He studied these things for a while, but could make no sense of them, and then toed through to the kitchen, which stood empty, the shades drawn, the refrigerator whirring, a single light under a cabinet illuminating a tub of sugar and a set of knives mounted to the wall on magnets so that they appeared to float.

The windowless stairwell was particularly dark. He hung onto the banister as he went up. Then the top step lay underfoot and the guest bedroom stood open and empty, the bed squarely made and desolate. The door of the master bedroom stood ajar and swung under his hand. The shades drawn, the room lay in dim grey illumination, its objects defined by shadows. After a while he could see Heather asleep in the bed. He felt he could hardly breathe and feared he would inadvertently gasp or cry out. For minutes he stood. Then he moved into the room, aware of the sounds he made — the brushing of the creases of his clothing, the crackling press of his feet into the carpet, the tiny grinding of his joints. He stood beside the bed, then eased down until he kneeled on the carpet. She slept on her stomach, her head turned so that the right side of her face pressed into the pillow, exposing the scar on the left side. Her hair spread wild. Her lashless eyelids appeared frail and naked as an infant's, but her face was lined in a way that made her seem tired even as she slept. He reached toward her, but stopped short. The bed sheets were twisted tight around her. Laundry sprawled at the foot of the bed, and a half-dozen coffee mugs crowded the bedside table.

He was glad to watch her sleep and feared that when she woke she would send him away, because he had not saved Boggs, because he had killed Boggs, because he had left her for so long, because he had not called, because to be sent away seemed the least that he deserved.

Through parted lips her teeth showed dry and dull white. Her eyes darted under the lids. The scar on her skin seemed more shining and pale than he recalled. The room's shadows darkened.

Then her eyes opened; she gazed at him.

Time seemed to condense, gather and fall in tiny droplets. He kneeled trembling. 'Ellis,' she said, unsurprised. 'I've been so worried.'

'Boggs is dead.' His awareness concentrated in a little circle, of Heather, of the dark beyond gone blurry. 'He stepped into the highway.'

'They said you were there.' She touched his hand. 'I thought maybe at the funeral you would come.'

'I just drove. For days I didn't know what I was doing. Or I tried not to know. I was afraid if I came here you would send me away.'

She shook her head. 'Why?'

'You'll forgive me?'

'Forgive? There are a thousand things that we should talk about, and I don't even know what you're talking about.'

'Heather — '

'I thought about buying an RV like the one my dad had and going out to look for you. The same kind of RV so you would know it was me. But I guessed you would come back.' She spoke to the ceiling, turning to him only with glances, as if shy. 'Because you had said you would, and you're the kind of person who does what he says he will do. Even if you did say you would come back *soon*.'

'As soon as I could — '

'If I had a nickel for every excuse.'

'The road to hell is paved with nickels.'

She smiled a little. 'Yes.'

It seemed as if he could hear the faint, entropic noise of everything around him slowly corroding, oxidising, of the room's thin light minutely eating into the surfaces it touched.

Heather's features suddenly strained, and she rolled away. 'It's OK,' she said without looking at him. 'It's OK.'

He moved into bed with her. He nestled against her. He tried not to suggest to himself the question of how many times Boggs had lain in this bed.

After Boggs's death, after the police had
released him, he had begun driving without
any sense of intention. He seemed able to see
and to recall everything, and this was terrible,
and he wished for a catatonic state, a slipping
under the waters of consciousness. Only the
shaking in him had stopped, and now he
found he missed it. Otherwise he wanted
nothing of the world, but even as it feigned
indifference the lurid world impinged on him
constantly. He ate, he drank, he slept, he went
to the bathroom in gas stations and rest stops
and Taco Bells. His feelings were small,
constant and physical in their shifting, like a
leaf fluttering in his lung. He had loved
Boggs, but he loved Heather more passion-
ately, and recalling this pairing of facts stirred
certain notions to life, and at times he
screamed, beat on the steering wheel. But
these efforts made no difference to anything,
and when he stopped it seemed to be because
he had simply decided to stop.

One afternoon, as he drove a lonesome
stretch of two-lane between fields where
cotton tufted white like a scatter of snow on
low brown plants, the minivan's temperature
gauge began to climb. Soon the radiator spit
steam, and he had to be towed from the

roadside. While a mechanic worked to swap the water pump, Ellis asked what day it was. Two weeks had dissolved since Boggs's death. He went to a phone on a post near the road and, after several minutes of doubt, called the hospital.

'He's come out of it,' Mrs Dell exclaimed. 'He's really better. I've told him about you, about how you called, about your concern. He wants to meet you.'

This — he saw now — was obviously an untruth. But when she said it, he believed her and glimpsed something past his personal oblivion. He drove the minivan for a day and a half without rest to reach the hospital.

★ ★ ★

But now the jolt of purpose had faded. He moved in a strange world, filled with dark strangeness, and it was strange to be expected — by the implication of the progress of time, if nothing else — to continue with life and find ways to act. For three days he did not leave Heather's house. He wished he had come here sooner. He felt impossibly indebted. Here, for now, nothing needed to be explained.

Boggs had been cremated, Heather said, the ashes sent to his surviving aunt. She had arranged to have his convertible donated to a charity rather than shipping it back here, but the things piled over the living room floor were Boggs's things, or things that she thought of as his, which she could not bring herself to use or to trash. She asked Ellis if he would do something with them.

So he had a task. When she went to school to teach, he ranged the house, gathering: all the items in the living room, then the shoes and shirts and slacks in the bedroom closet — clothing that he had seen Boggs wear many times — and a pair of sunglasses on the dresser, toothbrushes in a drawer under the bathroom sink, a collection of pocketknives in the chest of drawers in the hallway, an assortment of baseball caps on the refrigerator, all into plastic garbage bags that he assembled in ranks on the back patio. The files of records and financial documents that Boggs had assembled were still stacked on the dining table. Ellis put them into a cabinet in the spare bedroom.

He told her what had happened, as best he could, the facts of the event, likely not much different from what the police had told her. The official report, Heather said, had labelled it a suicide. 'No,' Ellis said. 'What do you call it when a person loses at Russian roulette? He didn't look at the car that hit him. He didn't look to see if there was a car. I don't think he was aware of the car, except as a possibility. He knew there was traffic, which might or might not be able to stop for him. He'd done exactly the same thing a little while earlier, and got away with it. He took a chance. What do you call a person who does that?' He waited for Heather to say something, but she didn't. He said, 'I think there was a distinction in his mind.'

He told her that when he reached Boggs and found him dead, he had somehow bloodied his own face on the ground, so that the police believed for some time that he had also been involved in the collision. And that his own actions had even at the time felt light and insultingly comic.

He laboured to raise words. 'What's strange is that I have to work very hard to remember the collision,' he told her. 'James Dell still flips up onto the hood in front of me. But it's as if Boggs had stepped into a fog. I can remember details, but I have to concentrate, and even then the sequence doesn't flow, there are only some disconnected pieces, as if I had been told about it, no sense of having been there, and it seems I can't even feel guilty correctly.' As he spoke a prickling sensation of hot sand filled him grain by grain until he was choking and could say no more.

Over the days he grew aware — in a partial way — that Heather's constraint and quiet were a little strange, but he had his own impulse to silence, and he told himself that the silence between them was not uncomfortable, because of Boggs and everything now thick with Boggs's presence, because they both knew that in death John Boggs had spread himself everywhere. The idea that Boggs was simply gone was impossible to sustain. Unlike the dead man at the lake, who in his anonymity became a curiosity. Unlike Christopher, who Ellis had known well but had not understood, so that in death he became an object of the past.

And although they hardly spoke in the course of the evening, they still clung together in the night, they still made love, and he felt as if here they had come to a place of such unbounded emotion that there was nothing left to say.

In boxes in the closets he discovered hats and gloves and scarves, rubbers for Boggs's size twelve shoes, and a sunshade for his convertible's windshield. In the corners of the garage he discovered a dusty, half-empty pack of cigarettes, an extra set of tyres for the convertible, a few old T-shirts. He sifted and contemplated Boggs's collection of tools — wrenches, screwdrivers, hand drill, sander, pipe cutter, hammers, pliers, table saw, mitre saw — and then began putting them into boxes. From the basement he brought up cans of tennis balls, aluminum-frame tennis rackets, cross-country skis, a selection of paperback thrillers, AC/DC and Led Zeppelin cassette tapes, a box of model-railroad equipment. Most surprising, perhaps, was how little it all amounted to. A few bags. Boggs kept a messy desk at the office, but he didn't have much clutter at home. Soon Ellis was searching through closets for the fourth or fifth time, sorting item by item through drawers and wondering whether Heather would consider a ball-point from a Hyatt or a stray brown coat button to have been Boggs's. He peered under the bed and sofa, into the crannies of the furnace room, along the rafters of the garage. In a bin of unused flowerpots he found a hidden box of Boggs's keepsakes — tapes of a high school rock band, photos of a girl perhaps eighteen years old, strings of beads and shells, medals from youth golf tournaments, high school and college diplomas, and stacks of report cards. Ellis began to sort through the stuff, but then stopped and upended it into a garbage bag.

He also found hidden away — and, it seemed, forgotten — a couple of Heather's art projects. There were a few disposable coffee cups that rattled when he lifted them: each contained a paper diorama to be viewed through the hole in the lid. Octopuses hanging from tiny strings. A skyline of gold foil buildings. A dinosaur emerging from an outhouse. And he discovered a toy airplane, more than two feet long, which had been covered with delicately placed feathers. It looked like an airplane-shaped chicken, with a chicken's incompetence for real flight, and he adored it. Fearing Heather might throw them away, he left them where he had found them.

He discovered evidence of a house that had been divided for some time — many of Boggs's clothes were in the guest room. Dirty plates and glasses were stacked around the desk Boggs kept in the basement.

On the fourth day Ellis decided to take out this desk and the file cabinet beside it. He approached the task with some anxiety — he knew Boggs had kept copies of a number of work files in the drawers, and Ellis had a fear of those files, as if by a monstrous magnetism they might draw him into old nightmares. But when he opened the drawers, he found them empty. Heavy and bulky, the desk and the drawers could be pushed over the floor, but he saw that he could not move them up the stairs by himself. He retrieved a hammer and a pry bar from Boggs's tools, began yanking out the drawers, and found taped to the underside of one a broken, weathered plastic nameplate that said *airlane*.

He stood turning it in his hands for a long while, confounded. Eventually he carried it to the minivan and put it into the glovebox. He sat in the passenger seat, wondering, until, with a bellowing noise, a neighbour began mowing his lawn. Ellis locked the glovebox, retreated inside and took apart the desk with hammer blows.

★ ★ ★

Still time moved by like a slow wind, a large and invisible force, present in the nodding of grasses and the shaking of leaves, easily forgotten. He watched Heather and thought a great deal about the *airlane* nameplate, trying to derive its significance. *You ever talk to Heather about your brother's accident?* Boggs had asked.

'I feel ashamed all the time,' she said one evening. 'As if I'd been coated with something, plasticky or rubbery, shiny. Mint green. It's strange when no one else seems to

284

notice.' She looked at her hand. 'Do you still see my scars?'

'I haven't noticed them in a long time,' Ellis said. This seemed the only thing to say, even if it was not entirely true.

'I think I'd actually forgotten them for a while. I didn't think I ever would, but then I did. I know because now I see them again.'

He watched for her to throw things or claw herself, but she didn't move. He knew something undefined and emotional had shifted between them, and he tried to think through it carefully. But it was like trying to think his way to California.

In their long stretches of silence, he watched her take art books off the shelf — Rothko, Still, Motherwell, Johns — and turn through the images, her expression unaffected by whatever she saw. Sometimes she spent hours with the TV on and a page before her, doodling dense tangles of lines, craggy, elaborate constructions: leaves, machineries, mazes, branches, flowers, tangles of wire, heaps of rope, blending into one another from edge to edge of the page.

* ★ ★

The shattering heat of the shower poured on him until the hot-water tank had been

285

exhausted. He set himself into jeans and a T-shirt, socks and shoes, and with these tasks completed sat on the bending edge of the bed. Heather would not be back until five or six. Sunlight cut between the leaves outside and set a shifting pattern of shadow on the wall. He watched it move until the last of it seeped off the wall onto the floor. Then he went into the bathroom to pee and then the kitchen and ate a couple of slices of plain bread. At the bottom of the sink lay loose puddles of water, evaporating. All around, dust settled. He swept the kitchen floor — as he had done the day before, and the day before that — and gathered a few crumbs into a dustpan and threw them away. In the living room he turned through a magazine — not reading, but watching how the glare of the light moved over the gloss of the pages as he manipulated them.

At noon he poured a can of soup into a bowl, microwaved it, ate, washed the bowl and spoon by hand, dried them, set them back in the cupboard. He sat with the jobs section of the classifieds and read through it but marked nothing — he was either under-qualified or overqualified. He went to the computer that Heather kept in the spare bedroom and opened a new document to begin working out a résumé. He'd put his name at the top of the page before he realised that the mouse pad beside the keyboard, showing a brown mouse with a red ribbon around his neck, was the same one that he had given to her in the museum years before. It disoriented him badly.

Finally he aimed his gaze at the screen and tried to consider whether he should provide as his address this house or his apartment, until his eyes felt dried by the steady glow of the screen, and he turned it off. Darkened, the dust captured on its surface could be seen. He attempted to examine it, mote by mote. He shifted his fingers. He seemed to feel something, but was it large or small, was it guilt or grief? Did these two actually feel different from each other, or were they only two labels applied to the same thing depending on context?

He sat on the floor, trying to detect the impression of the bones of his spine one atop another, the press of his lungs into his ribs, the taste of the top of his mouth against his tongue, the flickering contact of his eyelids when he blinked, the fall of his hair against his scalp. If he concentrated hard enough perhaps he could even sense the hair growing from the follicles, the smell of himself lifting from himself, the noise of molecules of nitrogen and oxygen bouncing off his eardrums, the cells of his body slowly creating and destroying themselves.

Certain thoughts worked through his mind on long, spiral paths. Christopher became James became Boggs, and other accidents that he had worked on pressed into his attention, photograph images, the scents and winds and landscapes of accident scenes, a family scattered dead over the road and the crushed tow-truck driver and the little girl killed by a family of geese and the man who backed away from the burning van while screams still sounded inside — which was exactly what Christopher had failed to do. It shocked Ellis to realise this. How strange he had never made the connection.

He did not know what to do with the questions that the *airlane* nameplate forced him toward. Apparently Boggs had gone to see Christopher's car. Why had he done that? Had he done a reconstruction of Christopher's accident? Why? What had he found? Ellis didn't want to look into any accident, he didn't want to reconstruct anything, and he absolutely did not want to consider or reconstruct Christopher's accident. But it seemed the only way to discover what Boggs had known. Did it matter what Boggs had known? He wasn't sure. But the question presented itself again and again, summoning itself up as if by the same mechanism that the image of James Dell on the hood still made itself known. He could only guess that it related to Boggs's conversation with Heather beside the golf course.

When Heather arrived home she moved around to redistribute the same items she had collected that morning — cellphone, keys, purse — then went into the bedroom. He heard the lisp of her skirt's collapse on the floor and a drawer opening as she pulled out jeans.

She sat beside him. She asked how his day had been. He spoke of what he had seen in the paper and online, of thinking about his résumé. She nodded. 'What happened to Boggs's files in the basement?' he asked.

'I took all that to the office and told them this was everything I had of John's work, and I didn't want anyone from there contacting me again.'

She rested one hand on his knee, and he studied her veins and tendons, the faint small hairs, the irregularity of scarred skin near the base of the thumb. He asked about her day, she described the variable moods of children, and then they sat touching lightly while the traffic in the street buzzed. She asked, not looking at him, 'How long will it be like this?'

'What do you mean?'

'You don't see anyone but me.'

'What about you? How do you feel?'

'I'm so absolutely fucking angry with him,' she said.

It seemed odd to him that it really hadn't occurred to him to be angry at Boggs.

'How long?' Softly. Her hand on his leg did not move away and neither did it tighten.

Feeling the question was unanswerable, he did not answer. He saw behind her, perched in a far upper corner of the room, a spider. It crept an inch down the wall, then returned to where it had started. Then he was aware again of her attention on him — it seemed to have tightened, and he observed suddenly how strange he was becoming. Had become. He bore responsibility, too, for her quiet. He had reduced her to quiet doodling.

Her fingers tightened slightly on his leg, then lifted away.

She stood and went out of the room. A cupboard door clattered. Ellis lifted a hand and held it, testing its heaviness. With a tap of noise a glass was set on the counter. Water hissed into the kitchen sink.

'I'm sorry,' he called.

She reappeared and stood looking at him. Not unkind. Not without patience. But looking. And he felt something in himself hiding. He wanted to ask her, What am I hiding? What is wrong with me? He recalled how, when searching for Boggs, he had wished to somehow pry under his rational processes. Maybe now he had succeeded, but if so it had been a foolish thing to hope for, because under them lay, it seemed, nothing.

When she turned away he was startled, as if he had forgotten the possibility of movement.

At dinner Heather lit two squat candles on the table that burned with tiny steady globular flames, and they ate Italian takeout with the television on, tossing its shifting light on the ceiling. In bed he clasped lightly around her back until she seemed asleep. With eyes clutched shut he waited for sleep, thinking of her attention on him. Not without patience, but with limits.

★　★　★

The first time he set out, he drove north a few miles, then turned in at a park that he knew and sat for some hours at the edge of a lake with a swim area to watch the children scream and splash one another. Behind him mountain bikes came down a rocky trail with the noise of rolling typewriters. As the day leaned into dusk the bikes grew fewer and the swimmers exited until the lake water lay smooth, and he sat alone in the bluish light that hovered off the water and recalled the dead man that he and Boggs had left, and who might still, for all that he knew, lie there undiscovered, because in the aftermath of Boggs's death he had never mentioned it to the police.

The second time he made it to Coil. He circled on the roads, peering at the park, the strip malls, the old buildings in the old centre of town, many shut and boarded. Much of the local commerce had shifted to chain stores and restaurants around an interstate exit a couple of miles to the west. But the high school appeared unchanged, the library likewise; he avoided the street where he had grown up. In only a few minutes he was carried through town and out into the surrounding fields of corn and sugar beets. He discovered a new golf course — a startling open space of deep green and lifeless flags.

He turned back and stopped in front of a store that sold pet supplies. It stood in the place of a baseball-card shop that he remembered, and he sat not looking at the intersection where his brother had died, then stood out of the minivan and approached the intersection and with his hands in his pockets looked at the place. East across Mill Street lay the gas station where Heather had watched the accident, now a green-and-white BP

— he studied it with a sense of unease. Whatever it had been back then, he felt pretty sure it hadn't been a BP. Cattycorner from where he stood spread the trees and grass of the park that had held his favourite swings. The trees looked older and fewer now, and a weirdly rococo gazebo had been put up to rot. And south across Main Street lurked, presumably, the house where he had once lived; the tall fencing that ran alongside the street had been replaced, now even taller, painted a red brown. The lane counts on Mill and Main had not changed, but the lights suspended overhead appeared new, and in the years since the accident how many times had the asphalt been resurfaced, the kerbs rebuilt, the lane lines repainted? The entire pattern of it could have shifted several feet. The parking lot he stood in had a new kerb cut near the intersection. To what extent was this no longer really the place where Christopher had died? To a great extent. But there was no other place.

He didn't want to be doing this work again. But he thought of the *airlane* nameplate and went forward. He paced the distances across the lanes, from light pole to kerb edge, from kerb edge to street sign, measuring a yard with each step, a simple skill that Boggs had made him practise. Boggs had also given him a five-pound sack of sugar and told him to test its weight at arm's length, then gave him a desk lamp, a laptop computer, a brake drum, and asked of each, 'More or less than five pounds? Guess the weight?' Soon they descended to the basement garage where Boggs attempted, with loud failures, to juggle wrenches — the memory of the odour of motor oil and sawdust and the riotous clanging of the wrenches became suddenly so vivid that Ellis had to stop a minute and breathe.

He ripped a page from the back of the minivan's owner's manual and sketched the intersection in ballpoint and labelled it with his paced measurements. He added notes on light timing and traffic flow, and amid this work he noticed a new sensation — relief. As if he had swum nearly to the point of exhaustion, of drowning, but now his feet had found land. This work. How easy it was to move here. The relief unnerved and disappointed him.

Eventually he looked up and saw a woman, in sweatpants and a T-shirt snug enough to show the roll of her belly fat, standing outside the pet supply store, watching him. She smiled and moved to the side window of the minivan and tapped. 'Ellis Barstow!' she exclaimed as he rolled down the window. And he said hi, but who was she? Without provocation she talked about teachers he remembered and some of his friends. She mentioned Christopher, solemnly, and glanced at the intersection. She seemed his own age, more or less, but her weight had bagged into small jowls that exaggerated as she frowned. A spray of curling thin brown hair imperfectly covered her pink scalp. Ellis said little to encourage her, and finally she said, 'You don't recognise me, do you?'

He smiled and shook his head.

'Kari Butters.'

Even this did not help. But he said, 'Oh, yes, Kari. Of course.' And because she still had a look of expectation, he added, 'Wow.'

She mentioned other people, one feebly familiar, but more that it seemed to him he had never heard of before in his life. He nodded dumbly. He tried to subtract the jowls, subtract some wrinkles from around her eyes. But the effort gained him nothing. She talked on, faster and faster, and suddenly she said, with forced enthusiasm, 'Well, how about you? What are you up to? What do you do?'

'Nothing,' he said. 'Nothing right now.'

She waited.

'I'm between jobs,' he said. 'Between things.'

With a little clawing motion she burst into talking about a couple more people. He felt like a disappointment. Soon she looked over to the pet store — Kissing Kritters — as if it had just now appeared, cast out a farewell and fled.

He was glad to drive again. The land streamed by and he worked out a sense that some of the people she had mentioned had been a grade or two below himself, and if she were also from one of the lower grades that might explain how she had been so aware of him while he could not recall her at all. Or perhaps Christopher's death had made everyone aware of him. Nonetheless, he had a feeling of precarious nullity: the place where his brother had died was no longer the place where his brother had died, and Kari Butters indicated a world that had once been his life and yet now he hardly recognised it.

When he reached the house and found Heather there, he embraced her with an urgency that he saw startled her.

That night he lay naked beside her, and he recalled that she had never answered his questions about Christopher's accident, but he also hated to be holding any secret from her. Having begun this examination of Christopher's accident he felt himself in the midst of a betrayal that he could hardly afford

296

when without her he might dissipate, a phantom of smoke, an odour of tyre rubber.

★ ★ ★

On the interstate the next day he passed signs and exits, fields and woods that should have been perfectly familiar from the day before and yet much of it appeared strange and newborn. Then, in Coil he had to stop and think for several minutes to recall where to find the police station.

Like the high school, like the library, the police station had not changed: an almost windowless beige brick building, its function named across the front in aluminum letters. He had entered it only once before, years ago, on a grade school field trip led by a teacher named Mrs Hose — *with a hair out her nose,* went the playground chant. The children were fingerprinted onto souvenir cards, and they peered into a holding cell. He had been disappointed that it had no steel bars, only pink walls. Pink, said their guide, a woman who normally sat at the reception desk, was soothing.

He wasn't sure that it wasn't the same woman, now much older, who sat at a desk by the door and nodded and darted glances at him while he explained his purpose. The accident report that he wanted was very old, she said, and it wouldn't be here but at a document-holding facility maintained by the county. She drew a map on the backside of an 'Emergency Preparedness' brochure, lining roads and highways atop a bulleted list of first-aid items.

Her route took him through the intersection where Christopher had died and onward between two silvered lakes under a vast cream sky, through cow fields, and along the edge of a regional airport where prop airplanes came down and went up with dragonfly noises, to a warehouse with a bank of offices stretched along the front. Its gutters sagged and the appliqué window tints had bubbled. A receptionist sent him to a heavy, balding, moustached, cubicled man in beige pants and a mauve shirt who listened to what Ellis wanted, spent a few minutes peering into an old, DOS-based program on his computer, wrote down a number, said, 'Please wait here,' and went away.

Ellis studied a photograph on the desk — two fat children grinned before a pull-down backdrop of washed-out blue — until he wanted to smash it. The man returned with a manila folder. He said that he could xerox the text of the report for ten cents a page, but the photos would have to be sent to the photo lab for prints, which would take several days.

He went away to copy the report, and Ellis sat with the stack of photos — color glossy 4x6s. Minutes passed while he sat not looking at the photos, thinking only of putting them aside, standing and leaving.

Then without any conscious prompting his attention settled onto them. The first photo, mostly black, showed a view straight down at an asphalt road surface with someone's black shoe — probably the photographer's — gleaming in the corner, and he could not tell if the photo was taken in error or if it was supposed to show something on the road that could not be seen, a tyre mark, perhaps. The second photo offered only more black and a double yellow lane line crossing it diagonally. In the third photo shapes could be made out — a lamp post, a portion of a parked police cruiser, and in the middle distance a burned vehicle bellied on the street, an overhead light reflecting weakly from the patches of unburned paint on its front end. Between the burned car and the camera lay a blanket-covered shape that was, almost certainly, Christopher, and Ellis experienced a surge of feeling that he had not prepared for. A ferocious hot pain. He set the photos aside. He had not taken them up again when the fat man returned with his copy of the report. Ellis gave him a cheque and asked to have the photos mailed to his apartment's address.

★ ★ ★

He had not been to his apartment since the day after the accident with James Dell. The silent grandfather clock, the shelves of books — everything here held a layer of dust, which obscurely pleased him, and he tried to disturb it as little as possible. He sorted the mail heaped under the mail slot — junk mail, magazines, catalogues, bills, overdue notices — and when he found the photos he opened the envelope quickly, to pre-empt hesitation, and turned through the images. The pain that had caught him the first time he had looked at them did not resume. Christopher's body was visible in just three photos and was never the centre of focus, only a thing under a blanket in the middle distance. Ellis looked at it calmly. Why? He didn't know. Was this how he should have felt when he first saw the photo? Or had the feeling before been the true feeling?

The evidence in the photos seemed generally as he had expected — short tyre marks left by the *airlane*, a point of impact indicated by a spill of fluid and glass in the middle of the intersection, two cars standing at their points of rest, police and fire vehicles scattered around the periphery, everything muddled by the surrounding murk of night. Strange to see how long ago it all appeared — the boxy cars, the men with shaggy hair and moustaches, a sign in the background offering a gallon of gasoline for less than a dollar. It had been an Amoco station — so, he and Heather had both been wrong. He went back and forth through the photos, thinking, If you look long enough you will see something new. He didn't; but when he finally set the photos down, the objects of his apartment appeared strange, as if their dirt and wear had been caused by someone else.

Working between the photos, the police report and the measurements he'd made at the intersection, he built a diagram of the scene in his computer. He drew dimensionally correct icons to represent the cars at their points of rest, then he studied the damage on each vehicle and the tyre marks on the roadway to estimate their orientations as they collided and set the icons at the point of impact and at maximum intrusion with a couple of inches added to account for restitution — his brother's *airlane* striking the left rear-quarter panel area of the other vehicle at a little less than ninety degrees, the result of both vehicles swerving too late.

When he finished, the diagram showed an overhead view of the lane lines, the kerbs, the poles at the corners, the two cars at the instant of impact and the positions where they had come to rest. This was, in a sense, the place where Christopher had died.

He copied the scene diagram into a specialised accident reconstruction program called PC-Crash — when he started working with Boggs he had thought a lot of jokes would come of the name, but it had only become part of the background: *chair, calculator, email, PC-Crash*. Within the program he created representations of the two cars that included suspension character-istics and passenger weights — he tried for a minute to remember what Christopher's weight might have been, but finally settled for using a published statistical average. He set the simulated vehicles onto the icons at the point of impact, adjusted their velocities, steering angles, brake factors and restitution. Then he ran the analysis and watched as they spun away from the impact toward the rest positions. The *airlane* overshot its mark by a dozen feet, while the other vehicle didn't go far enough and ended up facing the wrong way. He began to make adjustments. Velocity. Steering angles. Brake factors. Restitution factors. Small changes sometimes resulted in large effects in post-impact motion, but after a couple of hours he had refined the model so that the vehicles spun away from the point of impact, scrubbed speed off as they went round and rocked to a stop exactly on the icons where he had marked the rest positions.

He ran the model a few times, and the accident enacted itself again and again in shifting pixels, perfectly silent. The computer offered that at impact Christopher's car had been travelling at 42.3 mph; the other car at 49.1 mph. By hand Ellis calculated his brother's initial velocity before he had begun laying down tyre marks, and came up with 46 mph, give or take a couple of mph, a speed not unexpected on that road, a speed that might even be considered cautious, since Ellis had observed many vehicles breezing through at around 60 mph. Perhaps Christopher had slowed while he was involved with some distraction. But one might formulate endless speculations.

He had no evidence whatsoever as to whether Christopher had entered the inter-section under a green, yellow or red light. Witnesses often provided the only available evidence about light timing, and here the witness statements recorded in the police report, from the occupants of vehicles that had been approaching the intersection, were all against Christopher. The report mentioned that Heather had been at the scene at the time of the accident and described her injuries, but it didn't include any witness testimony from her.

He tried to think, what had he gained from this analysis?

Nothing presented itself. This sort of analysis was needed to make a credible presentation in a courtroom, but he probably could have estimated the results to within a few mph beforehand.

Could Boggs have seen something in this that he had missed?

He turned through the photos again. It seemed perhaps the *airlane* had come to a stop a few feet further off the kerb than he had represented it in his scene diagram. He moved the point of rest in PC-Crash and began readjusting parameters. It took him an hour to clean up the simulation again, but in the end it only made a half an mph of difference.

He went through the photos yet again, and again, until although his eyes focused on the images he seemed not to see anything, and he was tempted to think that by memorising them completely he might forget them.

He returned to the house. He was lying flat

on the floor when he heard Heather's car in the drive. Seeing him, she started, then laughed. 'You're all right?' She passed through the room, her steps jarring faintly through the floor into his skull. After a few minutes she returned, barefoot — he couldn't see her feet but knew by the sound.

'Can you get up?'

'It's all right,' he said.

'I find you like this,' she said, 'and I worry that you've been on the floor all afternoon.'

'It's only been a moment,' he said. 'It's not uncomfortable.' Sun through a window beat warmly on his foot and ankle. He monitored the effort of the rise and fall of his chest as he breathed. 'It's a very nice floor,' he offered.

She frowned, but sat cross-legged beside him.

He felt his heaviness pressing him to the floor and, in a way gratifying to observe, it held him here and his weight implied his substance, his existence.

He pushed himself up — surprising how little effort it took — and put his head in her lap. She stroked the hair at his temples. 'You're OK,' she said, in a tone that didn't seem to seek an immediate response. He closed his eyes and lay feeling his weight and her fingers and thinking to himself that he loved her. And, he didn't quite trust her. He wanted to ask her about that, but the words too were dense and did not like to rise.

★ ★ ★

The next step would be to go to see his father, but he hesitated.

He made coffee and watched the arabesque of the milk and its subsequent slow diffusion. He put ice in a glass of water and grew lost in the transmutation of solid into liquid. Everything worked this way, one thing always becoming another, powered by entropy. In the nights when he rose to pace the house it contained a faint, nameless smell that Boggs must have carried on his clothes, because at times it sucker-punched Ellis, forcing memories of awful vividness. And despite a general sense of slowness, whenever he looked at a clock minutes seemed to have passed with startling speed.

'My brother — ' From time to time those two words came of themselves into his mind, the beginning of a sentence or thought that went no further. Sometimes it felt like a message delivered incompletely, sometimes it felt like a failure in himself, and sometimes he seemed to be thinking about Christopher only to realise that the image he had in his mind was of Boggs. And he still saw the form of James Dell strike the windshield and press into it and saw, or imagined — because he knew that he had shut his eyes — the glass flex and the cracks form and run to all directions like a growth of shining crystals.

Heather asked what kind of jobs he was looking at. Engineering, he said, the only field he had qualifications in. 'Accident reconstruction?' He said no. They ate dinners with the television on, so that the quiet would be less conspicuous.

As far as he knew, his father still had Christopher's *airlane*. To see it he would need to see his father, and he didn't want to see his father.

In the mornings he woke before her, but waited, listening to her slow breath. Eventually she pulled up her legs and curled her face down toward them, as if in a last effort to gather into sleep and fend off the day. Then she stretched. He rolled over and moved to hold her a minute before she slipped out of bed. He made coffee and put on a kettle of water for her tea while she showered. He stirred milk into her tea and handed it to her while she ate a bowl of cereal. He asked about what she would do that day. As she finished a bowl of cereal, her spoon knocked noisily against the bottom of the bowl. She carried her bowl to the sink. She moved toward the front door, efficiently gathering her things along the way. He watched her go with a knife working inside himself.

★ ★ ★

Heather had given him a cellphone, so that she could reach him, and he had had his old number reassigned to it. It surprised him every time it rang.

'I'm having a bad time,' said Mrs Dell. 'I don't want to bother you. But I thought it might help to talk.'

He went to visit. Although Mrs Dell's house stood directly beside an industrial-looking railway embankment that crossed the road on a concrete bridge, her neighbourhood was filled with pleasant little houses on large lawns. Mrs Dell's was a yellow house with green shutters behind tall trees and several flower beds — a patch of hostas under a blue spruce, towering sunflowers near the road, clusters of roses and others around the house. The rubber mat at the front door said 'Welcome', and a brass plaque attached to the door frame said 'Solicitors will be composted'. He rang, and she opened the door squinting into the sun glare and smiling with the corners of her lips. She appeared puffy under the eyes. But she had her hair neatly in place and wore pants, blouse and vest in matched patterns of white, grey, and black. She led him into a pink sitting room shadowed and crowded with photos and knick-knacks, set him on an overstuffed love seat, and sat across from him on the front edge of a high-backed wooden rocking chair, leaning with her elbows on her thighs. She began to say something, then laughed, looked away, began again. 'This is silly. I shouldn't have dragged you here.'

He shook his head. 'I didn't know you were a gardener.'

'Only a few flowers.' She looked at the window. 'The hostas have a slug problem. The thing to do about slugs is to put out pans of beer, and they will drown themselves.'

'My mom liked flowers,' Ellis said. 'But when I was growing up the entire lawn around our house was covered with concrete.'

'A city?'

'Small town, a sort of semi-rural place. Dad worked for a concrete contractor.'

'He paved your yard?' She looked shocked.

'Dad never could get the screws in his head all tightened down. Once I went outside and found a gas-pump nozzle stuck in the gas tank of his car, hose hanging down. He'd forgotten to take it out at the gas station and just drove away. It might have been in there for days if I hadn't pointed it out.'

She sat blinking, as if trying to remember if she had ever done such a thing.

Ellis said, 'When I told him about it, he said, 'I thought something sounded funny.''

'Well,' she said, 'we all have our quirks.' She twisted a foot against the carpet. 'Can I get you a drink?' Ellis refused. She nodded. 'I should be glad he's gone, really. He met a woman who throws pottery.' She glanced around. 'Well, maybe he's known her for a while. She makes it, I mean. The pottery. Her hands are ugly things.' She smiled as if for a camera. 'Oh, it's true he never totally lived here. Maybe he told you that. He had his own place, but he stayed here. He'd come here crying like a baby, and I'd take care of him. A lot of drama. Eventually, he'd leave, then a couple of days later he'd come back. He didn't have anyone else to take care of him. Maybe now the potter is taking care of him.' She shrugged. 'Do you understand? I thought you might understand, somehow.' She nodded her rocking chair. 'Why did he do this, now? What's wrong with him? How can I help him? I thought maybe — He was very moved by your visit. He didn't have many friends.'

'I don't really have any insight — '

'He often hides what's in his heart. But

310

there was a connection between you, wasn't there?'

Ellis shook his head.

She stood and made little fluttering gestures. She said, 'Should I give up hope?'

Ellis didn't dare say a thing.

'Shouldn't I?' she said. 'But if I could, wouldn't I have years ago?'

'Maybe a little time apart from him will help,' Ellis said, then regretted having said it. For a time he watched her as she paced. 'I'm sorry,' he said.

'He's old now, of course,' she said, 'but he was a good-looking young man.' She retrieved a photo from the clutter on a shelf. 'That's him with his brother,' she said. 'His brother died several years ago of a stroke, unfortunately.' Two young men, probably in their twenties, stood holding each other around the shoulders and lifting champagne glasses, wearing matching black suits and ties, one with a moustache and the other O-ing his mouth as if singing. Either one could have been a plausible younger version of James Dell. Ellis hazarded, 'He's the one singing?'

Mrs Dell sat again in her rocking chair and gazed at the ceiling. 'He hated singing.'

Ellis wasn't sure how that answered the question. He didn't ask. It seemed he might only, somehow, grow even more confused,

311

and he didn't know if he could bear that. At the top of the window he saw a long series of coal cars creeping silently by on the railway embankment.

When he stood, she stood, and he stepped forward and awkwardly accepted her embrace. Returning to the minivan he saw, under the blue spruce, two pans of standing beer. He stopped at a gas station, then steered for the interstate. The sun made a white smear in a silver-grey sky. He passed over a stretch of roadway dark and shining with wet, but he saw no rain. The exit ramp lifted the minivan upward as if to launch it into the sky. He would see his father.

★   ★   ★

Because until now he had avoided it, he went first to the old house. The white siding had been replaced with pale blue and — absurdly, he thought — a wagon wheel and ox yoke had been nailed to the wall on either side of the front door for decorative effect. The TV antenna that he had climbed no longer existed. Grass, shaggy and weedy, had replaced the concrete lawn. A pair of maples he had never seen before reached up twenty-five feet or more. The driveway lay empty, and he could see nothing in the windows. Strange to think of strangers living here, but his family hadn't been the first to live here, either.

He stood out of the minivan, crouched on the kerb, put a hand in the lawn. Surely, he thought, remnants remained here — paint under the paint, holes patched in the drywall, scratches in the floors, fragments of broken concrete buried in the lawn — by which a former life could be reconstructed. As he crouched with his hand pressed to the grass, watching the house, it seemed his parents might walk out, or Heather, or Christopher, or himself, now, or now, or now.

He stood and brushed the clinging grass from his hand and saw that the impress of the grass remained in the skin. He walked to the park, which lay nearer than it seemed in his memory. The swings had been taken out and unmarked turf lay where the scalloped places under them had been. In the intersection moved traffic. Blue pickup. Silver coupé. Yellow school bus. A green convertible — not Boggs's.

As he walked back to the house no one was around, except in the vehicles on the road, and he felt as if moving on foot made him strange and atavistic. From the minivan he watched the house a while longer, then turned the ignition.

His father's house lay a dozen miles to the west, and Ellis drove slowly that way, following first along a river, then down a long straight two-lane interrupted now and again by stop signs at the intersections of narrow dirt roads spanning off to perhaps a house, a farmer's field access, a fishing pond, a patch of private hunting preserve. After a signpost indicating the county line, the roadway became an assemblage of patched cracks and potholes that set the minivan's panels and joints rattling in bright percussion and the steering wheel shaking in his hands. Weeds flourished to the edge of the asphalt and infiltrated its cracks. He passed ragged houses with missing roof shingles, listing into their foundations, wood trim rotting, lawns decorated with tyres and broken concrete. In front of one house a tall woman with a sledgehammer laboured to destroy something on the ground.

He turned onto a dirt-and-gravel road that rolled below the van more smoothly than had the patched asphalt. On either side lay open fields, but the road was lined with oaks and maples that reached over the road so that he seemed to be passing down an arbour. Dust pulled up off the road accumulated on the rear window in a brown fungous pattern. Tunnelling under glinting leaves with the tyres murmuring on the gravel, he felt he would be content to drive on and on and on this way and never arrive.

He slowed approaching the driveway, wallowed up to it, turned in.

The solitary object of any size on the horizon was the house, a two-storey clapboard farmhouse, grey neglect gripping its edges. When he stopped at the end of the drive he saw behind the house a long, metal-roofed shed and, on open ground a little further away, a solitary white toilet. Past the toilet lay only open field, ploughed into parallel furrows and abandoned to low weeds. In the distance ran a trace of fence and low green brush along it, demarcating the next field. The land fell gradually toward the line of the fence and rose again on the other side. Where the land appeared to stop, the sky began with a ridge of clouds the colour of used motor oil.

He stood out of the minivan and kicked through untended grass to the front porch — a pair of naked two-by-fours held up one corner of the porch roof, and missing posts gap-toothed the surrounding rail. Here and there on the floorboards stood empty beer bottles, a sprawling water-damaged phone book, a half of a Clorox bottle filled with rusting nails.

When he put his fist to the door, no one answered. His minivan was the only vehicle in the driveway. He sat on the porch steps to wait.

He destroyed without energy or malice the first half-dozen mosquitoes that came to him, then gave up and let them have what they wanted. Gnats swarmed in clouds over the grass. He closed his eyes, rested his head on his arms.

He woke with a jerk as a long Oldsmobile drew up. It parked behind the minivan, and his father emerged: his father with a paunch, shoulders fallen, bagged under the eyes, hair receded and feral, but unmistakably his father, with his father's large hands and his high cheekbones grown even more prominent, the staring dark eyes a little watery. He wore a button-down shirt of startling white. He crossed half the distance from the car, stopped in the grass, and said, 'Is that you?' He raised a hand and pointed at Ellis, as if to clarify.

Ellis felt confused by the question which, in its literal sense, seemed to allow no negative answer. He stood and opened his hands. He said, 'I need to see the car, Dad.'

His father came forward with a tight smile, staring. Small sharp wrinkles rayed from under the lobes of his ears. His arms, above the big hands, were thinner than Ellis remembered. 'Boy,' he said. 'A surprise.' He twitched and stepped back and looked around the yard. He laughed. 'Let me get you a beer.'

His father let him in and passed into the kitchen while Ellis waited in a dark living room where, as his eyes adjusted, the furnishings materialised slowly and silently in their places. Heavy curtains were pulled, but a vertical slat of light penetrated and illuminated spiralling dust. An unnerving sense of familiarity seized and held him for some seconds before he understood that these furnishings, although in a new context and new arrangement, were known to him: he had grown up with these chairs, these end tables, this sofa, this coffee table, this bookshelf, this wall mirror with the thick carved frame, its silver now spotting and browning, holding a distorted version of himself — his aged self examining a mirror where his younger self had once examined his younger self.

The sofa and chairs, all in their original upholstery, were dirty, sagging, blackened along the front edges of the cushions and arms. Scratches and stains marked the coffee table. One of the shelves of the low bookcase had been replaced with a plank of particle

317

board that sagged alarmingly under a pair of pickle jars filled with coins.

His father gave him a bottle of beer and Ellis said, 'You've kept everything.'

His father glanced around. 'It's a little old, I guess, but nothing wrong with it.' As if to demonstrate functionality, he sat in one of the armchairs.

'Have you seen a tall bearded man here?' Ellis asked — the same question that he had put to any number of cashiers and clerks, and asking it again seemed to frame him once more into that long pursuit. As if Boggs had arranged things so that he would be pursuing him all the rest of his life. 'Have you?' he asked.

'My son died in that car,' his father said.

Ellis shook his head. 'He didn't die in that car. He climbed out and got himself burned and died in the street. And you had two sons. You might say, 'One of my sons died.''

'Tell me something,' his father said, staring. 'Of your life.'

'Tell me about the big bearded guy. I know he was here. I know he looked at the car.'

His father didn't answer.

Ellis looked at the furniture again and hated it, hated the mindless, numb inertia that kept it here. 'Did he tell you who his wife was?'

'Why are you here?'

'I need to see the car.'

'Why?'

Ellis stood over the coffee table and vaguely tried to recall which of its nicks and scratches had been there when he last saw it. 'That's a reasonable question, but it would require a lot of background, and it doesn't really matter. I have a suspicion. That's what it amounts to.'

'You mean, to explain you'd have to tell me something about your life.'

He reluctantly met his father's gaze. The pouches below his father's eyes sagged as if they stored coins.

'Well, your friend was here,' his father said. 'He talked for quite a while. Friendly guy. He did, in fact, tell me who he was married to. Had some interesting ideas about this and that. A little full of himself. I showed him the car. He wouldn't tell me much about you, though.'

'Can I look at the car?'

A fly noised a circle somewhere overhead. His father shifted and drank. 'I ran into someone who knew Heather's dad the other day, at Pep Boys. I was buying lifters for my trunk lid. This guy said Heather's husband is dead. Hit by a car. Is that true?'

'It is. Can I look at the *airlane*?'

When his father only stared, Ellis turned and went to the window and pulled the shade aside. He had to keep a grip on his anxiety and impatience. He felt he might begin to scream. But he sipped his beer.

His father said vaguely, 'It's funny.'

Ellis looked at him.

'You can look at the car if you'll do something for me. Two things.'

Ellis waited.

'Tell me something about yourself. And then listen while I tell you something.' A meekness shaded his father's stare.

'All right,' Ellis said. 'Fine.'

A quiet.

'Tell you something?'

'Please.'

Without intention, Ellis sat. The feel of the chair under himself was familiar. 'I hated my brother.'

'You didn't really hate him,' his father said. He pulled at the sleeve of his strangely white shirt.

'I did.'

'Christopher was in a bad position, between myself and his mother, sent back and forth, never allowed to settle and get comfortable with anyone or learn to trust anyone. Maybe he wasn't your friend, but he was your brother. You looked up to him, you

320

envied him, you wanted him to give more of himself to you than he did, and that angered you. But you didn't hate him. If you think so, it's an idea you've developed since then, and it's my fault. I can see it's my fault.'

'You're constructing fantasies and blaming yourself for them. I hated him because he was a jerk.'

'I didn't understand what I was doing to your relationship with him. I rarely understand what I'm doing, I guess.'

'You have no idea how I felt, Dad.' Ellis was angry with himself for allowing a conversation he had wanted to avoid. He looked at his father's receded hair, tendrilling and floating a little up and down as he drank his beer. Was this truly his father? His father, certainly, but transformed by years, and so was this in any meaningful way the man that he had grown up with? 'I'm living with Heather,' he said. 'I've been involved with her for some time, since before Boggs died. He killed himself. He stepped into moving highway traffic right in front of me.'

'Ah,' his father said.

Ellis straightened and remembered straightening exactly this way in the same chair long ago.

'I'll tell you this,' his father said. 'I love you.' He examined his shirtsleeve in silence.

'But I realise I've never been able to properly manage that emotion.' Silence. 'You were easy to love and Christopher was hard to love, and maybe that was the problem — I overcompensated. I don't know. Some years back, I had a girlfriend, a waitress with three kids. I liked her a lot, I was fond of her kids. One day she asked if I would pick up the youngest, a boy, from day care and drop him off at a friend's where he would stay a couple more hours until she got off her shift at the restaurant. So I did. Picked up the boy, drove him to the friend's house, nudged him in the door. I was backing out of the driveway when a woman came charging out of the house, yelling. Took me a while to figure out what had set her off. What it was was, I had brought the wrong kid. To look at him, it was perfectly obvious, and I knew the kid well enough, there was no excuse for it. So I took this boy back to the day care, where everybody had been going bonkers — police, a fire truck, my waitress girlfriend and other people, all running around, yelling at each other. My girlfriend's boy, feeling guilty that he'd missed his ride, had hidden in a closet, under a pile of blankets, and it took a while to find him. And the parents of the boy I had taken were screaming at anyone who stood still to listen. They let me have it. My girlfriend was practically having seizures. A mess. I apologised of course, but that was it, I never saw her again. I thought about it a lot, and I realised that I just never learned how to do anything properly. I can't even see things properly. I miss the obvious. It's sabotaged my life.'

Ellis waited. When he moved his foot a board creaked and it sounded explosive. He felt sad and heavy and weary and impatient and indifferent — he had heard from his father a number of similar stories with the same conclusion, and nothing ever came of it, no change of temperament or behaviour. The most surprising part of this one was that his father had managed to find a girlfriend, if only briefly. In the kitchen the compressor in the refrigerator kicked on and whirred. His father finished his beer, stared at him for a full minute, then stood and led him outside and around the house to the shed where he turned a key in the lock and slid the door aside. It moved with a sound of corroded steel bearings and revealed a space filled high and wall to wall with dusty and haphazardly stacked objects, many of them familiar — the brass coat rack, the child-sized desk, the crate of board games, the lamp made out of driftwood, the iron headboard, the steamer trunk painted green. His father heaved out two full garbage bags and revealed the hood of the *airlane*, standing at the centre of the clutter like an icon in a shrine.

The two of them stepped over a box of slot-car tracks and squeezed past a cupboard that Ellis recognised from the old kitchen. Leaning into the trunk of the *airlane*, his father grunting through his nose, they pushed it into the daylight. The damaged chassis caused it to move on an arc to the right, so that when they stopped it pointed toward the toilet standing at the verge of the open fields, and Ellis realised that the toilet, too, he knew. 'You took the toilet.'

'The bank got the house,' his father said, 'so I took out everything. Took the hot-water tank. Would have taken the furnace, but it wouldn't fit through the doorway, and I didn't have time to rip out the door frame.'

'You have our old hot-water tank?'

'Started leaking a while back. It's in the shed there somewhere. Might be useful some day.'

'How?'

'Could need a part out of it.'

'Why is the toilet out there?'

'Weather won't hurt a toilet. Ceramic. Washes right off.'

'You've lost your mind,' Ellis said, and his father smiled.

Dust on the car's upper surfaces had been disturbed here and there by the brushing and pressing of hands — presumably from Boggs's visit. Wires spilled from the broken headlamp openings. The wheels were overtaken by rust, and the tyres were flat and cracked. Looking at the damage across the front he could see already that the estimate of the angle of impact that he had used in the PC-Crash simulation had been off by a few degrees, although it seemed unlikely to make much difference. The *airlane* nameplate was missing from the left front fender.

He retrieved a pen, notepad and three disposable cameras from the minivan, and he borrowed an old, worn retractable tape measure from his father; he could not recall if it was the same tape measure that they had had when he was a boy. He would have preferred to have several tape measures to provide measurements relative to one another, but his father only had the one. He found just inside the shed door a sack of wooden golf tees — he'd never known his father to play golf, but he didn't ask — and used them to mark points in the grass around the car and measured straight lines between them.

He followed the same protocol that he and Boggs had developed over the years. He checked and noted vehicle make, model, year, ID number, wheel and tyre sizes, transmission type, brake type, overall width, overall height, overall length, axle positions, tyre conditions, brake-pad wear. At every six inches across the front end he measured depth of crush relative to the rear axle position, first at bumper level, and then again at hood line. The air was ripe with humidity, and as he made notes sweat fell on the page and glistened there in wet blisters. His father stood watching, then went to the toilet and sat facing the open fields, elbows hitched up a little as if he might giddy-up the commode into the distance.

Ellis stood fussing with one of the cameras until he realised that he was hesitating, unsure he wanted photos of this car. He circled, taking photos from each side and each corner, from low and high, then moved in and snapped close-ups of the wheels, licence plates, vehicle ID number, the place where the *airlane* nameplate should have been, broken headlamps and windows, then focused on the damaged area at the front and took photo after photo at every angle, nearer and further, with and without measuring tape for scale. A gust of wind ruffled his notes and made the trees along the road silvery and flickering. The clouds on the western horizon were closing in, black, rigged with claws of vapour. He tried the driver's door but it would not budge, so he opened the passenger door and slid over to the driver's side — he had to cram himself, thighs nudging the steering wheel, knees into the dash. He sat gripping the steering wheel. Then he took up his pad and noted the mileage, the fuel level and that the gear shift was in neutral. The dash appeared largely undamaged, though now riven with age cracks. He twisted himself down under the steering wheel to look at the foot pedals — wear of use looked normal. Remembering the headlamp bulbs, and wondering if they were on at the time of the collision, he climbed out but couldn't find either of them. They might have been lost in the collision, or put into police storage somewhere, or possibly Boggs had taken them. He drew out the driver's seat belt and examined its length and found a transfer marking where the belt had locked and pulled a little plastic off the D-ring during the impact. He took a photo of it, leaned across the front seat and pulled out the passenger belt, and it also bore a transfer mark.

A transfer mark on the passenger-side belt.

Ellis stared at it for a long while, then let the belt run back on its retractor and stood out of the car. His hands had picked up a layer of grime from the car, and he saw it in great detail — the grey thickest on the pads of his fingers, thinner down through the joints and onto the palm.

A transfer mark on the passenger-side belt.

He crawled in again, pulled out the passenger belt and examined the mark and then looked away and then re-examined the mark: a small black line across the width of the webbing, almost as if drawn there with a crayon. But it matched the colour of the D-ring, and when he pulled the belt away from the D-ring the impress of the belt into the plastic could be seen there. He photographed both — transfer mark, D-ring.

'Got to put the car back before the rain,' his father said behind him.

'A minute.'

Sometimes load markings could also be found on the belt latch plate, but here he could not see one on the driver's side, and on the passenger side he could only see a very faint marking that might have been a manufacturing effect. Inconclusive. He crawled into the back seat, which had only lap belts — no D-rings, and therefore no possibility of transfer marks. He checked the latch plates, but there were no indications of loading. He returned to the front passenger-side belt and looked at the transfer mark there one more time, felt its texture, turned it in the light. He let the retractor take the belt back. He stood out of the car. 'Dad,' he said.

Side by side they put hands on the damaged sheet metal and leaning and straining they rolled the car back. His father slid the shed door shut and set the lock, then started toward the toilet. He said, without looking around, 'I'm sorry that your friend is dead. I liked him.'

'I'm going to get going.'

'Find what you wanted?'

Ellis didn't answer. His father turned to look. 'I need to think,' Ellis said.

'You always did.'

They watched the weed-infested fields and the sky, which darkened further, the reaching, dark cloud masses now advancing with visible speed. A wind pressed, died, then renewed violently. Ellis put his notes in a back pocket and stood hesitating. Odours rose of dust, manure, mud. His father sat unperturbed on his toilet. A piece of paperboard went by bouncing and spinning, and the wind took dust off the fields and streamed it through the air, making Ellis squint and blink. He wasn't sure of what he was seeing until it had come halfway across the fields: the leading edge of the rain, perfectly defined, a curtain in the air, and below it the field turned black. The sight of this vast motion held Ellis until, although it seemed to be very slowly crawling over the open fields, the rain suddenly hit him with heavy cold droplets. A gust soaked the length of him. He squinted at his father — at times in the past he'd been convinced that the root problem of his life was that his father loved Christopher more than himself. But perhaps his father in his self-pity was right, and everything could be explained by errors of incompetence.

Then his father looked at him through the rain and howled, cheerfully, like an ape.

Startled, Ellis ran.

In the minivan, his father was visible through the windshield, radically distorted by the water moving on the glass, glowing in his white shirt. He remained atop the toilet and his white arm waved high in the air, like a captain committed to going down with the ship. Ellis waved, but his father almost certainly could not see the gesture. He backed the minivan to the road. The wipers flopped water aside but could barely keep up. The muddy gravel road spattered into the wheel wells. He drove slowly and watched the road and wanted to watch the gravel stones in the road, to watch each drop of water on the windshield — he did not want to think about the transfer mark on the passenger belt of his brother's car and its meaning.

Abruptly he cleared the rain. Traffic moved densely on the interstate. Now the afternoon sun, which had stood over his right shoulder in the morning, stood again over his right shoulder. He powered the windows down and air entered clamorously.

Boggs would have seen the same thing. It meant that a second person had been in the car. Who?

He didn't know that it had been Heather.

He followed the paired doors of a semi-trailer for miles and miles. At a certain distance from the rear of the trailer, he could glimpse the heavy-lidded eyes of the driver in the jittering side-view mirror.

The police report didn't say anything about a second person in the car. Why would the second person have been covered up?

He discovered that he had passed his exit. To keep driving — to drive and drive and drive — seemed simple and enticing. World passing without consequence. But he took an exit ramp and turned back.

On the night of the accident he had assumed that Heather had been a passenger in Christopher's car, until her father told him that she had been at the gas station.

If she had been driving —

The front seat of the *airlane* had been close

against the steering wheel.

He manoeuvred through roads and turns, returning. He carried his notes and cameras into the house and went to the computer to pull up a reference website — the designed distance between the wheels of the 1970 Fairlane was within a half-inch of the distance that he had measured on the driver's side of his brother's car. That distance had not been altered by the collision: the dash had not been pushed back toward the seat. Rather, the seat had been slid forward, for a driver shorter than he was, or Christopher had been.

He looked through the police report again, for any suggestion of a second occupant. There was none. An officer that Ellis did not recognise had signed the report. It did note that Heather's father had been first on the scene. Certainly he had been there, because Ellis had seen him. Perhaps he had not been able to author the report because his daughter was involved. But surely he had had input.

Ellis called the police station at Coil. A woman's voice told him that the officer who had signed and filed the report had died several years ago, of a heart attack, only months after his retirement. The woman's voice caught, and Ellis murmured condolences.

He took the police report and his notes and cameras to the minivan and put them into the glove compartment and locked it. Why did he feel so ungainly as he moved? As if the earth were teetering under him. He returned to the living room. He sat.

If other explanations existed for the evidence on the seat belts, those explanations did not rise to mind. Typically in such cases he would have talked to Boggs for a fresh perspective. Boggs had known all of this. He had seen the same evidence. What had led him to it? Something Heather said, perhaps. It would have been like him to decide to investigate some small contradiction in whatever she had told him about the accident. Or, just curiosity.

If she had been driving the car, why hadn't she told him? The question was critical, and Ellis tried to focus on it. Of course she had held some of herself from sight; in the nature of their affair a lot had been obscured. Yet he thought he had understood her, essentially, if not entirely. Perhaps he had been wrong. What had he known of her relationship with Boggs? She'd said little about it. But he had not asked. She had said that her marriage was a mistake that she blamed on herself. And what had she meant by that? He had no idea. How, after all, had she come together with him? He had been someone other than Boggs, and he had desired her, and she had felt herself linked to him by — what?

Rain again, darkening the windows, thrumming on the roof, sloshing in the gutters. He watched a droplet work slowly down a windowpane, the shift of the light it held. He tried to think what he should do, of confronting Heather — an idea like a balloon at the end of a string, he pulled it toward himself, then it rose a short distance away again.

He sat in the living room until late, waiting, listening to the air conditioning turn itself off and on. The rain had stopped. The hour when Heather usually returned went by and in agitation he checked the windows whenever a car passed. Finally he went to the toilet, then lay down and curled on the hard tile of the bathroom floor.

Eventually he stood again and went upstairs to the bedroom. Startled, he stopped — a shape lay in the bed.

At the sound of his step she shifted a little. 'Love,' he said. 'You've been here all this time?' he asked. She was silent. 'Where is your car?'

'It broke down,' she said. 'The engine just stopped.' Her hand, lying atop the bed sheets, opened and closed. 'I got it towed, and then I was late and stressed. I couldn't face school, not another day of it, so I took a taxi home. I thought you'd be here.'

He understood that she was frightened of him, and that she had been for some time now.

'Where were you?'

'I've been in Coil,' he said.

That night he lay gathering a hatred of Boggs. He could not believe that Boggs had not envisioned this course of events.

★ ★ ★

He lay beside her until morning, then he said, 'I have to show you something.'

Her station wagon was already repaired — an ignition coil replaced. They retrieved it, and then she drove. He was struck by the fact that she almost always preferred to drive. The route to the interstate through familiar end-to-end suburbs spanned past. Tuxedo shop. Liquor store. Laundromat. Starbucks. Church. Chiropractor. A build-your-own-teddy-bear shop. Jiffy Lube. Walgreens. Babies R Us. Bed Bath & Beyond. He had not ridden in the passenger seat of a car in a long time, and it felt unnatural and dangerous, travelling down the roadway without steering wheel or pedals, without control. Strip mall abutted strip mall to create a continuous path of commerce over the land. Heather wound up the engine and pushed into the interstate lanes. Ellis asked, 'Do you still think about Christopher?'

'Are we going to talk now?' she asked. 'Have a conversation?'

'Do you?'

'Of course I do.'

'Do you think often of the accident?'

'No.'

'You don't.'

'I hate to think of it.'

'So you just stopped?'

'I'd say it's something that I've learned.'

'What do you remember?'

'I don't like to remember.'

'Why have we never talked about this?'

'There are a lot things that we haven't talked about. Maybe you've noticed.' She looked at him, her expression closed and ungiving.

'Heather,' he said, and hesitated, and the two syllables stood open, an empty vessel. They were the last spoken for several miles.

But then he asked, 'Will you tell me what you remember about Christopher's accident?'

'Why?'

'Heather — please.'

'I walked from school to the gas station to buy a 7-Up and to call my dad for a ride. And

I was standing in the parking lot when I heard the brakes and turned and saw one car slam into another.' She spoke flatly. 'There was an enormous explosion and a fireball. When it had settled down and my eyes readjusted, I saw that the car was Christopher's. I ran to it. By the time I got there, he was already out, and he went to the other car.' She stared ahead. 'There were screams and it was hot and Christopher went into the car and came out with someone, and the fire was spreading and he went in, and the fire and smoke were everywhere, and he was trying to go in even further. He kept trying, and I was screaming at him to come out. Then he just stopped. I tried to pull him out. Someone dragged me away.'

'Did you call your dad from the gas station?'

'What?'

'You said that was the reason you were at the gas station.'

'I was waiting. I knew he wouldn't be home yet.'

'Did you buy the 7-Up?'

'I guess so, yes. I remember the cold of it in my hand when the heat of the explosion pushed out over me.'

'How long did it take you to recognise the *airlane?*'

'I don't know. Why?'

'Where was Christopher when you first saw him?'

'This is a strange conversation,' she said.

'Did anyone else get out of the *airlane*?'

'Oh God. Ellis — '

'Were there two people in the *airlane*?'

'Did John tell you to ask these questions?'

'Well, there were two people in the car at the time of the collision.'

'Did John tell you that?'

'I looked at the car.'

'You think I was in there? That's what John thought.'

Ellis said nothing.

'I wasn't,' she said.

'Who then?'

'Christopher was alone.'

'These things are never knowable to one hundred per cent certainty,' Ellis said, 'but the evidence is pretty clear. Someone sat in the driver's seat and someone else sat in the passenger seat. Both wore seat belts. I think you were in the car. In fact, you were driving. And your dad manipulated the accident report.'

She pulled to the side of the road and stopped, tyres scraping on the gravel, and she bent forward and gasped.

'Isn't that right?' he asked.

'I watched from the gas station with a can of 7-Up in my hand. You have no idea how much you sound like John.'

It is over, he thought, this is the end. He breathed shallowly and she stared at the steering wheel and time passed.

'Do you want me to drive?' he asked.

She opened her door, stood out of the car. He thought she might walk away, but she circled the car, and he stood out and circled the car, and he began to drive.

★   ★   ★

A boy and an older man — presumably the boy's father — huddled together over something in the lawn, a white-and-red cylinder with tailfins.

'What are they doing?'

'Water rocket.'

The father began to work a small hand pump.

'No concrete,' she observed.

'You remember.'

'Of course.'

'Do you know the difference between a cheeseburger and a blow job?'

'No.'

'Then let's go get lunch.'

She glanced at him, but her expression

didn't change. She said softly, 'You were afraid of me.'

'When's the last time you were here?' Ellis asked.

'Before the accident.'

'When?'

She sat looking at the house. 'I met him here earlier that day, I think.'

'You left with him in the *airlane*?'

In the lawn, the boy and his father stepped back, and in a shrill voice the boy shouted, 'Ten! Nine! Eight!' At zero, the rocket shot into the sky.

'I don't remember.' She sighed. 'That ox yoke is ridiculous.'

'But you think you got out of his car at some point and went to the school and then went to the gas station and waited there for your dad to pick you up.'

Something crashed just above their heads, and Ellis threw his hands up. Heather screamed.

'The rocket,' Ellis said.

'I think my heart really stopped.'

The boy and father came running, and the father took the rocket off the roof of the car, grinning and mouthing, 'Sorry.'

'But why would you go back to the school?'

'I had friends in choir. Maybe I met one of them. I don't know.' The father and son crouched to prepare a second launch. They stepped back and counted down, but this time the rocket only lifted a foot or so before it flopped over, geysering.

Ellis drove. Again the road reduced to a cobble of asphalt patchwork. Again he took the dirt road under the trees. Turning in the driveway he said, 'This is my father's house.' He stopped behind his father's car. 'The car is here.'

'What car?'

'Christopher's. The *airlane*.'

'No.' She shook her head with a jerk. 'Are you kidding?'

'It's here because my dad is completely crazy.'

They stood on the porch, and his father opened the screen door. He let the door slap into his shoulder and his gaze shifted between them. He seemed to be wearing the same clothes he'd worn the day before, with the same or an identical white shirt, clean and pressed.

'Dad, this is Heather.'

'I remember, of course.'

'Hi, Mr Barstow. It's nice to see you again.'

'We need to see the car, Dad.'

'Do you want to?' his father asked Heather.

But she was staring past him. 'Is that the same sofa? And chairs?'

His father reached and with awkward gentleness, with the fingertips of one hand, touched her on the shoulder. Then he turned. 'I'll get the key.' He could be heard in the kitchen rattling jars and drawers. Ellis again looked over the living room's wretched objects. Heather pushed a fist into the sofa. Then his father reappeared, holding the key in one cupped hand. He led the way toward the shed, but Heather veered off and stopped near the toilet and stood looking at the fields while Ellis and his father again slid open the shed doors, again slithered through the clutter to the rear of the vehicle, again strained to move the car on its rotten wheels into the sunlight.

Ellis then stood beside it, watching Heather. Blue sky topped the open fields, and there rose neither wind nor the sense of imminence that the weather had provided before.

Finally he crossed the open ground and asked her to come. He brought her to the passenger side and pulled out the seat belt and showed her the trace of plastic it had pulled off the D-ring, then asked her to lean inside to see the matching impression in the plastic of the D-ring itself.

She looked and offered no comment.

Then he asked her to slide over into the

driver's seat. 'How is the steering wheel?' he asked. 'The pedals? Are they too near? Too far?'

'No.'

'You see?'

She only sat. He didn't know what to do now, and she said nothing.

After a minute he climbed into the passenger seat to sit beside her.

'We used to fight in this car. Christopher did let me drive occasionally. For some reason he always wanted to fight when I was driving.'

'What did you fight about?'

'Which party to go to. Dumb things like that. Whose fault it was that we were lost. That was pretty common. We made long trips into the countryside until we had no idea where we were. One time I got out at a farm stand and the woman there referenced all these towns and roads I had never heard of, and eventually it came out that we'd gone almost two hundred miles and had actually crossed the state line.'

'That seat is set for you. Maybe you were at the gas station earlier on the day of the accident and transposed the memory.'

'I remember the heat of the explosion. I remember stumbling on the kerb as I ran.'

'The collision would have thrown you

forward, the belt would have held your torso, but your head would have snapped down, your arms and hands would have been thrown forward, your legs probably gone up into the dash, probably bruised. And maybe the next day you had bruising along the line of the belt. Maybe your neck hurt.' They sat facing forward and gazing at the space where the windshield should have been, and it struck Ellis as a terrible arrangement for a conversation. But perfectly common. 'There would have been a flash of light and heat through the broken windshield. The spin of the car throwing you into the door, the shrieking of the tyres, the lurching stop.'

'I told John that I had nothing to say about it. I don't.'

He stood out of the car and after a minute wandered to the house. From the kitchen he looked back through the window. She was still in the car. He found his father in the living room, slouching back in one of the chairs, eyes closed, lax, looking dead.

I hate him, Ellis thought.

But the thought passed; it wasn't true. He didn't even dislike his father. His father made him uncomfortable. He didn't want to allow himself, however, to develop dislike or hate out of a resentment of discomfort, the proximate cause of which was his father.

'You're not dead,' Ellis said.

His father's eyes opened. 'Don't think so, but you never can tell.' He lifted his head into an awkward angle. 'Strange to see her again, isn't it?'

'I've been seeing her for a while.'

'Great.'

'You don't know anything about it.'

'What are you showing her?'

'She says she wasn't in the car.'

'So?'

'She was. She was driving.'

'Really?'

'Both the driver and passenger seats were occupied at the time of the accident, and the driver's side is positioned for a person her size.'

His father's eyelids lowered shut again. 'It happened a long time ago.'

Silence.

'I thought you would have more to say. Christopher was your favourite.'

Slack, dead-looking, his father said, 'I love you.'

'All right.'

'You don't believe me.'

'All right. I believe you.'

'I love you, and I know you know I love you. I guess that must be enough. You love her?'

Ellis turned away and came out of the house. Heather had wandered into the fields. He waited for her to turn, so that he could wave for her to come back, but she did not turn.

The furrowed soil crumbled underfoot. Low weeds snagged his shoes and cuffs. His lungs laboured to move the heavy, humid air, and he had the feeling that if he tried to shout to her the words would hit the air and fall to the ground. She stood motionless, looking away toward the line of the fence and the brush growing along it, arms hugging herself, posture tense. And what did he want from her? He only wanted an acknowledgement of the facts. A life without access to facts felt to him like a life without anchors.

Was this what Boggs had intended? To punish the two of them? Or to reveal a truth to a friend?

'Heather,' he said.

'You whisper my name that way,' she said, 'and I feel as if I've embarrassed myself, like I've forgotten to wear pants.'

He laughed a little hysterically. She held a dandelion gone to seed, and she was picking it apart, letting the seeds fall down a languid, angled path. He circled to stand in front of her, downslope. By the fence — three strands of rusting wire sagging between greyed posts

— a trickle of water gurgled between weeds.

'John could have done it,' she said. 'He could have made a mark like that on the seat belt.'

'Boggs?'

'He would, too.'

Would he? Could he? Ellis hadn't thought of such a thing. But he said, 'No. It would have been extremely difficult.'

'John could do anything he set himself to.'

'He couldn't just draw some crayon onto the belt. You saw the D-ring, the plastic had clearly transferred from the D-ring. There would be two ways to do it. One would be to somehow heat the D-ring to the point of melting and then pull the belt over it, and you'd have to experiment with the heat level and practise the movement of the belt to produce an effect that looked right — it would be hard. The other way to do it would be to pull the belt as hard as it would be pulled during a collision. But it's not as if anyone has the arm strength to just reach in and do it. Extreme forces are involved. You'd need to create some mechanical device, an original design and fabrication. And then you'd have to bring it into the car and operate it and at the same time hide it from my dad. It doesn't make sense.'

'It was a used car when Christopher got it.

It could have been in some other accident.'

'The driver's belt showed only one mark, and it would show two if it had been involved in two collisions.'

She cast down her shoulders. 'What are we to each other?' she asked. 'I don't even know.'

'You don't remember the accident at all?'

'I remember it. I remember it just as I told you.'

'You don't have any doubt.'

'It's what I remember.'

'But what do you believe?'

'What do you want me to do, Ellis? What do you want me to believe? Tell me. I'll try. That little black mark is the truth? I'll believe it. Should I tell you that I remember it as you described, the seat belt on me, my limbs flying, all of that? Then everything would line up with the evidence and that would be that?'

'All I know,' he said, 'is that when we worked our cases, we always discounted witness testimony. We set it aside entirely, if possible, and worked from the physical evidence. People will tell you they saw a car shoot a hundred feet into the air like a rocket and flip a dozen times end over end before coming down undamaged on its wheels — stuff that's not remotely possible in the real world. The physical evidence is objective.'

'Physical evidence,' she said. Her tone

348

might have been the same if she had been echoing the phrases of a gibbering lunatic.

'Verifiable facts and analysable traces of events as they actually occurred, outside the subjective manipulation of memory.'

'You think that I killed those people and your brother.'

'I'm asking you what you remember. You really don't have any doubt?'

She stepped a little distance from him. 'It's like you're asking, *The world ended yesterday, don't you remember?*'

'All right,' he said, 'what do you want to do?'

She looked at the turned earth at their feet. He awaited the answer with fear.

She said, with exhaustion, 'I just want to eat something.'

She drove them back into town — he had a feeling of hurtling down the road with insane speed yet watching it pass very slowly — to Devito's, an Italian restaurant and pizzeria where his family had sometimes gone. It still stood in its place in the middle of the town's single central block. The storefront windows to either side, however, showed only plywood. He saw no one he recognised at the old tables, which stood in an arrangement unchanged since he had eaten at them as a child, and he watched for one of the old waitresses — now in bifocals, short hair and gaudy lipstick. But the girl who came to the table was only a couple of years out of high school and nervous, touching her ear and trying to smile by straining her lips into a rictus. The tables and chairs and wood panelling and green-glass light fixtures were all just as they had been when he was young, when this place seemed fancy and sophisticated. But the salad bar now seemed classless, the water came in plastic cups, cheap silverware sat beside paper napkins. Down the centre of the ceiling ran a strip of fluorescent lights. It was merely a neighbourhood restaurant, more or less a dive.

They ate quietly.

'Maybe,' he said, 'if we look at the photos, something will stir up in your mind.'

She shook her head.

'Boggs said that if you look at the photos long enough, you can always see something new.'

'Sounds like John.'

They were quiet.

'You expect too much,' she said.

It seemed to him, however, that all he ever did was to passively accept the rough world. He paid, and when he came outside she stood on the sidewalk, looking at the street as if a secret door might open there. It occurred to him that she could have fled, and she had waited. A couple of cars floated down the street, lamps glowing in the twilight. The row of buildings across from them stood dark, the windows boarded or hung with For Sale and For Lease signs. Across the railroad tracks and down the street, the True Value remained, the pharmacy, the grocery.

He had to force his thoughts slowly forward. 'Will you drive through the intersection?' he asked. 'It might bring out some memory. Have you driven it since the accident? Since Christopher died?'

She stepped down the sidewalk.

He followed. Already she was opening the door of the station wagon. As he approached, the engine ignited, and before he pulled the passenger door closed behind him she began reversing. 'Heather,' he said. He watched her steer into traffic. 'Heather.' She took them west, out of town, the night-time road streaking under the headlamps. She turned and turned and soon they drove on unfamiliar roads where cars were scarce. A few houses stood far back from the road, deep in the murk, a window or two glowing. A massive green John Deere tractor tilted on the road shoulder, abandoned. She slowed for an intersection, and low branches groped past the stop sign toward the car.

He saw that they had circled. Coil lay ahead of them now. They passed an abandoned motel, a used car lot, a bar called the Best Place. As they heaved and thudded on potholes and patches, Heather leaned forward, right hand flexing.

Two-storey houses on festering lawns. A church fronted with a wide parking lot. A low bridge with concrete rails flaking and showing rebar. Most of it looked just as it had when he was a child, returning from the mall in the back seat of his mother's car. They passed the high school. The road here ran with two lanes in either direction, sparsely trafficked. A Buick with red cellophane taped over a broken tail light slowed and turned without signalling.

'How fast was Christopher's car going before the crash?' she asked. 'Do you know?'

'Forty-seven, forty-eight, around there.'

The lights of the intersection shone a quarter-mile ahead. He saw Heather settle the speedometer between 45 and 50 mph. At the intersection, the green light dropped to red. A little white Plymouth rolled to a stop in the right lane, but the left lay open. A couple hundred feet from the cross street she still held speed, and finally he understood. He could grab the steering wheel, but he could see nowhere safe to redirect the vehicle. To reach a foot over to the brake pedal he would need to remove his seat belt. He said, 'Heather.'

'I want to know.'

'I didn't mean this.' Although at the same time, he wondered if something might be gained, a more authentic version of the experience.

'I want to know,' she said. 'Don't you want to know?'

The car bellied into a low place, then rose into the intersection. He felt brightly calm, aware, a passenger, he could do nothing. He started to lift his hands to brace against the dash, but remembered the airbag that would explode from there and let his hands drop.

This accident felt different from the others, from the accident with James Dell, which had moved slowly before him while every detail caught him with surprise, and from the accident that killed Boggs, which came in an instant of distraction and finished even before he understood that it had begun. Here he felt no surprise and as he faced the oncoming event without surprise an awareness rose of how time might be subdivided, of his mind ranging forward as if all of it were preordained. And maybe it was — probably it could all be calculated already.

His left hand, thrown out, came awkwardly

against Heather's chest. A green Ford Explorer passed just before them, left to right, the driver peering at them through his side window, a large bald head with eyes tight, mouth tight, right hand risen as if to fend away, and in the window behind him a boy of seven or eight with brown bangs over his eyes, grimacing. Crossing in the opposite direction in the far kerbside lane moved a beige Saturn driven by a tall man, his head nearly into the ceiling, watching straight ahead, apparently oblivious, while in the passing lane came a red Chevy pickup. A horn sounded — the Explorer's, although the Explorer had already safely passed by.

As they crossed the first lane he saw that they would miss the Saturn, but the Chevy pickup would be very close.

Headlights on the left, bright. Noise of the road under the tyres. Motion, shrieking, vehicles locked into their trajectories.

Heather had not touched the brakes, and in this she had it wrong: the driver of his brother's car had braked. She looked straight ahead while he looked past her profile into the pickup's headlights, incredibly near, as if in the car with them. Shrieking. The pickup braking, shrieking, how long had that noise existed? The gaping chromed grille of the pickup. Heather's profile passed in front of the second headlight. He could not see the pickup's driver, could see nothing past the lamps and the grille. The lamps passed behind the B-, then C-pillars, and the light thrown into the wagon flickered. Perhaps it would pass behind them, by an inch or two, he thought.

Then the horrendous clash of sheet metal on sheet metal in mutual forced distortion, and the wagon lurched right, and Ellis felt himself twisting, one shoulder biting into the seat belt while his chin slammed down into the other. An instant later the wagon was free of the Chevy, the noise of the collision ended, replaced by the scream of the tyres rubbing sideways and of chassis components biting into one another, the wagon spinning. His chin came up, and already he was being pulled in the other direction, toward the door. Lights streaked out horizontally. Objects moved across the windshield — a parked car, a lamp pole, the canopy of the gas station, the fence. His body hit the door while time subdivided ever more finely, into a desert of sand, and then smaller yet, as if he might approach death with the assurance of never reaching it. He recalled once, at some event where they were all together, Boggs had asked a simple question about Christopher, and neither he nor Heather answered, and Boggs said, 'When you get like this about it, I begin to wonder if he ever really existed at all.' But he did exist, and now he didn't, and that was what had always been incomprehensible, even if he was a jerk.

The station wagon lurched and heaved as it came into the kerb, and Ellis glimpsed a wheel, broken free, spinning into the air and away into the dark. The wagon's yawing movement was stopped, but it continued to slide sideways, scraping bare metal over concrete. He could not bring his head around to see where they were going, saw only where they had come from, a spectacle of sparks streaming up in their trail. Heather had her eyes closed. Another impact pressed him hard against his door. Darkness shuddered up. He could not breathe and could not see. Everything rushed toward ending, and again the phrase *my brother* —

★   ★   ★

He touched something human with his left hand. Heather moaned. A network of cracks shone in the windshield. Beside him stood a white vehicle, only a few inches from his window, some enormous thing, a pickup or SUV. The station wagon had slapped sideways into it. He looked for his left hand

356

and saw it clutching at the fabric of his own pants. 'Heather,' he said. He could not get out through his door, because of the vehicle beside it.

'Yes.'

'Can you open your door?'

'I thought I would remember,' she said. 'I really thought I would. I was terrified that I would remember. But I didn't. I don't. Did you?'

Did he? Did he remember driving Christopher's car into the intersection? No, he'd never driven Christopher's car. No. He felt a lurch of nausea. But no. The driver's seat of the *airlane* — he recalled — wasn't set for his height. 'No,' he said. 'No.' He unbuckled his belt, leaned across her, opened her door. An excess of adrenalin made objects vibrate. 'Can you climb out?'

She did. And he crawled over her seat, put his hands on the concrete and pulled his legs out. Slowly he stood. He examined his right arm where it had hit the door, but there was no blood, only dull pain. Heather looked fine. The vehicle that had stopped their movement was an empty Suburban. Ellis smelled faintly the acrid scent of gasoline, and he took Heather by the hand and led her away from it.

The Chevy pickup that had hit them stood

on the road's shoulder, and the driver emerged from it with a cellphone pressed to his head. A couple other cars had stopped. 'Are you all right?' someone called.

Ellis nodded.

He felt tremors passing through Heather. He sat with her on the kerb. 'When the cops come,' he said, 'tell them that you just didn't see the light.'

She turned to regard him.

'You don't have any idea if it was red or green or yellow,' he said. 'A lapse of attention. It happens all the time.'

'I'll never drive again,' she said.

Ellis shook his head. 'You can't live in this country without driving.' Traffic, working around the pickup, resumed its movements. The lights overhead changed. The air stank of scorched brake pads and smoked rubber.

★ ★ ★

The police released her late that evening. He drove a rental car; she fell asleep in the passenger seat. He passed the exit for her house and went on. For half an hour he fought exhaustion and drooping eyelids. Then the sense of fatigue passed and he grew alert, open. He stopped at 2 a.m. for gas in an island of fluorescent glow, crowded with vehicles and silent drivers. Heather didn't wake. Interstate miles passed. She slept with her head slumped to her shoulder.

Dawn was marshalling when her shoulders and hands twitched, after which she was still for another ten minutes. Then she groaned and winced as she lifted her head. She blinked at the road. Ellis said nothing. 'Where are we?' she asked.

The eastern sky, in his mirror, lay awash in shades of pink and lilac. 'I'm not exactly sure,' he said. 'Does it matter?'

Flat land streamed by. She said, 'Pull over.'

'Here?' He let the car slow and stop on the shoulder. She looked decided: the muscles around her eyes relaxed, her lips set — a look that pushed him down like a hand on the head of a swimmer. She stood out and closed the door and walked away, a figure diminishing, then vanishing, under the blush of dawn light.

He watched the traffic and the road and the landscape — the road ran straight to disappearing in either direction and on either side the land opened, the trees a distant effect clutching the horizon, except, across the highway, a single old oak, like a thing that would be there forever. He went through everything again. Could he be wrong about Christopher's accident? An error in multiplication, a detail missed in a photograph, a cop sliding seats around — it was possible. Could she be right? Could he have been in Christopher's car? It was insane to think so. If that were true, anything might be true. But perhaps anything might be true.

He discovered that he was sweating and he ran down the windows, which alleviated the temperature only a little and brought into the car all the furious noise of the highway, the wheels beating on the asphalt and the trucks clanking and the air pushed before one vehicle and sucked behind another so that at times it howled as it was torn in two directions.

Not knowing what to do he waited. If she had said anything he would have had no hope — if she had said go on, if she had said goodbye, if she had flicked a hand in gesture, he would be without hope. But she had said nothing, and so he would wait.

A double-trailer truck went by, the air shuddering behind it. A series of silver sedans passed one after another like a beaded necklace dragged over the ground. Midday, he stood out of the car and went a little distance off the side of the road to pee. And then examined the roadside gravel, with greater and greater care, studied it stone by stone. But if traces of her steps were there, he could not see them.

Had Boggs foreseen all of this, or something like this? His gaze drifted to the oak across the highway, to its intricate, indifferent manner of occupying space. A cement truck passed, its barrel striped like a colossal peppermint candy. Had Christopher foreseen this? A lawless unreality hung like a purple fog at the limit of vision. How long should he wait? He thought of trying to follow her, as he had tried to follow Boggs. But Boggs had wanted him to follow. She did not. Yes? Or, was he only too tired? Of course, she would be right to leave him. For a time he cried out amid the roaring traffic noise and swore he would wait until he saw her coming — a figure resolving out of the far distance. He would wait. He would wait and wait and wait. He could only wait.

He waited into the afternoon with a headache scraping his eyes. He was also hungry — a dull, ridiculous sensation.

If he sat here long enough, he thought, he would see an accident occur.

For a long while he watched the oak, its solidity flickered by passing vehicles, and when he turned forward again he saw her.

He held his breath. He could see her. Coming out of the wavering distance, beside the flashing traffic. Stooped a little. Limping a

361

little. Watching him as she came.

When she reached the minivan she opened the door and sat beside him. Smelling of sweat and exhaust and faintly sweet and of herself. Scarred. Without eyelashes.

Not saying anything. But here.

'Love?' he said, and abandoned all the rest, turned the key and began to drive again.

We do hope that you have enjoyed reading this large print book.

Did you know that all of our titles are available for purchase?

We publish a wide range of high quality large print books including:
Romances, Mysteries, Classics
General Fiction
Non Fiction and Westerns

Special interest titles available in large print are:
The Little Oxford Dictionary
Music Book
Song Book
Hymn Book
Service Book

Also available from us courtesy of Oxford University Press:
Young Readers' Dictionary
(large print edition)
Young Readers' Thesaurus
(large print edition)

For further information or a free brochure, please contact us at:
Ulverscroft Large Print Books Ltd.,
The Green, Bradgate Road, Anstey,
Leicester, LE7 7FU, England.
Tel: (00 44) 0116 236 4325
Fax: (00 44) 0116 234 0205

Other titles published by
The House of Ulverscroft:

SILENCE

Jan Costin Wagner

In Finland a young girl disappears while cycling to volleyball practice. Her abandoned bike is found in exactly the same place that another girl was assaulted and murdered thirty-three years previously. The perpetrator was never brought to justice and the authorities suspect the same killer has struck again. An unsettling crime — particularly for someone who's carried a burden of guilt for years . . . Investigating, Detective Kimmo Joentaa is helped by his colleague Ketola, who worked on the original murder. As the ripples from the impact of the new disappearance spread, Kimmo discovers that the truth is not always what you expect.

INTO DARKNESS

Jonathan Lewis

Lying facedown in Docklands mud, saintly Sir Tommy Best, Britain's best-loved entertainer and tireless charity benefactor, is found dead. His guide dog, Suzy, is found cowering a mile away. With no clues or witnesses to the killing, the case is assigned to the brilliant DCI Ned Bale. But police dog-handler Kate Baker, believes that Suzy holds the secret of her master's fate. The public turns the wharf into a shrine and the tabloids bay for blood. Meanwhile, the police suspecting that Sir Tommy wasn't all he seemed, must retrace, step by painstaking step, his last walk into darkness . . .

BLOOD IN GRANDPONT

Peter Tickler

When a woman is stabbed to death in an Oxford car park, a revealing photograph on her mobile points towards a crime of sexual passion or revenge. But as DI Holden and her team investigate further, it seems that things might not be as clear cut as they first appeared. Then another body is found in the Guardian-reading, Labour-voting area of Oxford known as Grandpont, adding a whole new dimension to the case. Now, as the complications pile up in Holden's professional and personal life, finding the killer becomes more than a matter of life and death . . .

ALL THAT FOLLOWS

Jim Crace

Leonard Lessing is a jazzman taking a break. His glory days behind him, his body letting him down, he relives old gigs and feeds his media addiction during solitary days at home. Increasingly estranged from his wife Francine, who is herself mourning the sudden absence of her only daughter, Leonard has found his own safe, suburban groove. But then a news bulletin comes that threatens to change everything. A gunman has seized hostages a short drive from Lennie's house. His face leaps out of the evening news — and out of Leonard's own past . . . Leonard has a choice to make.

CRACKS

Sheila Kohler

A beautiful schoolgirl mysteriously disappears into the South African veldt. Forty years later, ten members of the missing girl's swimming team gather at their old boarding school for a reunion, and look back to the long, dry weeks leading to Fiamma's disappearance. As teenage memories and emotions resurface, the women relive the horror of a long-buried secret, which hides the tribalism of adolescence — and the violence that lies in the heart of even the most innocent . . .